Legend at

Keith R. Rees

Published in the USA

Amazon Kindle Direct Publishing

P.O. Box 81226

Seattle, WA 98108-1226

http://www.kdp.amazon.com

Printed in the USA

Edited by Keith R. Rees and Sherrie Keenan

Cover Design by Keith R. Rees

Cover Image (with permission) by

Nathan Anderson, Unsplash.com

Back cover image by Keith R. Rees

13-digit ISBN: 978-1-080-53547-7

First Edition: January 2020

Other Titles by Keith R. Rees

Specter in the Glass – *PARANORMAL FICTION*
One Night in Bangkok – *SCIENCE FICTION*
The Lunas - FICTION
The Hana Sun Does Shine - POETRY
Take the Water to the Mountain - FICTION
Shaking the Tree - FICTION
The Brazilian – FICTION
Legend upon the Cane – HISTORICAL FICTION
Quill and Ink - POETRY

For my dad, Richard L. Rees

With a special dedication to the people of Alto, Texas. This area was devastated by two tornados on the afternoon of April 13, 2019, just a month before the writing of this novel. This tragic event did enormous damage to the area, including Caddo Mounds State Historic Site along Highway 21 (part of the El Camino Real). The annual Caddo Culture Day event was taking place when the storm unexpectedly came upon the hundreds of visitors there. May the Lord lift those who lost their lives and help heal the injured and their families and loved ones.

Prologue

The history of the Caddo Indians in North America is profound and vibrant with roots that go back as far as the ninth century. The first signs of this great nation of Native Americans were seen in the lower Mississippi Valley around 800 A.D. Their territory included parts of Mississippi, Louisiana, Arkansas, Oklahoma, and East Texas. In ancient days, the Caddo culture was known for its religious belief in Earthen mounds built over those who had passed on to the afterlife. Evidence of these mounds are still seen today in parts of East Texas.

At the height of their prominence around 1200 A.D., the Caddo Indians numbered more than a quarter of a million people. In Texas, they were known as one of the most advanced Native American tribes of their time. As time went on, and with the discovery of the New World by European explorers, the Caddo began to split into smaller tribes in numerous areas in fear of these newcomers. In the forests and rolling hills of East Texas, there lived many factions of the Caddo, including the Hainai, Nabedache, Nacogdoche, Nasoni, Nadote and the Nadaco (also known as the Anadarko) Indians. Collectively, these small off-shoots of the Caddo were part of the Hasinai culture and all of them spoke the same language, albeit in various dialects.

In the days of King Louis XIV of France and King Phillip IV of Spain, there was the France-Spain War which lasted for twenty-four years until it finally ended in 1659 with the signing of the Treaty of the Pyrenees. War had ended in their homelands, but expansion in the New World was well underway and the race was on to claim as much of the new territory as possible in the name of both sovereignties. France expanded by way of the southern Gulf coasts near Mobile and New Orleans. While the Spanish explored northward by way of Mexico and into New Mexico and Texas. The common divider in the New World between the two countries was the Sabine River which runs between Texas and Louisiana. Many times, soldiers and explorers from both countries ventured into adversarial territory but each time they were thwarted. Tensions remained high between them until trusted and secure trade routes could be established.

One such trail that greatly eased these tensions was known as the Old San Antonio Road, or King's Highway. The more common name for this route was the El Camino Real. It was started by a Spanish explorer named Alonso DeLeon. He was charged with finding safe passage from locations on the Rio Grande River to East Texas with the intention of forming Spanish missions in these areas. However, his efforts were short-lived and further attempts were not made again until after the start of the 18th century.

History was made in 1716 when this crucial trade route was aided significantly by the many factions of the Caddo Indians and a determined French explorer named Louis Juchereau de St. Denis. He had already established trading posts at Natchitoches as well as Mobile and New Orleans. With the aid of the Caddo, the resolute St. Denis made a successful push into East Texas and on down to Mexico along this famed route. However, upon his arrival, St. Denis was imprisoned, but he was able to secure his release after agreeing to help the Spanish re-establish the El Camino Real and start Catholic missions in East Texas. St. Denis would be accompanied on these missions by the Spanish leader, Captain Domingo Ramon, and the courageous friar, Father Antonio Margil de Jesus.

This is a companion story, or sequel, to the book *Legend Upon the Cane* which told of the relationship of St. Denis and the chief of the Nashitosh Indians, Natchitos. As is known from that story, the legend tells of how Natchitos and his twin brother are instructed by their father to split the tribe and travel in opposite directions for three days. This story is a fictional account of true persons and events that revolve around the twin brother named Nakahodot.

After traveling west from the Sabine River for three days, Nakahodot and his new tribe arrived in a densely forested area alongside two narrow creeks. The small tributaries would become known as Banita and Lanana Creeks. Their tribe would settle in this area fifty miles west of the Sabine River and one hundred and fifty miles north of the Gulf of Mexico. The forests were lush and thriving with wildlife and seemed quite suitable for Nakahodot and his tribe. Little did he know, that the land he had settled upon would one day play a critical role in the history of

Texas and America. In the years that follow it would become known as Nacogdoches, the oldest settlement in Texas.

Chapter 1

A lone Indian brave danced by the firelight on the crest of a small hill. He was dressed in full headdress and his chants were lifted to the Heavens and stars along with the sacred smoke from the fire.

A nervous Chief Caddo paced feverishly outside a small hut. Beads of sweat formed on his forehead as his pace quickened with each turn. From time to time he would stop and listen for any sign that his wife's agony had finally ended. With each cry that he heard from Aiyana, he became more and more worried.

Chief Caddo's closest friend, Atohi, tried to calm him. He had gone through the same ordeal just a few months before with his own wife, so he gave his friend the requisite sympathy. "Chief, you must not worry yourself so much. She will be fine, my friend."

Just as he had said this, they heard another loud cry from within the hut. Aiyana was in terrible pain. Caddo grabbed Atohi by and arm and responded in panic, "Her cries are worse by the minute. I need to help her." He made a move for the door flap to the hut, but Atohi blocked his way. "Move, I tell you. I must get in there!"

"Patience, my friend," Atohi assured him. "Have faith in White Owl. She's delivered every child in this camp for the last ten years. Your wife is in the best of hands." Atohi tried his best to lead Caddo away from the door. "Please, come and sit with me by the fire."

Atohi sat on a log next to a small fire Caddo had built just outside his home. Normally he wouldn't have such a fire in the open. Only the sacred fire on the hill was permitted during such a time, but Caddo used his position as his reason to have one of his own on such a night. Otherwise, he would be by the fire in his home, or at the very least, in the smoking hut. However, for Caddo, as well as Aiyana, this was no ordinary night. For the first time in his life, it was his turn to pace around nervously as he waited for his wife to give birth to their first child.

"Come sit down," Atohi pleaded once more. "You have built a nice fire out here. The least you could do is come and enjoy it. When this is all over, we will share a smoke to mark the occasion."

To Caddo, the only thing better than a good fire was a good smoke. He smiled at his friend's kind proposal and answered, "All in good time. I think..." He trailed off when at that moment he heard a faint cry come from within the hut. No longer did he hear the frantic, painful cries of his wife, but that of an infant.

He rushed over to the door and as soon as he reached for the flap, White Owl emerged with a weary look upon her face holding a water skin. She nodded to the anxious Caddo that he may go inside.

Caddo knelt next to his exhausted wife and smiled at her. "Your eyes are shining brightly this night, my wife," he said to her sweetly. "How brave you are."

Aiyana weakly produced a smile for her husband and motioned to the infant in her arms, saying, "Here is our son."

He caressed the side of her face with his broad hand, then reached to gently take his son into his arms for the first time. Before he could take the child, pain shot through Aiyana's body and she arched her back, wailing in agony. Startled, Caddo jumped to his feet just as White Owl came rushing back into the hut.

White Owl quickly took the child from Aiyana and placed him on a small bed of soft pelts and grasses. She instinctively knew what the problem was and rushed Caddo toward the door.

"You must leave now," she commanded.

"Why? What has happened?" Caddo asked frantically.

"There is still another! I must attend to her now." White Owl pushed Caddo through the door and rushed to her side and wiped the sweat from Aiyana's face. "Easy, my child, easy. I will stay with you. I will not leave your side." She called out loudly to Caddo and Atohi who were both just outside the door, "Fill some more water skins. Bring them to me quickly!"

"I will!" Caddo answered back.

Atohi ran with Caddo toward the river and asked as he jogged, "What is it? Is she alright?"

"There is another baby. My wife is going through a terrible ordeal." He tossed a water skin to Atohi as they reached the water's edge. A light rain began to fall as they quickly filled the sacks with water. "I never knew she would have to go through so much. I am afraid she will die."

"Do not lose hope, great friend," Atohi replied optimistically. "Women have had twins before and lived to tell stories about it. Aiyana will have a story to tell after this night, I assure you."

"I hope you are right. Come, let us get these to White Owl." The men ran back up the slope toward the tribal camp and set the water skins just inside the hut but neither dared to go in.

Caddo kept his vigil outside the hut in the light rain the rest of the night. Hours past and Aiyana's ordeal continued ceaselessly. The fire he had burning outside smoldered in the darkness and rain. Soon, the rain stopped, and the eastern sky began to glow with the first hint of dawn. As he wearily paced outside the hut with his eyes closed, he finally heard the faint cry of another child. His eyes darted open at the sound. A thoroughly exhausted White Owl opened the flap to the hut carrying an empty water skin and nearly fell into Caddo's arms.

"She is alright?" Caddo asked her. She nodded and motioned for him to go inside. He entered and saw his first son sleeping on the fox pelts and then he spotted his second son lying next to him. He was wide awake and cooing softly as his arms and legs flailed and kicked about. Caddo looked at both his sons with astonishment and pride.

Then he knelt next to his wife who was asleep and completely drained. "My lovely Aiyana," he spoke softly to her. He placed his hand on hers. "Rest now, my wife. I will not leave your side."

Three days later a great bonfire celebration was held, as was the custom, for the arrival of the chief and his wife's twin sons. Aiyana had regained her strength and was able to attend the ceremony that would commence with dancing and singing. It was the tribal celebration in which names would be given to the newest members of their tribe.

Caddo stood before the people and said, "The 'great spirit' has come upon our village and blessed us with the arrival of not one, but two sons. We welcome them to our family with dancing and the sacred smoke that will lift their names to the realm of the 'great spirit'. Let the names of my sons now be spoken."

Aiyana handed him the first of their two sons. Caddo held him in his arms and said, "My son, since you came into this world as the sun set over our lands, I shall call you Nakahodot."

He handed Nakahodot back to Aiyana then took their second son from her. "My son, since you came into this world as the sun rose over our lands, I will call you Natchitos.

Caddo sat next to his wife who held their two sons, and the dancing and singing began. He smiled at his wife and thought how lovely she looked as she held them. The celebration would go onto in the rest of the night.

The years passed and the twin sons grew into fine young braves. Like his brother did each morning to marvel at the sunrise, Nakahodot would do the same in the evenings watching the marvelous sunsets over the Sabine River valley. Every evening at dusk, young Nakahodot would find a good spot on a hillside and take in the wonderous beauty in the sky. His father would smile with pride at his dedication to such simple pleasures. When he could, his father would often join him in watching the sunsets. Nakahodot would wonder aloud where the sun went each night. "Father, why does the sun go down in one place and rise in the opposite direction?" he would ask.

"The sun moves around us," Caddo would explain, "you can see that, right? It rises in the east and moves across the sky during the day, then sets in the opposite direction in the west. We see the same movement of the stars and the moon at night."

This perplexed Nakahodot greatly, as it seemed where they lived the ground was always flat. "I wonder what it looks like underneath us when the sun goes around while we sleep."

"Who knows?" his father would always answer. "Imagining such things is an excellent way to tell stories around a fire, I always say."

Although they were twins, one could easily tell one brother from the other. Natchitos had long flowing dark hair just like his father. However, Nakahodot had long flowing hair that was fair and light in color and shimmered in the bright summer sun. When they were boys, the other young braves would tease him because of his light hair. Nakahodot would grow angry with them and defend himself fiercely despite the others playful teasing. Playful or not, he never did like it and his father would often have to step in to keep a brotherly scuffle from escalating.

"You should not tease your brother," Caddo scolded his other son and his friends. "Enough of this folly and get back to your chores."

One of the tasks of becoming a good hunter was to take care of the spears that were used. They needed to be sharpened on a regular basis for hunting wild game and for fishing.

Nakahodot and his brother went back to a pile of spears that awaited them. He shook his head dejectedly and grabbed one from the pile and began to file the spearhead. "I don't like you making fun of me," he told his brother. "You are always getting us into trouble. Now look at how many we must sharpen today."

Natchitos gave his brother a playful shove, "Move over and hand me one of those."

"You move over," Nakahodot retorted, "and give me some room. One of these days I am going to be chief and you will have to do what I say."

Natchitos laughed and said, "Well, today is not that day. Move over and give me that stone." He reached over and grabbed the filing stone that Nakahodot was using.

"Hey, I was using that!" Nakahodot griped. He quickly swiped it back from his brother. "Get your own."

Natchitos smiled and produced a filing stone of his own and grabbed one of the spears. "Who says you will be chief, anyway? Did you just come up with this yourself?"

Nakahodot answered very confidently, "Who else can it be? I am the oldest. End of story."

"Oldest?" Natchitos asked dumbfounded. "Ha! You are the funny one. You are not even a day older, if that. So, what of it?" He got to his feet and stood tall with his spear held tightly before him. "You do not even have dark hair. *I* will be chief." He thumped his chest with his fist and shouted, "I am Chief Natchitos, warrior of the rising sun!"

The same time Natchitos was putting on his manly display, three young squaws, Ayita, Calanele, and Taima were passing by carrying baskets of vegetables. Nakahodot had an idea and with a sly grin he gave his brother a quick shove while he placed the handle of the spear between his feet to trip him. Natchitos went tumbling to the ground and landed with a thud. Nakahodot began to laugh and point at him, saying, "No, you are the warrior with his face in the dirt!"

The girls giggled as they continued walking by. When Natchitos realized the girls had seen him fall to the ground, his face turned red with embarrassment. He quickly tried to redeem himself by throwing a handful of dirt at his brother but Nakahodot ducked out of the way easily as he continued laughing at him.

"Nice performance, brother," he chuckled some more. "You should do your act in front of the whole tribe one night."

"You keep laughing," Natchitos countered, as he got to his feet dusting off the dirt. "I will get you back one of these days."

Each year, the twin brothers continued to learn the ways of the Caddo with their father as their mentor. Chief Caddo was the mentor for many of the young braves in the tribe that were close to the age of becoming men. It was his duty to get them prepared to be leaders themselves. He taught them many different skills in farming and hunting, as well as how to build their homes from trees and grass thatch and mud. He and the elders of the tribe also taught them how to fight and defend themselves in case they were ever faced with battle. Each young brave became quite skilled with a bow and arrow as well as the spear. They taught them how to use daggers, or hand darts, to hunt small game. All the braves were tested carefully with each weapon on how to use them and how to hunt with stealth as to not alert their prey.

In the brothers fourteenth year, the chief decided it was time to take the young men on a great hunt far from home. It would be unlike the daily hunts they did near the village. It was early spring, and the wild game would be more plentiful in the warmer days. After another long winter, it was necessary to go hunting deep into the woods to replenish their supply of game for the tribe. The braves sat around a small fire early one morning, readying their weapons for the coming trek to find wild game.

"It is a fine, crisp morning we have," Chief Caddo commented as he observed each young brave in their tasks. "A good morning for a hunt." Atohi and two other elder braves, Tuari and Lanu, looked on as well. "Our brothers in the caravans tell of black bear and deer. The 'great spirit' may even lead us to buffalo."

Lanu raised an eyebrow at hearing this and asked the chief curiously, "Do you really think there will be buffalo this year?"

Caddo winked at him, so the boys would not see, "You never know, Lanu. This could be the year we come across a great herd."

"Yes. A great herd of buffalo awaits us somewhere out there," Lanu answered in understanding of Caddo's hopeful optimism. He knew better though. It was rare to see buffalo anywhere near the river in a such a warm and humid climate. He knew their best bet for large game would be deer and black bear.

"Have you ever seen buffalo, Father?" Nakahodot asked as he sharpened his spear. All the boys waited patiently for the chief's response. It was a question they were eager to hear him answer.

As the chief examined a quiver stocked with arrows, he calmly replied, "Of course, I have. I will never forget that day either. I was just a little older than you young braves are now." All of them stopped what they were doing, including the men, and listened to the chief's story. "There is a very sacred place, many days journey from here by foot. Perhaps you could reach it in three or four days on horseback. The forests on the way there are so thick in some parts, one can barely see the sun on a clear day. One day, long ago, I was on a hunt with my father and several other braves. We had walked for days in search of large game, but we were finding nothing, as the days were still long and dry and lingering on from a harsh winter. We walked and walked until we came upon a great clearing. From one moment to the next, the tall, thick forest was behind us. There, before us, was a beautiful, rolling green prairie as far as the crow flies. Before we could stop and take in all the beauty of this new land we had found, we heard the roar of thunder. The sky was clear though, the sun was shining brightly over our heads. In an instant, we saw an amazing sight. There before us was a great herd of buffalo who had also found this great stretch of land to graze upon."

The boys, and even the men began to murmur in awe of what a sight that would be. Nakahodot especially was most curious. "Is that really true, Father?"

"Oh yes, it is true," Atohi answered for Caddo. "I was with your father on that same hunt. He still has a buffalo hide of mine I have been trying to win back form him for years now." Everyone chuckled at knowing how fond the chief was of the betting games the men played.

"Ah," Caddo continued, "perhaps your luck will change one day, Atohi." He looked over at his son and answered, "Yes, the story is true. We were blessed with many buffalo that day. More than we could carry home, as I remember. So, yes. You never know when we might find another herd of those magnificent beasts. Until then, we must focus on what we do know in these areas. Rabbits, foxes and squirrels are necessary but keep a sharper eye out for deer and black bear."

One of the brother's closest friends, Tooantuh, smiled at hearing of the black bear. "I will be the first to find a black bear. Natchitos and I know the best place for it." He slapped Natchitos on the shoulder for reassurance. "Right?"

Natchitos nodded confidently, "Of course, we do."

"What do you know of black bear?" Nakahodot objected. "I do not think you are such an expert. I bet I can find a black bear before you can."

"No, I will!" shouted three other younger braves. They were Pakwa, son of Atohi, Ayashe, son of Lanu, and Tuwa, son of Tuari.

Caddo beamed at the braves enthusiasm. "I see we have some spirited competition going on already. That is good. One knows how soft a rabbit's pelt is, but a black bear? Oh, yes. A black bear skin is very soft as well. It would take a dozen rabbits to match one good black bear skin. I agree, this would be an excellent find for the hunt."

"Black bear are always a better prize in the fall just before they sleep for winter," Tuari reminded Chief Caddo. "Too scrawny in the spring."

Caddo nodded in agreement but countered, "The hungrier the bear, though, the harder the fight he will have in him. We must be alert, men. Never get caught in the wilderness alone. Always hunt together."

As the braves got to their feet, Nakahodot gathered his quiver filled with arrows and flung it over his shoulder. The quiver was made of carefully washed goat skin and laced intricately with equally strong leather strands. On one side of the long, narrow pouch were drawings of large game, including deer and bears. On the other side was a single drawing of a red buffalo.

"That is my quiver you have there, brother," Natchitos said casually. "You may borrow it for this hunt, if you like."

Nakahodot frowned at him. It was a conversation he was tired of having. "It is *not* your quiver. I made it myself and put my markings on the side. The red buffalo shows that it is mine. It shows power and strength, just like me."

Natchitos disagreed, saying, "No, mine was the one with the red buffalo. Yours was the one with the tiny little frog on the side, because you hop around like this." He crouched low to the ground and began to hop around like a frog and make the sound of one as well. All the other braves laughed at his antics. "You always let the squaws order you around. You hop at their every command." Natchitos kept hopping around, making fun of his brother.

"Stop your teasing," Nakahodot complained as he shoved his brother over. Natchitos rolled on the ground still laughing at him. "You do not even know how to make the red color to paint the buffalo. You would not even know how to find the right flowers to make the color."

Natchitos sat on his rear end, still laughing at his own theatrics and began pretending he was gathering flower petals. "He picks the little flowers and puts the petals in his light hair..." The braves laughed even harder at his teasing.

Nakahodot's face turned bright red as he became more and more angry and embarrassed. He leaped on his brother like a panther. Natchitos braced himself but kept laughing. "Oh no, the blonde toad is leaping again!" He fended off his brother and they both went rolling over the ground. The other boys looked on laughing like hyenas. Caddo noticed what was going on and stepped in, barking at his second son, "Enough! Get on your feet." The boys immediately obeyed their father and stood motionless, staring at the ground. "Now let us go hunt like men. It is time to put this kind of foolishness behind you."

Caddo looked over the braves one last time. When he was satisfied that they were ready, he motioned toward the squaws. Aiyana and several other squaws were waiting patiently for the chief to signal they were ready. They brought them plenty of food and water skins to carry with them to last them during the hunt. "We will go then, yes?" All the braves and elders nodded. "Alright. Let us go hunting."

The hunt began and as the hours passed, the braves were finding some good catches in rabbit and squirrel. Pakwa was the first to strike a deer. Atohi smiled with pride in seeing how skilled his son was with a bow and arrow. Caddo noticed as well, the young braves exceptional skills.

Nakahodot and Natchitos were exceptional at having a keen eye and spotting prey even in the thickest of brush. They were becoming excellent trackers and could point out a target for the other men to take aim. Caddo beamed with pride as he watched the younger generation in his tribe sharpen the skills he and the elders had taught them.

As the day wore on, they had many kills and the tally was growing for them to take back to the village, but still they hadn't come across any black bear. The braves began to hunt in pairs but kept within sight of the other hunters as they traversed the forest. Nakahodot walked with his father as they slowly continued the hunt. His mind wandered as they walked, and he thought about many things. He thought about the story his father had told them about the buffalo.

"Father," he asked, "what was sacred about the land where you found the buffalo? Was it because of the great hunt that day?"

"No," Caddo replied in a hushed voice. "We learned that the land was sacred to all our Hasinai brothers. In ancient times, our ancestors did not leave the deceased in the forest as an offering to the 'great spirit' as we do now. Holy men would instruct the warriors to place their deceased on the ground outside of the trees in a clearing. Then they would gather the ground around them. When another would pass away, they would place them on the same ground next to the first and gather more Earth around both the deceased, and so on and so on. People would bring offerings, such as personal belongings like a dagger or pottery and bury them along with the dead, so they could use them in the afterlife. Soon, as more went on to the 'great spirit', the mounds would become higher and wider."

Nakahodot listened intently. His thirst for knowledge was always insatiable and he was eager to learn more. "You actually saw this ancient place?"

"Yes," Caddo continued, "we had come across one of these sacred mounds. That is why we took care not to hunt on the burials, but away from them. When the elders saw the mounds, they gave us explicit instructions to leave them undisturbed. If we would do this, our hunt would be blessed."

"I would like to see this great place," Nakahodot thought aloud. Then something else occurred to him. "Father, why do we not practice this type of burial any longer?"

Caddo thought for a moment in answering his inquisitive son. "No one knows why cultures change throughout the centuries, but we must do as we are shown. But we also show respect and reverence to those who have gone before us, even if their ways sound foreign to us."

Suddenly, Caddo stopped walking and held up his fist to signal the others to stop and be silent. He sensed something, or someone, in the area.

Nakahodot's heart began to pound in his chest. He had no idea what had alerted his father. "Bear?" he whispered.

Caddo looked all around through the dense forest in the late afternoon sun. Without warning, an arrow came zipping through air and splintered into a tree only feet away. He put up his arm to keep his son from advancing. "Stay here. I must see of this." He walked over to the tree and pulled the arrow out and examined it. He immediately recognized it and said to himself, "Nadaco." He called out to his son and told him to spread the word. "It is the Nadaco."

Caddo stood and waited patiently for the chief to make himself known. Caddo knew they must have been following them for quite some time.

From the thick trees emerged a young warrior no more than twenty years of age. He wore a single hawks feather on his head band. Caddo recognized the young brave immediately.

"Lahote, it is I, Chief Caddo." He observed him carefully. There was a change in the young man since the last time he had seen him that he knew that could only be of great significance. Lahote stepped closer and stood only about ten feet away from the chief. "I see the boy I knew in the man before me. Greetings. I hear in the winds from our brothers that you are now chief. I built a sacred fire to honor your father when I learned the news of his death."

Several other members of the Nadaco tribe emerged from the woods behind Lahote. Caddo's hunting party also arrived to greet the other tribe. Caddo handed the arrow back to Lahote who quickly slipped it into his quiver. The young warrior finally spoke. "I am Lahote, chief of the Nadaco. Greetings to you great Caddo."

"We ask your permission to hunt in your forest," Caddo answered. "We bring offerings to share with you." He motioned for Atohi to bring some of their catch. Atohi brought three rabbits and gave them to Caddo. "Please accept this offering. Let us build a fire so we may share them. Come, sit with us."

Lahote raised his hand to decline. "There is no need. We accept your offering though. You may continue your hunt and have safe passage back to your village. Instead, I come to give you a warning."

Caddo looked at him curiously. He was not accustomed to another chief turning down a friendly meal during a hunt to celebrate the catch. "What is this warning?" he asked.

Lahote did not hesitate and answered firmly, "Word is spreading from our brothers to the south and the east. The white explorers are being seen with more frequency in their lands. Have you seen the white men?"

"I have only heard stories from my own elders of times past. In all my days I have never seen such a man."

"It is my advice that we do not take up with these white men. We cannot let them come and steal our crops and horses. I hear this is all that the white man comes for. I ask that you send word if there ever is a time you see such men." Lahote had one of his men come and take the offering of rabbit. "I will do the same for you if that day comes."

Caddo was bewildered with the young warrior's impatience. He felt as if he was withholding something. "Have you encountered the white man in such a way? Did they take things from you?"

Lahote responded, "I have not, but I feel the day is coming."

This astonished Caddo greatly. He was perplexed at how a chief could come to a conclusion so hastily. He feared something had happened to his Nadaco brothers. He asked Lahote, "How can you make such a decision if you have never seen nor spoken with a white man?"

Lahote side-stepped the question however and answered, "The talk is becoming louder about these intruders. I will fight to protect my people from them. I urge you to be just as vigilant."

He motioned for his braves to turn back. "I have given you the word I came to deliver. We will leave you in peace, Chief Caddo." With that, Lahote and his men disappeared into the woods.

Caddo stood dumbfounded as he watched the men walk away. He undoubtedly knew his own men and sons were waiting for his response to such an unusual encounter. He quietly contemplated what had transpired and decided to keep his thoughts on the matter private for the time being. He turned to his hunting party and they all stared at each other in silence, eagerly awaiting him to speak. It was not the way they had expected their hunt would end. Caddo observed the tally of what remained of their catch and nodded with satisfaction. "That is enough for today," he finally told them. "We will head back to our village."

Chapter 2

Spring had returned in earnest alongside the river. Caddo had discussed with the tribe elders the events that occurred in the forest with the Nadaco, but nothing more was decided on the matter. The weather was ideal and there was much work to be done. The tribe was busy each day preparing the lands that surrounded them for the new crops. While the men worked in the fields, squaws busily cooked meals, fetched water, and cleaned pelts and set them out to dry.

As Caddo's wife, Aiyana, worked hard in the mid-morning sun, she heard a familiar sound in the air high above their beehive-shaped homes. She stopped scrubbing the fresh rabbit pelts for a moment and looked up into the sky, shading her eyes. A smile appeared on her face and her spirits lifted at the sound of the birds chirping as they sailed overhead. She got to her feet and looked around for one of her sons. She spotted Nakahodot carrying some brush from a nearby field and called out to him. "Naka, come here! I have a small job for you." He immediately trotted toward his mother carrying the brush under his arm.

Tooantuh saw Nakahodot run to go help his mother and shook his head. "There he goes again. Running off at the sound of any squaws command," he said to Natchitos.

"Let him be," Natchitos shot back. "My mother is not any squaw. You know that. If it is my mother that calls him, then he should go. What would my father say if we disobeyed our mother?"

Tooantuh was not convinced though. "He still runs off to do women's work. No young squaw will respect that. My father says it is almost time that we must choose a squaw. Believe me, I would not let Ayita see me doing women's work."

Natchitos knew it was futile to try and argue with his friend. He slapped him on the arm and said, "So, it is true then. You have your eyes set on Ayita." Tooantuh nodded proudly. "A very nice choice, indeed. I would not worry about my brother though. Forget it and let him be. Come on, let us go."

Nakahodot approached his mother and asked, "What is it?"

"Remember the long pole you cut for me from the tree I had you take down last winter?" Nakahodot recalled what she was referring to and nodded. "It is time to stand it up in front of our hut. Out in the open. I will help you dig a hole for it."

Caddo noticed his wife and son digging a hole to erect the long piece of wood lying next to them on the ground. "Ah, my beautiful bride wishes to brighten our village even more, does she not? I have seen the swallows as well, my wife. Your eyes are sharp as they are beautiful." Aiyana gave him a playful wink and a smile.

"Naka," Aiyana said, "go and fetch the gourds that we hollowed out last fall. We will lash them to the top." Her son obeyed and immediately ran to go get the gourds.

Caddo looked around for more help. He spotted his other son and Tooantuh. "You men, come over here and help." They quickly dropped what they were doing and ran over to the chief. "Once the gourds are lashed, carefully lift and place it in the hole." The boys did as he said and slowly raised the long pole with its gourds fastened to the top and slid the pole into the ground. "Fill the dirt around it so it can stand tall and firm."

Caddo put his arm around his wife and commended her. "You will bring the purple swallows back to our village. I think this is a fine idea. It has been years since we have done this. A wonderful idea, indeed."

"They will bring good fortune with their colorful plumage and their delightful chattering," Aiyana beamed. "I have missed that lovely sound. Our crops will be blessed this year, and this will give our feathered friends a wonderful new home."

After the martin gourds were raised and the job was done, many came around to observe and admire the small tower that was built for the arrival of the birds.

Natchitos gave Tooantuh a playful jab in the shoulder and said to him, "You are good at women's work." Tooantuh laughed and punched him back.

Nakahodot came up to them and commented, "I have asked father if we can go on our own hunt after the work is done."

Tooantuh looked at him surprised. "*You* asked this?"

"Yes," Nakahodot answered. "Are you not disappointed we did not find any black bear? I think we should go and hunt again."

"Father said we can do this on our own?" Natchitos asked curiously.

"Yes," he said again. "Are you coming or not? We will see who will be first to bring home a bear."

Tooantuh and Natchitos were both impressed with his courage. "I think this a good idea," Tooantuh said. "The sooner we get our work done, the sooner we can go find out who is the best at hunting bear."

After their chores were done, the braves set out on their hunt for black bear. Pakwa, Ayashe and Tuwa went along with them. Tooantuh instinctively took to the front and led the trek.

"How do you know where you are taking us?" Tuwa asked him.

"My father has shown me the area where it is known for black bears. We must look for signs of them on the forest floor. Look for tracks and scat as well."

Pakwa laughed and said, "We will look for the tracks and let Naka look for the scat."

Nakahodot picked up some mud and flung it at Pakwa. "Hey, I found some. Here, catch it!" Before he could jump out of the way, the mud splattered all over Pakwa's vest. He looked appalled and recoiled in disgust thinking he had bear scat all over him. Nakahodot laughed out loud and said, "Oh, I am sorry. Maybe that was just some mud." The rest of the boys laughed at Pakwa as well.

"Keep quiet," Tooantuh instructed. "We are getting near I think." He stopped by one of the tall pine trees and observed the trunk. "Look at the claw marks on the tree." Indeed, the tree had many long claw-like scratches and scrapes in the bark. The other braves grew nervous at seeing the first real evidence of a bear. "I think we should split into groups of three. Keep a sharp eye in every direction and be very quiet. Pakwa, you go with Ayashe and Tuwa. Naka, you come with us."

As the braves stalked farther into the forest for bears, the trees and brush became denser. The tall pines towered high above, easily reaching as high as fifty feet. The wind gently pushed the treetops in the hot afternoon breeze and the branches crackled overhead as they swayed from side to side.

Tooantuh signaled to Nakahodot and whispered, "Go and check that out-cropping over there. We will go look by these rocks. Stay low and quiet." When Nakahodot was out of sight, Tooantuh said to Natchitos, "Come. We know exactly where to go now."

"We must be careful," Natchitos warned, "we do not want to scare him too much."

"I know. We are just having a little fun. Come on, this way."

Nakahodot looked over the small out-cropping but saw nothing. He decided to go back to where he had left his brother and Tooantuh, but when he arrived, they were nowhere to be seen. He crouched to the ground and put his hand to his chin. He wondered to himself why they would leave him alone when they knew they should all stay together during a hunt. *They are hiding from me on purpose*, he thought to himself. He stood and continued searching for them. He found the pile of rocks that Tooantuh had mentioned before. He observed the ground to look for their tracks and determine their direction.

As he followed their tracks, he came to a small incline that was covered with brown leaves and pine straw. At the bottom of the incline there appeared to be a wall of vines and vegetation of all kinds growing everywhere. The ground was rocky and muddy and was harder to get good footing. As he got closer, he saw that the vines were covering the side of a small hill. Then he noticed a small jagged entrance amongst the vines and rocks to what appeared to be a cave.

He stopped at the entrance of the cave and looked at it curiously. He hesitated at going in and decided to call out for his brother. He whispered as loudly as he could, "*Natchitos.*" He stepped closer to the cave entrance and whispered again, "Tooantuh?" At seeing how dark it was inside the cave, he decided that his companions couldn't have possibly gone in. He carefully studied the ground some more and saw their moccasin tracks at the entrance. *Maybe they did go in there*, he thought to himself.

He took a deep breath and decided to look inside the cave. Just as he stepped into the cave entrance, he heard a rustling sound behind him. He heard the paws of an animal slowly tromping through the leaves and straw on the slope. Nakahodot froze in place and turned his head slightly to see what it was. To his surprise, it was not an adult bear as he suspected, but two small black bear cubs. The curious little animals stopped when they saw Nakahodot and clumsily stood on their hind feet before tumbling over and rolling on their bellies. The small cubs let out a faint cry as they steadied themselves once again on their paws. Nakahodot smiled at their playfulness, but then a look of horror seized him. In the depths of the cave, he heard the low echo of a deep-throated growl. He knew in an instant it could only be the mother of the two cubs.

"Oh, no," he said out loud and quickly stepped out of the cave. "You fool, you are caught right in between them." His hands shook and sweat poured down his face. He took one step to the side to not alarm the little cubs any more than they were already. "I will let you two and your mother be."

He took one more step away when suddenly someone came dashing out of the cave. Nakahodot was shocked to see his brother dart past the cubs and straight up the incline. The cubs cried out loudly in fright as he raced by. In a flash, Tooantuh burst forth from the cave as well, running as fast he could.

"*Run, you fool.* Run!" he shouted.

Instinctively, Nakahodot made a mad dash in the same direction as Tooantuh and Natchitos. Before he knew it, a large adult black bear came pounding out of the cave, snarling and growling as she ran right behind him. Nakahodot shrieked in terror as the bear chased him up the hill. It was all he could do to keep her from catching him. He was astonished at how fast the big bear could run. As he ran past the piles of rocks, he saw from the corner of his eye both braves hiding behind them. He thought for a second the bear would turn to pursue them, but to his dismay she kept right on him.

"Keep running, Naka!" Natchitos shouted after him. "Find somewhere to hide. Play like you are dead!"

"Play like you are *what*?" Nakahodot shouted back at them as he raced past. He panicked as he heard the deep snarling and heavy breathing of the bear as it kept right on his heels. His eyes darted everywhere in the thick forest for a place to escape the agitated beast. He soon spotted a thick pine tree partially leaning over at an angle. He quickly ascended the tree and within seconds was over twenty feet above the ground.

"No!" Tooantuh shouted after him, laughing somewhat as he did. "Not up a *tree*."

Nakahodot, thinking he was safe, looked over his shoulder and shouted back, "Why *not*?"

Before they could answer, the angry bear had started climbing the tree right after him. Nakahodot's eyes widened in terror.

"*That* is why!" the boys yelled in unison.

The bear snarled and swiped at the branches as she quickly ascended the tree. Nakahodot looked about frantically for a way to escape. He was too high to jump and there were no lower branches to get to easily. In his panic, he had almost forgotten about his bow and quiver of arrows still flung over his shoulder. In his tight confinement, he desperately tried to pull the bow around and grab an arrow from his quiver.

Tooantuh grabbed Natchitos by the arm and yanked him to his feet. "Come on. I am afraid we have gotten your brother in a bad position. We need to shoot the bear."

"But what about the cubs?" Natchitos countered.

"No time to argue. We must move now."

As they dashed around the pile of boulders, they saw Nakahodot docking an arrow on his bow. Natchitos and Tooantuh both readied their bows and stealthily began to sneak up on the bear. The raging bear clawed at Nakahodot's feet as he desperately tried to stay just out of reach and to keep from dropping his bow. He braced himself as best he could and finally pulled back on his bow to strike the bear, when suddenly he heard his friends yelling down below, trying to get the bear's attention.

Natchitos and Tooantuh froze in their tracks when they saw Tuwa and Pakwa both struggling to hold a bear cub in each of their arms. They held the young bears high in the air, yelling for the mother's attention. The little ones squealed in their arms and flailed about. The mother bear growled in anger and immediately scampered down the tree. Nakahodot let out a huge sigh of relief as the bear landed on the ground with a tremendous thump. Tuwa and Pakwa flung the cubs safely to their feet and the little ones hastily scampered away. The two boys quickly darted in the opposite direction and hid behind the boulders along with Natchitos and Tooantuh. Just as they were hoping, the mother bear padded after her two cubs and caught up to them in an instant. Soon, the three bears headed farther into the forest away from the braves.

Natchitos patted Tuwa on the shoulder, "Quick thinking, you two."

Pakwa shook his head and added, "That was crazy. Those cubs are *tough* little ones. Look at how they scratched my arms. And he was *heavy*."

"It was very heavy and *mad*," Tuwa added. "I am not doing *that* again."

The boys emerged from behind the boulders just as Nakahodot was climbing down from the tree. Natchitos called out to his brother, "Naka, are you alright?"

"How did he end up in that tree anyhow?" Ayashe asked. "What happened?"

"They played a trick on me," Nakahodot answered. "I am fine though, but she scratched my leg." The boys looked at his leg and saw a small cut was just above his ankle. There was a single trail of blood trickling down to his foot. "I am lucky you two came along when you did. I was prepared to kill her even though I did not want to. The cubs would have been orphaned."

"We will take you down to the creek, so you can wash your leg," Natchitos suggested. "We should not speak of this to my father, though. Does everyone agree? Father would surely take a stick to me if he hears we are out here teasing a bear and playing stupid tricks on one another." He glared at Tooantuh and punched him in the shoulder. "And how do we explain how scratched they are?"

Tooantuh tried to act innocent and responded, "It was all in good fun. He did not get hurt. Good thing you are the fastest runner in the village, right Naka?"

The braves all laughed at his joke, including Nakahodot. Natchitos was not laughing, however. He stepped closer to Tooantuh and shook his fist at him. "I said, does everyone agree?"

"Alright, we agree," Tooantuh answered. "Calm down and put your fist away."

"It is alright, brother," Nakahodot assured him. "No one is hurt, and we will not speak of it. We will say we got caught in some thorns. Let us go to the creek and then go home."

Despite the incident with the bear and knowing that his brother and the other braves had tricked him, Nakahodot was very keen on being competitive with them. He enjoyed the games they had at seeing who was the most skilled with a bow and arrow and with the spear.

One day after their work was done, the braves gathered around a large oak tree. The massive, sprawling, majestic tree stood over forty feet tall and its branches spread just as far all around it. Its mighty trunk was as round as five men and it made an excellent target for spear practice.

The six braves took turns at throwing spears at the center of the trunk from twenty paces back. Soon, a small gathering of spectators came to watch them as well, including the young squaws, Calanele, Ayita and Taima.

Nakahodot noticed Calanele right away, the squaw with which he held favor. He had been asking her ceaselessly for months if she would take a walk with him during the sunset, but each time she would give him an excuse not to. It frustrated him especially when the other braves would mock him for not ever getting her to say yes to him.

Tooantuh stood first to throw. "The center where the branches meet," he instructed. "The closest to the center wins." He was challenged by Pakwa first. Tooantuh was unquestionably the best at throwing a spear, so he was happy to accept a challenge from any of them. He would compete against them all to prove his superiority. He easily out-placed Pakwa, then Ayashe as well. Tuwa gave him a harder challenge but Tooantuh prevailed over him too.

Nakahodot knew his turn was coming but he was ever distracted by the presence of Calanele. She knew he was staring at her, but she pretended not to notice him. He tried to get her attention and whispered to her, "Calanele, will you walk with me this night?" She smiled slightly and turned away as if she hadn't heard him. He asked her again but louder this time. "Calanele, will you walk with me this night?"

Her face blushed in knowing the other squaws had heard him and she retorted, "Not if you throw badly, I will not." The other squaws giggled to themselves.

Natchitos motioned for him to take his turn. "It is your throw, brother. Step up."

Nakahodot's face was red with frustration and embarrassment. He studied the tree and saw that Tooantuh had struck just off-center of the tree. He concentrated on the tree and the spot he was aiming and steadied the spear in his hand.

Before he was about to throw, he heard Taima giggle under her breath, "Do not throw badly, Naka, or no romantic sunset." All the squaws and even the braves began to laugh heartily.

Nakahodot was flush with embarrassment. He angrily flung the spear as hard as he could. To his surprise, and to everyone else's, the spear thumped into the tree just inside Tooantuh's. He stood proudly as the crowd clapped for his excellent shot. Tooantuh was left shocked that he had been defeated.

"Nice throw, brother," Natchitos commended him. "Maybe your luck will change yet. But first you must face me now."

"Gladly," Nakahodot replied, his pride restored. "Take your best aim."

Natchitos sank his spear right into the center of the tree and he smiled in triumph. As his brother stepped to the line, their father approached the small gathering to watch the competition. Nakahodot took aim and threw his spear and it thumped precisely next to the other spear.

"They are even!" Caddo exclaimed. "Excellent throws, indeed. They must continue then until there is a winner. This time with a bow and arrow." He was encouraged to see the boys competing with one another and sharpening their hunting skills. More of the tribe gathered to watch the boys compete.

The two brothers looked at each other confidently. "We are getting a larger audience now, brother," Natchitos said. "Do not let them get you nervous."

"I would not dream of it," Nakahodot responded coolly. "Perhaps that is your worry."

"Now I will win my quiver back."

Naka smiled, saying, "You mean, if you win. And besides, my quiver is not yours to win."

"We shall see. I will shoot first." Natchitos took aim with his bow and zipped an arrow directly in the center of the tree. He looked over his shoulder and smiled proudly at Taima. She smiled sweetly back at him.

Next was Nakahodot. He shot his arrow and it landed equally next to his brothers.

"They are equal again," Caddo nodded proudly. "Now you will try your skill at a moving target. Come this way." The large gathering followed the two young men and the chief over to the area where the chickens were kept. Caddo observed the small collection of hens that were walking and cackling about. He pointed with his finger and told them, "The one with the black feet, make that hen your target. Hit that one and you can have a feast with your friends tonight by the fire."

Natchitos stepped forward to take the first shot. He stood about twenty paces away and followed the black-footed hen with his arrow aimed. The hen ran from side to side, pecking and clucking as she went. Finally, he took a deep breath and exhaled and then let his arrow fly. The arrow skipped off the ground at the hen's feet. The bird jumped away, cackling and flapping its wings wildly.

"Naka," Caddo commanded, "now it is your turn."

Without anyone seeing, Tooantuh snuck into the hen-house with an empty water skin. Nakahodot stepped forward and took aim at the same hen. He followed it closely as it darted back and forth in the enclosure. Tooantuh blew air into the skin until he had a nice round balloon. He smiled fiendishly as he took out his dagger and quickly jabbed the water-skin balloon. The loud bang sent the hens into a frenzy. Chickens, wings and feathers went flying everywhere. Even the crowd watching was startled at the loud noise. Some of the hens were so frightened that they flew right out of the pen, including the one with black feet.

Nakahodot kept his composure though and kept his arrow trained on the frantic chicken. The bird flew all over the courtyard, up and down and side to side. It flew behind him and landed on the ground and then up high in the air again. Nakahodot whirled around with his arrow, keeping dead aim at the mad chicken. The spectators gasped and ducked as the bird flew between them and Nakahodot's weapon, yet he kept his focus. Soon, it jumped one last time toward the pen and Nakahodot fired. In the blink of an eye, the arrow zipped and plunked right into the chicken in mid-air. The hen squawked loudly before landing on the dirt with a thud.

Makane, the tribe's medicine man and keeper of the chickens, came rushing out of his hut and yelled at the crowd and at Tooantuh, "Why are you scaring all my hens this way? Away all of you. Look what you have done!"

"That is enough for now," Caddo asserted. "My apologies, great Makane. We will gather them for you."

After the chickens settled and were back in their pen, Tooantuh's parents took him home to scold him. Caddo chuckled at his antics and shook his head as Tooantuh's mother dragged him away by the ear. Caddo looked at his two sons proudly and said, "You two competed well. I am proud of both of you."

"Thank you, Father," Nakahodot replied.

"I am glad everyone watching survived," Caddo joked.

Later that evening as the sun was going down, Nakahodot sat in the hut with his mother. "Why are you not at the fire with your friends celebrating with the feast?"

"I did not want anymore," he answered in a pouting voice. "They are always making fun of me, even in front of the squaws. I just get tired of it. The squaws even laugh at me."

"They were not laughing at you after you won today. Even the young squaws clapped for you."

"Yes, but they were laughing and teasing me before that," he complained. "Calanele thinks I am just silly. I cannot do anything right for her."

His mother shook her head and answered, "I do not think that at all. In fact, I think she is very taken with you."

"With me?" he asked flummoxed.

"I have eyes, do I not? I have seen the way she looks at you. I know what that look means, Naka. It is the look of a young woman who wants to walk by your side."

Nakahodot looked dejected and confused. "Believe me, Mother. I have tried to ask her that very thing many times, but she always tells me no."

Just then, he heard a voice call out to him from outside the hut. "Naka, are you there?"

He quickly got to his feet and opened the flap. He was pleasantly surprised to see Calanele standing outside. "Yes, I am here, Calanele."

"I will walk with you this night," she said firmly.

Nakahodot, looking stunned, turned to his mother who was smiling broadly. She cleverly asked, "You were saying?" She got to her feet and said, "I will get my shawl."

"*Mother*," he hissed at her, "she does not need a shawl."

"It is not for her, silly. It is for me. Come on, let us not keep her waiting." Nakahodot rolled his eyes. He should have known he would have a chaperone.

As the brilliant sunset sprawled colorfully across the evening sky, Calanele and Nakahodot walked slowly together down a path by the river. They made small talk with one another and enjoyed the beautiful display as they walked. Following close behind them a few paces back, were their mothers, plus nine more elder squaws from the village.

Chapter 3

It was late spring that same year and the purple martins were fluttering about the gourds, chirping happily and circling high above in the crisp, early morning air.

It was an especially anxious morning for one brave in particular, though. As he was the eldest of the braves who were close to coming of age, Tooantuh would be the first to ask permission to marry.

Natchitos and Nakahodot sat together outside their family's hut watching the birds circle and swoop all around the village, catching their morning meal of flying insects. They noticed Tooantuh walking swiftly, yet nervously across the village. They called out to him, "Tooantuh, come sit with us," but the young brave kept walking without looking up, as if he were on a mission.

Nakahodot suspected this could be the morning that Tooantuh had been dreading. "Will he ask Ayita's father today for permission to marry her?" he asked his brother.

"If he does, then that means our day is not far off," Natchitos answered.

"Do you think he will do it? I mean, what if he decides not to?"

Natchitos shook his head and replied, "I do not know. But his father will surely hear of it if he had already granted him permission to seek a wife. His mother will certainly hear of it. I hope for his sake that he gathers his courage."

Nakahodot looked deflated, as if he were the one being put to the nerve-wracking task. "So, we will have to do this?"

Natchitos chuckled and sympathized with his brother by patting him on the back, saying, "Do not worry, brother. You will not have to do it today. A few more walks with Calanele and you will be eager for the day to ask permission."

"Are you certain? You do not seem nervous at all."

"Of course, I am certain. You know the squaws talk amongst themselves just as we do. She likes you, brother. Do not worry. I have known for a long time that Taima is the one I will seek permission to marry. I am quite eager to speak to her father, Running Wolf. If only father would give me permission."

"You make it sound so easy," Nakahodot whined. "Just thinking of doing what Tooantuh is doing right now makes my stomach hurt." Natchitos laughed out loud at him.

Tooantuh gathered the courage to enter the home of his friend Ayashe to speak with his father, Lanu, to ask him for his daughter Ayita's hand in marriage. Tooantuh knew that the answer would not be given right away. If Lanu were to give his permission, on the third day, Tooantuh would find blessings outside his door. The waiting of the three days was more agonizing than asking the question itself.

Word spread quickly, and it seemed the entire tribal village was eagerly awaiting Lanu's decision. On the third morning, the restless Tooantuh emerged from his home to find blessings outside his door. The wedding proceeded, and the entire tribe gathered at the center of the village to watch the young couple marry beneath the gourds and the chattering swallows. A great celebration of food and dancing at the tribal fire followed and Tooantuh was relieved that he could finally take his new bride, Ayita, into his home.

Six months had passed, and the day arrived that the twin brothers finally came of age. The long hot summer gave way to a welcoming cool air. Aiyana was busy hanging pelts outside to let them air out. She coughed from time to time in the brisk air but continued working. Caddo slowly emerged in the early morning, stretching his back.

"As I get older, the harder the ground becomes," he complained to his wife.

"That is why I am fluffing out these pelts for you, my husband," Aiyana answered sweetly. She coughed a few more times as she hung another fox pelt.

Caddo hugged her shoulder and said, "You are always thinking of me."

"And your back."

He noticed how she kept coughing and said, "The cold air is bothering you? Shall I have one of the boys fetch a water skin for you?"

"No, I am fine. It will go away soon." She walked over to Caddo after she finished the last of the pelts. "You know your sons will be asking to sit down with you today."

"For what reason?" Caddo asked, feigning ignorance.

She placed her hands on her hips and countered, "Do not be nonsensical. You know how important this is to them. I want you to be serious. You are the chief and their father."

He chuckled at her impatience with him. "I know, my sweet wife. I have been waiting eagerly for this day too. I just hope they are brave enough to come."

"Oh, do not you worry about that," she assured him.

As Caddo and Aiyana expected, both brothers appeared soon to speak to him. It was customary to begin the inquest of approval at first light, so to have enough time to discuss their intentions with both their father and the father of their intended betrothed. To keep them waiting any longer into the day would show a sign of unwillingness to marry and disrespect to that family. Caddo had wondered why they were not in the hut when he and his wife awoke. He could only attribute their early departure to mere restlessness.

The two brothers approached their father and mother. "Father," Natchitos said, "I wish to speak with you."

Caddo keenly observed his other son and asked him, "And you?"

Nakahodot nodded reluctantly, saying, "I wish to speak to you too."

"Very well. We will talk inside. Come." Aiyana watched impatiently with a nervous smile as her sons followed Caddo into their home.

The three men sat around the small fire in the center of their home. "Sleepless night, was it for both of you?"

"It was sleepless for me," Nakahodot admitted. "He only came with me to keep me calm."

"Calm?" Caddo asked curiously, as if he didn't know why. "What is it that has you so uneasy?"

Natchitos couldn't wait for his brother to answer. He was about to burst. He was more than ready to ask his father's permission. "I want to marry Taima, Father," he blurted out. "I have come to ask your permission to speak with her father, Nashoba."

"Is that so? You are the eager one, are you not?" Caddo asked, trying his best to conceal his joy. He was elated with each second of the moment. He picked up the traditional calumet, something that was normally reserved for only the smoking hut, but today he had brought it over to their home to share with his sons. "Nashoba, the one that is called Running Wolf. He is not an easy man to convince. Are you sure Taima is the one you wish to marry?"

"Yes, Father. I am quite sure," Natchitos answered.

Caddo lifted the pipe before him and replied, "Then let us smoke on this agreement. I give you permission to speak with Nashoba." He took a long draw on the pipe and then handed it to Natchitos, and he did the same. Nakahodot observed them quietly as they smoked. He knew his turn was coming, if only he could muster the courage to ask.

Caddo turned to this other son and asked, "You wished to speak to me as well, my son?"

Nakahodot's hands shook as his nerves overtook his emotions. "Yes, Father. I...I do wish to speak to you." He hesitated some more and looked over at his brother. Natchitos nodded, urging him to continue.

"Go on," Caddo said, urging him as well.

"I...I would like your permission," he paused again, sweat beading on his forehead, "your permission to speak with Atohi."

Caddo nodded after his son finally got the question out. "For what reason do you ask this of me? Atohi is my closest companion. He will surely want to know why you seek an audience with him."

"Calanele," Nakahodot finally said. "I am in love with her. There is nothing I want more in this world than to make her my wife." Caddo beamed with pride in hearing his son's heartfelt words. "I ask for your permission to speak with her father, Atohi." Natchitos was surprised at his brother's newfound candor, but he smiled at him and wished he had used the same words as he did.

Caddo raised the pipe and said to Nakahodot, "Your words are sincere and the 'great spirit' has given you the courage to speak them. Let us smoke on this agreement. I give you permission to speak with Atohi." Caddo took another long draw from the pipe and then handed it to his son who did the same.

The two brothers immediately left to seek out the respective homes of Nashoba and Atohi. In no time, Natchitos asked Nashoba for his daughter's hand in marriage. Nakahodot, on the other hand, was more deliberate in his approach to Atohi. He finally opened the flap to Atohi's home and peered inside but saw that no one was there. He began to worry that Atohi may have become offended by being made to wait. He ran behind the hut and nearly bumped into Atohi who was drinking some water.

"You seem to be in a hurry this morning, Naka," Atohi said gruffly.

"I am sorry for running into you," Nakahodot clumsily responded.

"What has you in such a rush?"

"I was hoping to speak with you, if I may."

Atohi set the water skin down and looked Nakahodot over. "I was about to go down to the river for some fishing. Do you have your father's permission to speak with me?"

"Yes, Atohi. He has just given his permission. May I speak with you?"

Atohi took him by the arm and said, "Come with me to the river." They began walking toward the river as the sun rose over the horizon. "Your father has been my closest friend my entire life. He is a great leader of the Caddo. We have known each other since we were boys, just as you and Pakwa."

Nakahodot nodded and responded, "Yes, I enjoy hearing the stories that you and father tell of those days."

They stopped by the river and Nakahodot helped him prepare his fishing nets. "What is it that you wish to speak to me about?" Atohi asked.

Nakahodot cleared his throat, and said, "I came to ask for your permission to marry Calanele."

Atohi stopped what he was doing and seemed surprised at his question. "You wish to marry Calanele?"

"Yes, I do. I care for her very much."

Atohi smiled at him and said, "You find yourself in a unique position, do you not?"

"I do not understand."

Atohi continued, "I love my brother, Caddo. He is my friend and my chief, but I do not admire the decision he must make before he passes on to the 'great spirit'." Nakahodot suddenly knew what he was referring to. It was a question he had not given much thought until this moment. "You and Natchitos are twins. Whom do you suppose your father will choose to be his successor?"

"That is up to my father," Nakahodot answered. "I am prepared to do his will whatever he decides. I am proud to be his son and I will honor him regardless, but my first intention is to be a good husband to Calanele."

42

"You speak like a man now. It is good to see this. You are right that your family comes first, but you must also remember as chief, the entire tribe is your family as well." Atohi tossed the fishing net into the water and nodded in approval at its placement. He turned to Nakahodot and said, "You have given the answer I wanted to hear. I see wisdom in you. You will be a good husband indeed, Naka. I give you my permission to marry Calanele."

After three days, the two brothers found blessings outside their home from both families. After the great celebration of Caddo's twin son's wedding, they were permitted to take their wives into their homes.

Chapter 4

After their double-wedding, the twin brothers and their wives were rarely seen, if at all. It became an amusing episode with lines of well-wishers coming by to visit the newlyweds but instead ended up leaving food and drink outside their huts. Many would joke amongst themselves about how busy the four of them must be to not even come out for a little while.

Aiyana shook her head as she sat with her husband, saying, "I think your sons are enjoying married life." Caddo cracked a faint smile at hearing her comment on such a thing. "A little too much if you ask me. We have not seen them for weeks."

"How soon you forget, my wife," Caddo recalled. "No one saw us for a whole month after our wedding. My father had to finally talk me out with promises of a great hunt."

"That sounds like an excellent idea," Aiyana said smartly. "They may raise an entire nation if we do not get them out of there soon." Caddo tried his best not to laugh at her. "Tooantuh is an experienced husband now. He should get out as well. Take him with you."

"The chief has spoken!" Caddo laughed out loud and Aiyana frowned in response, slapping him with her shawl. He calmed down and replied, "Perhaps you are right. We should go on a hunt. Winter is not far away, and we should prepare." He got to his feet and patted his wife on the head. "What would I do without you?"

"Nothing apparently," she snickered.

Caddo went and found Tooantuh and the two went together to lure the twin brothers from their honeymoons. They stood outside the two hive-shaped huts that were side-by-side, and Tooantuh called out to them.

"Naka and Natchitos, it is me, Tooantuh. Are the busy bees at home?" He laughed at his own joke and Caddo smiled as well. "Will the queen bees release you for some fresh air today?"

Calanele emerged from one of the huts with a not-so-pleasant expression on her face. "Tooantuh, what a surprise. Did your queen already kick you out? My husband will be out in a moment." She acknowledged her father-in-law standing next to Tooantuh. "Good morning, Father. Naka! The chief is here to see you."

Just then Natchitos came out of his hut with Taima. "Good morning, Father. Tooantuh, what brings you here?"

"Chief Caddo has an excellent idea," Tooantuh answered.

Nakahodot finally emerged and said, "Father, I was thinking this morning of a hunt."

Caddo nodded in agreement, saying, "That is why we are here. My apologies to my new daughters, but we must prepare as winter approaches. Gather yourselves for a long hunt. I will take you to a place far away where you have never been. We will take the horses, for the journey is many days from here."

Both Calanele and Taima had sour expressions on their faces. They were not ready to let their husbands go for such a long time. They knew it was necessary for the tribe, however.

With the efficiency of a military garrison, the men of the tribe gathered at the outskirts of the village. The hunting party consisted of a dozen men and horses, leaving behind only a few of the elder braves who were too old for the ride. They said their goodbyes to their squaws and children and Makane chanted blessings for a successful hunt as the braves rode away.

They traveled west, and Caddo spoke as they rode on their horses at a steady pace. "I will take you to the sacred place that I spoke of many moons ago. If the 'great spirit' smiles on our efforts, we may come across the buffalo. Until then, we will hunt for what we can. We will build fires at night to ask the 'great spirit' to bring sacred smoke upon our hunt. May we return to our village with ample bounty."

The braves were intrigued and excited at the prospect of hunting buffalo. Nakahodot was especially interested in seeing the sacred lands that contained the ancient burial mounds his father had taught them about. He imagined how wonderous the land must be. He thought of rolling hills of green as endless as the horizon, dotted with the sacred mounds of their ancestors. He imagined seeing majestic birds soaring overhead and warm sunlight bathing the countryside with a mighty herd of buffalo thundering across a plain of vibrant green.

As they pushed farther west and after three days of good hunting, they found that the forests were not as thick, but the trees were still many in number. The terrain had become rockier and hilly as well. The hunters came upon a narrow stream that flowed to the south. Nakahodot was especially fond of the area. He found the smaller trees endearing and the babbling brook enticing. They spotted a small herd of deer in a clearing and were able to hunt several of them with success.

They watered their horses in the creek and Caddo said to his men, "We will camp here tonight."

The group of hunters gathered around the fire and shared a meal of one of their catches. They talked about the events of the day and thoughts of eventually returning home.

Caddo handed Nakahodot a piece of rabbit and commented, "It must feel good to get out for a while, you and your brother."

"Yes, it does," he answered. "The cool air and the stars appeal to me. But I am missing my wife already."

"Me too," Natchitos chuckled with a smile. All the men around the fire laughed at him.

Caddo grinned and added, "Those first few weeks with your new wife are always treasured ones."

Atohi nodded and said, "And tiring!" The men erupted in laughter again.

"And famishing," Lanu added.

Nakahodot's face turned red but he couldn't help himself and said with a sheepish grin, "But *very* rewarding." The crowd roared once more with laughter.

After the laughter subsided, they settled down and continued to share the rabbit and squirrel. The tone grew more subdued when Natchitos spoke up and asked, "Father, have you ever gone into battle?" Everyone at the fire quieted to a hush. They all wanted to hear Caddo's answer. Being the elders, Atohi and Lanu knew the answer all too well.

Caddo stared at the fire for a short while before he answered. The expression on his face was one of stoic sadness. He finally gathered himself to answer his son's question. "Battle is something that is never taken lightly," he began. "No brave wants to be drawn into a fight, but one must never lack the courage to do so. We are the protectors of our people, no matter what the circumstances are and no matter who it is that has drawn us into battle." He looked up at the blanket of stars in the sky and gestured toward them. "Our country is blessed with many of our brothers. We are scattered far and wide across the plains and mountains. Each was assigned to his own territory centuries ago by the 'great spirit'. If one of our brothers were to wage war on us, it could only be dignified with a just reason. To kill only for blood is not justified and there is no honor in it." Everyone was hanging on his every word. Nakahodot and his brother listened very carefully to him. They knew his words would be something they would need to carry with them the rest of their lives.

Caddo continued, "That being said, to answer your question, Son; Yes, I have had to go into battle. When I was a little older than you are now, I was married but still learning from my father, the chief before me. Being his only son, I knew the day would come when I would have to take his place. A great famine was sweeping over our lands and the rains had stopped. The wild game had left in search of water elsewhere and we were left hungry and thirsty. We did not live by the river as we do now, but by a few narrow creeks. When the creeks ran dry, we were forced to seek out our brothers in nearby villages. They were not as accommodating as they had been in the past, however. Hunger will drive madness into a man and his reason abandons him. When we approached their village to ask for help, they attacked us without warning. We fought bitterly with our brothers, and many hearts were left on the ground." Atohi and Lanu looked very sorrowful as they listened, recalling the horrors of that day. "What was left of our warriors, we returned to our village, but our hunger continued. Weeks later, as the drought persisted, another tribe came to our village, hearing rumors that we had fish. It was trickery though. Instead, they had come for the few horses we had remaining and to steal our weapons. Another battle ensued, and chaos prevailed. Very few of us survived that day, including your elders sitting here tonight. One day, you young braves will be the leaders of our tribe. Pray you are never put to the test."

The men sat silently for what seemed an eternity after the chief had finished speaking. Natchitos and Nakahodot sat quietly contemplating his words. They knew one of them would be chosen to replace their father upon his passing and then the responsibility of the tribe would be placed on one of their shoulders. It was something that weighed heavy on each of their minds, yet they kept their thoughts on the matter to themselves.

Pakwa sat quietly, finishing his leg of rabbit, when he saw something out in the darkness. He tapped Atohi on the shoulder and told him, "Father, look. I see a torchlight approaching."

Everyone looked in the direction of the firelight and jumped to their feet. Men grabbed their spears and bows and arrows and went dashing toward the fire, yelling and calling out with intimidation. Caddo and the elders stayed at the fire momentarily. He knew the younger braves were capable of handling the situation, but still he wanted to see how they handled themselves.

Nakahodot and Pakwa were the first to arrive at the source of the torchlight. They were surprised to see three braves walking together, the oldest carrying the lighted torch. They had markings on their chests and many feathers on their headbands. Only one of the younger braves carried a spear. It was the only sign of a weapon they could see.

"Come no farther," Nakahodot said, holding his hand up. "I am Nakahodot, son of Chief Caddo. This is our camp while we are on a long hunt."

The eldest brave answered him, "I am Uzumati. These are my sons. We come in peace."

Caddo's curiosity had gotten the best of him after he heard his son conversing with the outsiders. He rose from the fire and walked over to where they had confronted them. Uzumati stood tall when he saw him approach and signaled in the customary way with his fist to his chest, knowing that he was Caddo the chief.

"Great chief, I am Uzumati," he said to Caddo.

Caddo motioned for his sons to back away and answered, "I have heard this accent before. You are brothers of the Hasinai?"

"Yes."

"Of what tribe? The Nabedache?"

"No," Uzumati answered, "we are outcasts from the Arkansas. I am training my sons as trappers of wild game, but also as guides and interpreters." He motioned to the two braves standing beside him and said, "These are my sons, Bride les Boeufs and Trappeur D'ours."

"The Arkansas?" Caddo asked surprised. "It has been many moons since I last encountered brothers from the Arkansas. Why do you say you are outcasts?"

Uzumati answered very directly, "My people grew angry when I took up with the white men. I felt strongly about learning the white words to have better trading negotiations."

"You are a wise man," Caddo commended him.

"But my people did not accept the intrusion of the white men. I went into exile when they refused to let me continue learning the white man's words." He paused for a moment, looking at his sons proudly. "They have no mother now, so I have taken it upon myself to teach them what I have learned."

It was then Caddo noticed that the three braves were not alone. In the darkness of the lone torchlight, he could see the shadows of many men standing nearby waiting to approach.

"You are guiding someone now?" Caddo asked. "Who is standing back there in the trees?"

"Do not be alarmed, great chief," Uzumati explained. "I come with white explorers." A hush fell over the gathering of braves and they began to whisper to each other nervously.

Caddo was incredibly curious, but he noticed his anxious men. It was certainly not something he had expected. He took a deep breath and said to Uzumati, "Have your follower's approach."

Uzumati turned and called out into the darkness, speaking in a language none of the Caddo had ever heard. "Commander, you and your men may approach."

Nakahodot and the others brought more torches and they raised them high as the white men came forth. They stood silently as one by one, eight white men dressed in clothing that covered their entire bodies, came out of the darkness and stood before them. Many of them had facial hair and skin as light as any of them had ever seen. Their bodies were gaunt, and their attire disheveled in appearance. They were dressed in white shirts and dark trousers and wore boots rather than moccasins. The boots seemed to stretch high upon their legs. The Indians stared at their strange attire with awestruck expressions. Wandering nervously back and forth amongst the men were two wiry hounds that looked just as tired and hungry as the men.

Then one man in particular approached the Indians by himself, leaving his men several paces behind. He did not look disheveled as the others and wore his clothing neatly. His mustache was long and narrow and was neatly trimmed. He carried a feathered, wide-brimmed dark blue hat under his arm. Caddo assumed this was the leader of the small troop of white men.

Uzumati spoke to the short-statured man in his language, "Commander, this is the chief of the Caddo. This is his hunting party that we have come upon."

The man answered, "You are able to converse with him? Does he speak Iroquois by chance?"

"He speaks the language of the Caddo. I can converse with him," Uzumati replied.

The man turned to Caddo and said, "My name is Robert Cavaelier, Sieur de LaSalle. My men simply call me LaSalle. My apologies to the great chief on interrupting his hunting party." It was the first time any of the braves present had ever heard the words of a white man. Uzumati translated the words for them.

"I am Caddo, chief. These are some of the men of my tribe, including my sons Nakahodot and Natchitos."

LaSalle nodded in understanding as his own men waited impatiently behind him. "I see," he continued. "It is a pleasure to meet Chief Caddo and his men. Like he, I and my men are away from our home. We are merely fur traders, but I myself am an explorer first and foremost. We are simply passing through, charting and claiming this land for King Louis of France. My current expedition is in search of the Colbert River. However, right now my men are tired and hungry, and we ask if we may make camp for tonight nearby so not to disturb you and your hunters."

Caddo nodded in agreement, saying, "You may make a camp nearby. I will see to it that you are not disturbed."

"My many thanks for your kindness, great chief," LaSalle said in response. Uzumati handed him his torch and LaSalle ordered his men to gather their things to make a camp for the night nearby.

Caddo motioned to Uzumati and said, "Tell them to wait." He looked over to his son, Nakahodot, and said, "Go and fetch them three counts of our catch today and bring it to them." Natchitos and the others seemed surprised at such a generous offer but none of them dared to question it. Nakahodot ran quickly to their camp and retrieved two rabbits and a squirrel. He approached the French explorers and offered the animals to them.

One of the men, LaSalle's second in command, Pierre Duhaut, came out to meet Nakahodot. Nakahodot tried not to stare at the man. His foul and unclean scent became most evident as he handed the rabbits and squirrel to him. Nakahodot's senses alerted him as he felt the man's glare, there was something about him that he didn't trust. The hounds yipped and snapped at Duhaut's heels when the scent of the rabbits and squirrel met their noses. One of the dogs danced around Nakahodot's feet and snapped at him as he handed over the animals, but he batted his snout away. He did not care for dogs very much as it was.

"Merci," Duhaut said to him. He was indeed grateful for the generous offering, but he frowned when he saw Nakahodot swat the hound. Nakahodot nodded and immediately retreated, giving a contemptuous smirk at the dog as he turned.

His brother and the other braves surrounded him as soon as he returned and anxiously asked him, "What did you say to him? Did he speak in return?"

Nakahodot said in reply, "I said nothing, but when he spoke, I did not understand him. It sounded something like this, '*Merci*'. He smelled strongly though. He needed to wash in the creek badly. And why do they travel with those mangy hounds?"

Caddo said to Uzumati, "Come and sit with us by the fire. You and your sons must be hungry." Uzumati nodded in acceptance.

The three newcomers joined Caddo and his men by their campfire. They settled in as they all shared a meal of rabbits and gopher. Uzumati and his sons were grateful for the roasted corn as well. "You are most generous, Chief Caddo. Many thanks to you for this meal."

Caddo could tell it must have been a while since these men had had anything to eat. "How many days have you wandered the wilderness with these white explorers? Have you encountered trouble along the way?"

Uzumati chewed hungrily on an ear of corn as he answered, "We have walked for many weeks. The commander's methods are confusing at times, though. His sense of direction is often wayward. He does not know which way he is going many times. He was leading them to ruin for certain if we had not spotted your campfire."

"Are all the whites so sickly in appearance?" Caddo asked. His two sons listened very attentively as they ate. They were quite interested in hearing more about these strangers.

"I have seen stronger white men," Uzumati admitted. "This group is not well organized. Too much arguing. I sense revolt in the wind amongst them. The men do not trust the commander in his search for the Great River."

Caddo's eyebrows raised in curiosity and asked, "This is the river that they are seeking?" He knew the Great River from stories he had heard from other tribes in the area who had seen it in years past. "Why did they give the Great River a different name? And what did he mean by saying he is claiming this land?"

"LaSalle says he explores and claims land in the name of his leader."

"He has a chief, then?" Caddo was most curious. "Where is this man?"

Uzumati continued, "They have many leaders at different levels of importance, but the highest of them is called King Louis. He lives in a land called France. It is where these white men have come from and he is the one they explore land for in his name."

"How far is this land?"

"Far," Uzumati asserted. "They traveled for weeks across a vast ocean on large canoes called 'ships'. The ships carry many men and they are as long as thirty of our canoes. They rise above the water more than ten men high."

The men around the fire murmured amongst themselves in hearing everything that Uzumati was saying. The thought of having a floating canoe of such enormous size was beyond belief. Caddo thought carefully about what he was saying, though.

"They come in great numbers then, to claim land?" he asked. Uzumati nodded. He could sense the distress from Caddo as the chief took in all this new information. "How have our other brothers reacted to these men and their intentions?"

"Some resist them, and battles have been fought. But other chiefs have been more patient when they see that the majority of these men do not wish to fight, but to establish trade and learn from one another."

Caddo nodded, saying, "A good dialogue is important, I agree. I can see why they have chosen you now for this task." He stared at the fire for a short while and stirred the coals with a long stick. He then said, "We will talk on this more."

Nakahodot was chewing on a piece of rabbit when he noticed one of Uzumati's sons staring at him from across the fire. He had a feeling the reason had something to do with his hair. "What are you staring at?" he finally asked sternly.

Trappeur D'ours didn't hesitate in answering, saying, "What is wrong with your hair? Why does it look that way?"

The group of men grew quiet when Nakahodot got to his feet abruptly with a very agitated expression. "There is *nothing* wrong with it. This is how I am. Is there something else you want to say?" Trappeur D'ours sat quietly not responding. His father and Caddo watched carefully to see if the argument would escalate further. "Why do you have a strange name? We have never heard such names before."

"My brother is called Bride les Boeufs," Trappeur D'ours began. "The name means Buffalo Tamer. I am called Bear Trapper."

Nakahodot scoffed at him, asking, "Oh, so you think you are a great hunter? Did you give yourself this name?"

At that, Bear Trapper got to his feet and threw down the ear of corn he was eating. "I can trap any animal, big or small, and without spears or arrows or even daggers. What can you do with hair so light? The bears would see you coming from miles away." A few of the braves chuckled to themselves. This made Nakahodot even more incensed.

Natchitos decided to speak in his brother's defense. "My brother is a great hunter, too. And he is the fastest brave in our tribe. He can outrun a bear easily. I have seen it myself."

Bear Trapper laughed to himself and said, "The bear was probably made blind because his hair is so bright." The men laughed even louder.

Uzumati was not laughing, though. He noticed how Nakahodot was growing angrier. He stood and scolded Bear Trapper, "Sit down, my son." Bear Trapper immediately did as he was told. Uzumati said to Caddo, "You must forgive my son's arrogance and lack of manners as a guest. I will say from experience, as a part of the Arkansas, I was once in a great battle. The fiercest warrior on the battlefield that day turned out to be a brave with light hair. He was known as Fox Paw and his enemies feared him from that day forward. Stories are still told of this great warrior."

"I have heard stories of this warrior as well," Caddo agreed. He motioned for his son to sit back down. While the young men had been arguing, Caddo had been thinking more about what Uzumati was saying about the white men. "I have heard about the vastness of the ocean but have not seen it myself. I see it as a great strength in these people if they can travel on water for weeks on these ships and in great number each time. Do you think there are more of these white men that will come here?"

"The one called LaSalle tells stories of other white men that come from a land called Spain. He claims they are his adversary, but that they are also interested in exploring our lands."

"This land is across the ocean as well?" Caddo asked.

Uzumati nodded and said, "Yes. They come on ships carrying many men bearing crosses on staffs."

"Crosses?" Nakahodot asked perplexed. It wasn't his intention to interrupt his father's conversation, but he was very intrigued. "Why would they do this?"

"They say it is in honor of their god," he explained.

Caddo seemed confused at such a notion but was interested that the travelers showed reverence for a god in such a manner. "I will share this news with our medicine man, Makane. I am distressed however, at hearing that these men are coming in great numbers."

Uzumati agreed in saying, "It is why I have chosen this path with my sons. Good dialogue must be made with these men, so we can have good trade instead of war. But many tribes fear them and will not have the patience that is needed, in my opinion. Resentment will swell, and battles will ensue. I fear for all our people and our lands. That is why we must be wise in our decisions."

Caddo and the elders all nodded in agreement. "What you say is true, Uzumati." Then he spoke to the rest of the assembly before they broke for the night. "The hunt will continue but we will do so on the way to our village. The sacred mounds will have to wait for another day." Some of the men groaned in hearing this, as they had come very far but had not reached the sacred lands. "I must return to our village and speak with other leaders in our area about this matter. Will you continue with the French in the morning, Uzumati?"

"I am sending my son, Trapper, with the whites to continue searching for the Great River. I intend to return to the Arkansas with my other son beginning tomorrow. I feel more dialogue is needed with the elders, if they will accept my words. They must hear of what I have seen."

Caddo nodded and responded, "May the 'great spirit' guide you, great Uzumati." With that, the men retired for the night and slept around the campfire.

Early in the morning, Natchitos had risen before sunrise as he always had done and found a small mound that overlooked the babbling brook. He watched quietly as the eastern sky began to glow in light oranges and yellows. As he listened to the peaceful sound of the creek running by, he contemplated the coming day and the hunt that will point them back to their village. He also thought of the talk from the night before of how the explorers are coming in large numbers from distant lands and seeing them for himself for the first time. He found it to be very fortunate for his brother to have interacted with one face to face.

As the sky grew brighter, he suddenly heard a growl and the huff of an animal rushing toward him. Before he knew it, one of the hounds was running at top speed alongside the creek directly at him. The dog let out a deep-throated growl as he sped toward Natchitos. It huffed and huffed as all four paws dashed across the dust in full sprint. Alarmed, Natchitos jumped to his feet and took off running the opposite way. He had no weapon or any means to fight the animal other than his hands and feet and his wits.

Natchitos ran like the wind as the dog was closing in on him. He made a good run, but the animal was too fast. He knew the hound was close to leaping at him when he threw himself to the ground. In an instant, the snarling canine went soaring over Natchitos in a fruitless leap. Natchitos slid on his belly as the dog sailed over his head. He quickly got up and ran the other way as the dog skidded to a dusty stop on his haunches and then took off again after Natchitos. He knew he could not outrun the dog and would have to resort to fighting him off somehow. He desperately looked for any kind of weapon to use against the hound; a rock, a log, a tree limb, anything.

The dog barked and growled, snapping at his heels and Natchitos yelped with each nip of its teeth. With one final push, Natchitos ran as hard as he could to get farther out in front of him and then slid to a stop, spinning around to face the charging beast. He braced himself for the collision with the raging fury of claws, teeth and wiry fur. The dog leapt aiming directly at Natchitos' throat, when suddenly an arrow came slicing through the air and struck the leaping dog. The impact of the arrow sent the animal flailing and yelping away from Natchitos and plunging into the mud alongside the creek. Natchitos stood shocked and amazed, staring wild-eyed at the dead animal lying in the mud at his feet with an arrow in its belly.

Natchitos let out a huge sigh and relief and fell to his knees in exhaustion. He whirled around to see who his savior was and smiled appreciatively and with pride in seeing it was his brother Nakahodot.

Nakahodot strode calmly over to his brother, carrying the bow in his hand triumphantly. "Close call, my brother," Nakahodot beamed. "Lucky for you I came along."

"Yes, thank you. It was not the way I had intended to start out my day. A fine shot, indeed. Saved me from a lot of scratches and teeth."

"Or worse," Nakahodot added, offering to help him up.

"Still using my quiver, I see though," Natchitos joked. "Maybe I will let you hold onto it for the time being."

Just then, Duhaut came running up from the direction of the French campsite with a pained expression on his face. The two brothers were surprised to see one of the white men again. He came running up and skidded to a halt, observing the dead dog by the creek.

"What have you done to my dog?" he yelped in his own language.

They didn't know what he was saying but they knew what he *meant*. Nakahodot immediately spoke up, "It was going to attack Natchitos, so I shot him."

Duhaut knelt beside the dead dog and patted its head softly. He then got to his feet and fumed at Nakahodot. "Why have you done this?" he yelled again. "You wild *savage*."

Nakahodot stood tall in defiance to the man's anger. Natchitos grabbed him by the arm, however, and tried his best to lead him back to camp. Before he could, more men from both camps arrived at the scene. The sun had risen over the horizon and sunlight began to cascade over the grounds and through the trees. LaSalle and his men, as well as the Indians, looked on the escalating scene.

"What is going on here?" LaSalle demanded. "Pierre, why are you berating these young natives? I demand you stop this at once."

"I saw it with my own eyes," Trapper spoke in French. "The Frenchmen's dog went rabid. It chased after the dark-haired brother, but Light Hair struck the animal down with a clean shot from a hundred paces." He looked over at Nakahodot and commended him, "That was a lucky shot, Light Hair. You still look odd to me, though."

"You should not call me that. My name is *Nakahodot*," he fired back. "And luck had nothing to do with it."

Duhaut argued with Trapper, "My dog was *not* rabid."

"Mr. Duhaut, you will return to our camp at once," LaSalle repeated. "I intended to leave at first light and continue our journey to the Colbert. If the animal made such a charge, it most certainly was rabid." He turned to Uzumati and said, "Please tell the chief he has my most sincere apologies for the animal attacking his son." He produced three animal pelts and handed them to Caddo. "I offer these pelts in exchange for your kindness to us. We will leave you in peace and Godspeed you on your hunt."

Duhaut complained bitterly however, "You are always siding with someone else, Robert. You will not listen to any of us! We will never find that river under your authority, not this way we will not. We will die of starvation before we arrive there. Listen to me when I say we should return to the fort at Saint Louis." He looked back at his dead, four-legged companion and said mournfully, "And you let them kill my dog."

LaSalle pulled him aside and reprimanded him privately. "It is enough of your insubordination. Our trek will continue immediately, and you *will* fall into line."

The Indians watched as the Frenchmen walked away with LaSalle and their guide, Trapper. It would be the last time they would ever see the commander alive again.

Chapter 5

1688 - Three Years Later

As the seasons passed, the younger generation of the Caddo tribe matured more and more. Tooantuh's younger brother, Sitting Crow, had come of age and was married to Taini. Calanele's brother, Pakwa, had also come of age and was married to his chosen squaw, Mitena, one spring morning by the river. Ayashe and Tuwa were still awaiting their time to come of age and choose a squaw to marry.

Tooantuh and Ayita were the first to start a family of the three couples that were married three years prior. Ayita gave birth to their first born, a son. He was named Tokala, for the morning that he was born, Tooantuh spotted a fox trotting past their home.

Five months after Tokala was born, Nakahodot and Calanele welcomed their first child, a daughter. She was named Kewanee, for the day she was introduced to the tribe, a hen was seen at their door and never left their company from that day onward.

Natchitos and Taima were the last of the three couples to start a family. Their first born, a son, arrived a year after the birth of Tokala. He was named Anoki, for when he was an infant, he could never sit still.

Chief Caddo and Aiyana were very pleased with all the new arrivals, especially their grandchildren. Natchitos and Nakahodot began to teach their children the ways of the Caddo just as they were taught.

The sun grew hot that summer, and the entire tribe was tasked with collecting as much food as possible. The crops yielded little corn and beans and there was little squash as well, so everyone was sent out into the forests to forage for anything that could be used by the tribe.

What had begun as a nagging cough in the years prior for Aiyana, had now become a daily burden of terrible coughing and wheezing and a persistent fever. As the days wore on, she became weaker and weaker. Caddo kept a watchful eye over her and even asked his sons to look after her whenever they could.

Nakahodot emerged from his hut as did Calanele, who was holding their toddler Kewanee. The chicken that stayed outside their home scurried away from the door flap when they came out. "Will you search for berries with us today?" she asked him.

"You go on ahead of me," he answered. "I must check on mother this morning."

Calanele frowned at him as Kewanee played with her mother's braids. "You are always checking on her."

"She is ill. It is right to go and see her." He leaned over and kissed Kewanee on the top of her head, saying, "Do not eat them all, my little hen."

He headed for his parent's hut and soon spotted his mother coming out, hobbling as she walked. "Mother, can I come and help you?" he asked.

"No, I will be fine," she said. "I am getting myself together to go and find huckleberries. Where is my sweet Kewanee today?"

"She is with her mother looking for berries too," Nakahodot answered. She stumbled a bit and he quickly helped her straighten. "I will go with you, Mother."

"Good, you can be my eyes for me."

"Are you feeling any better this morning?" he asked.

She waved his concern away though, saying, "I am a tough old squaw. The cough comes and goes, but I can still do my part." As they walked through the forest, she gazed at her son with skepticism as she could tell his thoughts were elsewhere. "What troubles you, Naka? Your mind seems far away."

"Nothing is the matter. Why do you ask?"

She coughed a bit as they scanned the forest for the huckleberry trees. "You still do not have confidence in yourself, do you?" Nakahodot looked surprised at her question. "Here you are, a grown man now. You are even a father. Why do you not trust yourself?"

"What makes you ask me this, Mother? Of course, I have confidence in myself."

"You are still ashamed of how you look, are you not?" she finally asked, getting to the point.

"I have always had this hair, Mother. I am still Nakahodot. I am not ashamed of that."

"You should not be," she continued. "You think you are different and are faced with ridicule from any brave ignorant enough to speak so. It is their problem for being so foolish. Have you ever wondered why you have such light hair?"

He shrugged his shoulders and answered, "No, not really." Then he thought for a moment longer. Perhaps his mother had some wisdom he had not heard before. "Alright, tell me why."

"You never knew my father, your grandfather. He went to the 'great spirit' before I had come of age. It is not polite to speak of the dead, but I feel you must know this about him." Nakahodot nodded in understanding. "Mother always spoke of how handsome he was. And he was the fiercest warrior in the tribe. He could have been the object of ridicule, but no one dared to make fun of his appearance. He was a great leader, and everyone respected him. I only wish that I knew him longer."

"What was it about his appearance?" Nakahodot asked curiously.

"No one else looked like him because his hair was just as yours, my son. This is why you have hair as you do. Mother always told me that this trait skips a generation and that I should prepare myself if I were to ever have children." She stopped and put her hand on his shoulder. "Well, she was right. I had two sons and one indeed had light hair, just as his grandfather did." She looked at him squarely and said, "Never doubt yourself, Son. Be proud of your heritage and always fight for the good. Then you will be a great leader."

Nakahodot embraced his mother and thanked her for her wisdom. What he didn't know though, is that he didn't have much more time to have such talks with her.

He spotted some huckleberry trees in the cover of the thick forest. They were thin and spindly in appearance and stood no more than five feet tall. "Look, Mother, these have many berries on them." They spent over an hour gathering the berries from the two small trees and when they had picked them clean, they decided to head back to the village.

Aiyana handed him the skin she had filled with berries, but when she did, she fell to one knee. Her face winced, and she put her hand to her forehead.

"Mother!" Nakahodot called out. He quickly leapt to her aid and knelt beside her. He felt the heat emanating from her body. She was wracked with fever. "You are hot."

"My legs have given way," she weakly told him. "My strength has left me."

"I will be your strength." He left the skins on the ground filled with berries and lifted his mother into his arms. He carried her all the way back to the village. By the time they had reached home, she had fainted from the extreme fever. Her arms dangled at her side as he carried her through the village. People gasped when they saw her in his arms.

Makane saw them immediately and called out to White Owl, "Go to the chief's home quickly. I will find Caddo. Aiyana is ill and needs our help." White Owl immediately did as she was told.

Within minutes the entire tribe was aware of Aiyana's illness. Makane found Caddo and brought him immediately. From that moment on, Caddo never left Aiyana's side.

Days would pass, but the fever would not leave Aiyana. Makane built a fire in the center of the village and danced as he chanted. He chanted words of prayer in hopes that his words would be raised up with the smoke to the 'great spirit'. After four days of struggle, Aiyana passed away in the night. The entire village was filled with sadness and Caddo was inconsolable. He was so filled with grief that he couldn't even bring himself to carry her body deep into the forest in the solemn procession to lay her to rest. Instead, he asked his two sons to carry her to the forest for the 'great spirit' to take her away.

As they left their mother's body alone in the darkened forest, Nakahodot spoke to his brother, even though they were enjoined to silence during the ritual. "I do not like how we honor our dead this way, leaving them to be discarded by animals. She was our mother."

Natchitos knew they mustn't speak at such a time, but he answered his brother anyway. "I have thought of this as well, but it is who we are. We must honor our father and his request. For now, we must not speak further."

A period of three days was set aside to mourn Aiyana. The two brothers tried their best to console their father, but their attempts were futile. He would not eat, and he barely spoke. After the period of mourning had passed, Caddo summoned all the men and elders of the tribe at the center of the village for a meeting. They shared smoking pipes and passed a water skin around the circle as was the custom.

"I have only a few words to say," Caddo began with a look of perpetual sadness on his face. "I have thought for many moons now about what our brothers have said about the whites in our country. And I have thought about our own encounter with them in the past. Soon, I will decide about the future of this tribe. We must be wise in preserving our people and our heritage. That is all I have to say. Now, let us smoke and enjoy the fire."

The men murmured amongst themselves, but none dared to ask questions of the chief, but they knew change was calling in the wind. The only conclusion they could come to was that the chief would soon be naming his successor. Natchitos and Nakahodot both sat quietly as they shared the calumet with the others.

As summer gave way to fall, word spread one night that their beloved chief had become ill. His sadness and despair had consumed him in the months that followed the passing of his beloved wife and now he found himself gripped with the same fever that had overcome Aiyana.

Nakahodot sat on some pelts with Kewanee, playing a game with her. He would hold his breath and make a bubble with his cheeks and then she would push them together to make a popping sound as he blew out his breath. Kewanee would giggle happily each time. Suddenly, the flap few open and Calanele came rushing in, saying, "Get up, Naka. Your father is worse. You must go to him right away." He jumped to his feet and leapt outside. "You must stay with me, little one," she said to Kewanee.

As soon as he went outside, the cool autumn air caressed his face. He immediately saw Natchitos and joined him as they walked briskly toward their father's home. "What do you think it could be?" he asked his brother.

"His sadness is too much for him," Natchitos answered matter-of-factly. "I fear he is being called away from us."

They entered the hut and found Caddo lying on his bed, gasping for air. Makane, who had been attending to him, left the hut and let them sit alone with their father.

"Natchitos," he coughed, "stir the fire. I feel the cold coming in." Natchitos did as he was told. "Sit with me, my sons."

The two brothers sat in silence with their father all evening and into the night. After many hours of letting him rest, Caddo finally opened his eyes and spoke in a weak voice. "My sons, my time has come and soon I will reunite with your mother. My soul has ached for her and now it is time to meet her once again." They listened to him with sadness in their eyes. "The 'great spirit' has provided us a fruitful land by the river. I am grateful to have been sent here. It is the place of your birth. But now it is time for the tribe to find a new land." Nakahodot and Natchitos looked at each other with surprise. *Where could we be going?* they both thought.

Caddo continued, "Soon, you will both be leaders of the Caddo. My sons, I ask of you this final wish. On the day of my passing, I ask that both of you gather your family and their families and go and settle in new lands. Do not mourn me for three days. Instead, I ask for you to remember me in another way." Both sons listened intently to their father. "Nakahodot, I ask that you travel for three days toward the setting sun. On the third day, you will stop and settle in the new land and rear a tribe." Then he turned to Natchitos and said, "Natchitos, I ask that you travel for three days toward the rising sun. On the third day, you will stop and settle in the new land and rear a tribe. The 'great spirit' willing, you will both find your way to one another again, thus continuing the sacred bond of the Caddo. What I ask of you, was done by me, and my father before me. Now, I am asking this of you. This is the only way to ensure the lasting of the Caddo."

Both sons sat and thought for a long while about what their father had said. They both looked at each other silently, wondering what the other must be thinking, yet they only nodded to one another and their father.

Many moments passed, then finally Natchitos looked at the chief and said, "We will honor your request, Father. It will be done." Later that night, Chief Caddo breathed his last.

Chapter 6

As word spread of the death of their chief and the revelation of his final wishes, panic as well as sadness spread throughout the village. People wailed in mourning while others comforted them. Makane kept a solemn vigil at the central fire, chanting and tapping a single drum, in hopes that Caddo's spirit will follow the drumbeat and smoke up to the heavens.

Sensing the people's distress about splitting and moving the tribe, Nakahodot approached his brother as they observed the restlessness, asking, "Are you certain this is the right thing for us to do? Together we make a more formidable tribe, do we not?"

"We must honor our father in life and in death," Natchitos responded.

"Then we will make preparations immediately, just as he asked," Nakahodot told him. "When both tribes are ready, you and I will meet on this spot once more."

Natchitos agreed and then they both set out to organize their people into two new tribes. Nakahodot gathered Calanele's family and other extended tribal families. In all, they numbered about forty-five people. Natchitos in turn, gathered Taima's family and their extended tribal families. They numbered about thirty-five in all. The brothers assigned an equal number of braves to each tribe for substantial protection over them. Ayashe and Tooantuh's families were to go with Natchitos. Pakwa and Tuwa and their families were to go with Nakahodot.

While the two tribes organized themselves, Nakahodot slipped away from the village and ran quickly as he could deep into the forest alone. Even though it was a cool, autumn morning, sweat poured from his face as he ran. Soon, he arrived at the sight of where they had laid their mother's body to rest. With tears in his eyes, he quickly but carefully retrieved her remains. His hands shook as he took great care in wrapping the remains in animal pelts.

"I will honor you in the old way," he whispered, as he wrapped the last of her bones in the pelt. "You will find rest with

Father, together in spirit and in the dust. This is my pledge to you." After he was finished, he gathered the pelt and ran as fast as he could back to the village.

In the village, the tribes were assembling with the efficiency of a military garrison. However, Calanele was in a panic. She grabbed Pakwa by the arm and pleaded with him, "The people are getting worried. Go and find my husband. They must see him so that they will not lose faith."

Before Pakwa could answer, Nakahodot came up behind them, saying, "I am here. What is our status?"

"Everyone is ready," Pakwa answered.

Calanele pulled her husband to the side and chided him, "Where have you been? You must show them that you *are* the chief. And why are you sweating so?"

"Share this with no one. When the time is right, I will reveal my intentions for our new tribe. I have retrieved my mother's bones. She is coming with us."

"You *what?*" she asked aghast.

"I will no longer allow her to be left alone in such a way." He motioned to the makeshift cot where the body of his father lay, wrapped carefully in animal pelts. "I have placed them with Father."

"You wish to change the ritual for our dead?" She knew his objections to the practice but was still surprised at his hasty actions. He nodded to her assuredly. She understood and whispered proudly to him, "Your first act as chief."

"Second," he affirmed. "The first will be to take our people to the proper place for mourning."

She nodded in support of him, saying, "I will stand with you, Naka."

The entire tribe was now assembled into two separate ones and were ready to begin their three-day trek according to their chief's wishes. Spirits were high, but the people were understandably nervous. Many were sad at the thought of leaving their close friends behind. The eldest of the tribe were the only ones who clearly understood the reasoning behind such a decision.

Nakahodot and Natchitos again met at the center of the gathering and clasped their arms together in the traditional manner. Natchitos said to his brother, "May the 'great spirit' guide us and give us strength. He will guide us to the proper place for mourning. We will know when we have found it. Then, mourning will turn to joy."

"Father's wishes only left one omission, brother," Nakahodot responded. "He did not direct us on what to do with his body, but only to not walk him to the forest in procession."

"You are correct," Natchitos answered. "What do you propose?"

Nakahodot motioned to the ritual cot that contained their father and secretly their mother. "With your blessing, I wish to take his body to our new land."

Natchitos thought on the matter for a moment. He began to understand what his brother intended. He nodded in agreement and said, "A new place for mourning, then? You are right, Father should rest not alone but near his people. I agree with this. You have my blessing." With their arms still clasped, he shook his brother's hands once more, saying, "I will always think of you, brother. Whenever the sun sets, my thoughts will be with you."

"We will meet again in this life," Nakahodot replied, "you have my word. As sure as the sun crosses the sky, we will meet again. We will share campfires and talk not of how we died, but of how we lived. Go in peace, my brother."

With that, both men gathered their tribes and began their journey. Nakahodot traveled west and Natchitos traveled east.

With heavy and anxious hearts but with hopeful optimism, Nakahodot and his new tribe set out. The terrain west of the Sabine River was open and predominately flat for half of the first day. The prairie was vast and still mostly green from the ample rains that year, but as they day wore on, the hills became more numerous and the trees taller. They crossed many narrow streams along the way, so water was abundant. Braves took turns in groups of four in carrying the cot that held their deceased chief. Nakahodot noticed their hard labor and put himself on duty in helping to carry the cot.

The tribe came to rest by another of the many creeks. It was close to sunset and the people were exhausted. "We will make camp here tonight," Nakahodot instructed. He went off alone to be with his thoughts and to find a high place with which to watch the sun set over their first day of wandering.

When he returned, he instructed that a fire be made especially for a place to set the bodies of his deceased parents. "I will keep a vigil over the chief, so he will not be disturbed in the night." Pakwa and Tuwa also took turns in helping him keep watch.

The next morning, the skies were overcast, and the wind was bustling through the tall pines. From time to time, a light rain would fall on them as they carried on. The walk became more arduous as the hills became rockier. There were many trees that had fallen, and were laying in rotted heaps, so the tribe had to traverse around them before getting back on track.

It was close to mid-day when Nakahodot and the others noticed rustling in the brush nearby. Pakwa walked over to Nakahodot and said, "They are getting closer. What do you think they are?"

Nakahodot wiped the sweat off his forehead in the cool, yet humid air. "I am afraid they are wild dogs or perhaps coyotes. I think they can sense the body. We must be very vigilant."

"When will we know when we have found our new home?" Pakwa asked impatiently. He hoped to glean as must information from his new chief as possible. Since they were friends from childhood, he felt Nakahodot would naturally confide in him. He was pleased to see that he was correct.

"I will let you know my intentions." He leaned in closer to Pakwa and said, "Do you remember where we made camp when we came across the French?" Pakwa quickly nodded. "It is easily three-days walk to that site. I think it was my father's intention all along for us to settle there one day. It is why he showed us that area. If my instincts are correct, we will come across it tomorrow."

"I like this idea," Pakwa responded. "But what of Natchitos? He has not the luxury of knowing what lies ahead of him like we do."

"The 'great spirit' will guide him to the right place. I have faith in his judgement." He heard the animals getting closer and the people began to panic as the growls grew louder. "I am afraid we do not know *everything* that lies ahead." He called out to the entire tribe and yelled, "Stand your ground!"

In every direction, coyotes came darting from the brush, growling and snarling as they ran. There were dozens of them, and they had surrounded the entire tribe. Arrows flew, spears were chucked at the hungry, vicious animals. One brave was tackled, then another. With each attack, arrows were quickly shot into the rampaging animals. The coyotes yipped and snarled as they were cut down one by one. One lunged at Nakahodot, tackling him from behind. He cried out in pain as the dog scratched and clawed at his back. Its snapping jaws tried desperately to pierce his neck but Nakahodot fought him courageously. He maneuvered around on his back and held the beast with his out-stretched arms, fiercely fighting it off. Tuwa fired an arrow and sent the coyote tumbling and yelping to the ground. He helped Nakahodot to his feet and handed him a spear.

The children were crying, and the women were screaming, trying to do anything to scare away the attacking coyotes. Atohi scrambled his way over to the group of braves who were doing their best to fight off the remaining animals. He called out to Tuwa, saying, "See if we can get fire! Light the arrows that remain!"

Tuwa understood and immediately produced some flint and quickly tried to light a fire on some straw. The fire sprang to life just as another coyote plowed into him. Instinctively, Atohi grabbed a nearby stick and set it aflame, waving it in the dog's face. Instantly, the animal yelped and jumped away from Tuwa. "Spread the fire!" Atohi shouted. "Shoot it in their bellies."

71

One by one, the braves and even the women shot flaming arrows at the frenzied coyotes. The animals yelped and howled as they were struck. The ones that were missed ran away frightened deep into the forest.

Satisfied the animals were finally thwarted and his people out of danger, Nakahodot helped the men douse what remained of the fire. He checked every man, woman and child to make sure they were all safe. He paid no attention to his own wounds when he saw that some of the men had been scratched badly as well. Tuwa had a bite on his arm but was not serious.

The rain began to fall harder as the tribe re-organized before setting out again. "Naka, the children are frightened of moving on," Calanele informed her husband. She noticed his back and shoulders. "You are bleeding."

"I will be fine. The rain will wash the wounds. We must calm the children somehow. This is no place to make camp. We must get to better ground."

Calanele looked exasperated with him. She and many others were exhausted from the fight. "Do we know where we will stop tomorrow?" She hesitated for a moment and followed with another question. "*Will* we stop tomorrow?"

"I know where we are going, Calanele," he assured her. "You must trust me. I have seen it before." She regained her confidence after hearing him reveal his plan.

They marched on through the steep hills of the piney woods the rest of the afternoon. After the rain stopped, they lit torches to keep them at the ready in case of another attack. As the sunset approached, many were expecting that they would break for the night and make camp. They came upon a stream that flowed between two of the steep inclines and stopped to rest and fill their water skins. They watered the horses and tended to those wounded earlier in the day.

Nakahodot looked to the east, thinking of his brother. A tremendous and awe-inspiring full moon had just risen on the horizon. He could see the yellow glow through the treetops. *I wonder how he is getting along with his tribe as they move eastward?* he thought to himself. He hoped his fortunes were better than their own thus far. The attack by the coyotes was a frightful one but they emerged as one tribe still. *Surely, we will find rest by the day's end tomorrow.*

He walked back to the tribe and found them eagerly awaiting his word to make camp. After much careful deliberation, he announced to them, "I feel we have little choice but to keep moving. We are still in great danger of attracting wild creatures that undoubtedly sense the dead we are carrying." He looked to the heavens as pointed to the rising moon. "The skies are clear this night. We will have a sky blanketed with stars and a yellow moon to light our way. If we walk through the night, we will reach our new home by morning. If we make camp here tonight, we leave ourselves at the mercy of the forest."

The tribe looked at one another with weariness. No one had the energy to go any farther after such a tasking journey. Being the eldest, Atohi stood and said, "You see the condition the people are in. We are all tired. But you will make the right decision. You have led us this far."

Kewanee jumped from her mother's lap and walked over to her father. She raised her arms for him to pick her up. He smiled and gladly lifted her. She quickly hugged his neck and pointed to the sky and called out, "*Niish hak'aykuh!*"

He laughed and said, "Yes, my little one. It is a yellow moon of the harvest. We have brought our bounty from the harvest with us on this great journey."

She kept pointing toward the sky, repeating the word to herself, "*Niish...niish.*"

He set her down and said to the tribe, "Let us share a meal with a fire for a few hours. When the moon is fully risen, we will set out to find our new home. As the moon moves westward, so shall we."

The tribe was all in agreement. A nice meal and long rest would be just what everyone would need to get through the night. They all agreed that the sooner they arrived the better.

After they ate, they lit torches and carried them at the head and the tail of the caravan to keep animals at bay. The bright light of the moon served as their best guide however. They trekked onward by the light of the full moon until morning. From that day on, their final push toward their new land was known as *'E Kajika Niish'*, or *'The Journey of the Full Moon'*.

Early morning light began to appear on the horizon behind them. Children slept on their mother's backs or on wooden rickshaws that were being dragged by two men at a time. Everyone was beyond exhausted as they stepped slowly through the dew-covered forest floor. A light fog had crept through the tops of the trees that were now less in number. The hills had become more manageable and their leader could sense they were getting close to familiar territory.

The fog was in scattered patches everywhere and even though it was not raining, it felt like a mist on one's skin. In the misty-morning forest, Nakahodot caught sight of smoke fire. He raised his hand for all to stop.

Tuwa approached him quietly and in a weary voice asked, "Naka, what do you see?"

"Over there, above those trees," he whispered. "Someone is disguising their smoke inside the fog. For a moment, I saw firelight." He looked back at his drained tribe. "Tell everyone to put out the torches. We will walk on."

"I know the creek you are seeking," Pakwa asserted before he walked back, "it is just over that ridge."

"You are correct, my friend."

They quietly reached the small ridge just beyond where they saw the smoke. He looked around as closely as he could, but he no longer saw the billowing smoke. The sun had begun to rise but the fog lingered all around the area. Up ahead was the same creek where the dog had attempted its attack on Natchitos a few years before. Nakahodot nodded as he scanned the landscape. Calanele came up behind him to ask why they had stopped again. She looked over the mostly rocky area that was dotted with a few small trees, but otherwise very flat and quite hospitable.

He noticed as she came alongside him and said, "We have reached our journey's end."

She looked over the land once more and saw the narrow creek up ahead and gave it a look of contempt. "We are going to live *here*?" she asked. "Naka, I cannot even bathe in that creek. It will not cover my shoulders. There will be no privacy."

Nakahodot was so tired. With one look his wife had dismissed the land he had chosen for his new tribe, but he was too weary to even argue with her.

Tuwa came up behind him as well and tapped him on the shoulder. "There is something in those trees," he warned him.

Nakahodot saw it too. "Calanele," he whispered, "get the others and have them hide amongst the brush over there. I will take Pakwa and Tuwa to see what or who this may be. Whoever had that fire going, they are still here." She did as he told her and quickly and quietly herded the rest of the tribe out of sight as best as she could.

The three braves walked slowly toward the trees where they saw the rustling. Nakahodot pulled the branches away and leaned inside. Before he knew it, a hand was placed over his mouth and he was pulled backward.

"*Shhh*," the voice said. "Keep your men out of sight." The hand lifted from his face and he turned to see who it was. Nakahodot was stunned to see Trapper crouched low to the ground. "Squat down beside me," he whispered again.

Nakahodot whispered back to him, "That was your fire, was it not? What are you hiding from?" Trapper pointed with his finger past the clearing and beyond the creek. "What do you see?"

"A war party," Trapper responded. He wasn't going to mince words. "Wichita. They number about twenty. They have been gone from their tribe many days now. They are far from home and becoming desperate."

Nakahodot looked on with astonishment. *What next?* was all he could think. "Have they spotted you? What do they want?"

Trapper shook his head, "I do not think so. What they want is what you have. They have been tracking you for days. They know what you have with you. Your supplies, weapons, whatever they can take. I am certain they will want your horses as well. They will stop at nothing to get them too. They know you are vulnerable with your elderly and women and children."

"They have been tracking us? How do you know all of this?" Nakahodot asked bewildered.

"I know it because I have been tracking *them*," he flatly stated. He looked over at Nakahodot and asked, "Why have you come back here?"

"It was my father's wish before he passed. He has sent us here."

"Your father has sent you here to die. If a war party returns empty-handed, they will live out their days in disgrace. They are here to fight or die. The only response you must have is to fight back." He looked at the two braves crouching next to Nakahodot. "From the looks of your tired men, you are no match for these warriors." He gave Nakahodot's hair another contemptuous glance. "I see you still have your light hair. You are chief now, correct? What of your brother?"

Nakahodot scoffed at him, saying, "Do not worry about my hair or my brother. He has traveled east and is chief of his own people now. And my light hair will be staying on my head this day, I assure you. We did not come all this way just to die."

"That is the spirit," Trapper chuckled. "Think you still have some fight left in you after all, do you?"

"Yes, I do." Nakahodot thought quickly to form a plan of battle. He had to get back to his tribe to warn and organize them. Yet, he still could not understand why Trapper remained in this area and why he was alone. "What happened to the French? Why are you by yourself?"

Trapper wiped the sweat off his forehead and said, "They turned on each other. They are all dead."

Nakahodot shook his head. The statement left more questions than answers. He had more pressing matters at the moment, though. He grabbed Pakwa by the arm and said, "You men, come with me." The four men quickly scurried their way back to the brush where the rest of the tribe was hunkered down.

"What is it?" Calanele hissed. "Who is out there?"

Nakahodot answered directly, "We are going to be attacked by the Wichita. We must gather our weapons immediately. Protect the children!"

Atohi and Tuari hurried over to the horses and mounted them. As soon as Tuari whirled around on his horse, an arrow struck him in the shoulder. He wailed in pain and the horse reared back on its hind legs.

They heard war cries and without warning, the Wichita came dashing out into the clearing, firing arrows and chucking spears directly at them.

"Get down!" Nakahodot yelled. The women grabbed children two and three at a time and hid behind tree stumps and fallen logs as best they could. Nakahodot released arrows one by one in rapid fashion, striking down warriors with each one. "Charge them on horseback!" he called out to Atohi.

Atohi steadied Tuari and his mount and gave him a spear. Tuari barely clung to the animal's mane with one hand and the spear in the other. The pain from the wound had seized his body. "You can still *fight*," Atohi pleaded with him as arrows zipped past them. "Come on!"

The two men bravely rode together and leapt over the tree logs with a head-on charge into the open. The remaining attackers spilled onto the battlefield with war cries. Nakahodot and his men followed the charge and pandemonium ensued.

Pakwa was tackled by a warrior and was pinned to the ground. His attacker smacked his face with one hand and produced a hatchet with the other. Just as he was about to thrust the hatchet into Pakwa, an arrow pierced his skull. Pakwa immediately threw the lifeless warrior to the ground. He whirled around to see Nakahodot crying out triumphantly. He screamed at Pakwa, "Keep fighting!"

Several Wichita slipped through the melee and headed straight for the rest of the tribe's hiding place to steal their possessions. They took no mercy as they fired upon the women and children. They let out blood-curdling screams as some were struck in their arms and legs.

Nakahodot and his men were all engaged in hand-to-hand combat, yet he heard the screams of their families. From out of nowhere, Trapper came dashing into the fury of the helpless being attacked, brandishing a long sword. The stunned attackers were no match for the slicing blade as he cut each warrior down effortlessly. The strange weapon surprised the women too, and the children scattered in hysterics.

Calanele screamed in horror as Kewanee ran away toward the chaotic fighting. The frightened and crying child ran helplessly, not knowing where to go.

As Nakahodot shot another warrior down, he caught sight of his child wandering aimlessly amongst the madness. "Kewanee!" he yelled.

One of the last of the Wichita saw the child gripped with fear, crying toward her father. He quickly surmised it was the chief's daughter and decided to take no mercy on her. He pulled a hatchet from his side and called out in a loud war cry. Then he ran as fast as he could straight toward Kewanee. Calanele's eyes widened in horror as she witnessed the warrior heading straight for Kewanee to slaughter her. From the corner of her eye, she spotted a spear on the ground and quickly dove for it. In one motion, she flung the spear as hard as she could over the head of her frantic daughter. Just as the warrior was about pounce on Kewanee, the spear buried into his chest, sending him flailing backwards. The fighter let out an anguished groan and blood spurted from his mouth as he hit the ground with a thud.

Calanele cried out in triumph, "*No one* will get *my* child!"

The last of the Wichita was cut down by Trapper with the sword. It was a weapon his companions had never seen before. He stood proudly as the last of their enemies had fallen.

Kewanee ran to her mother and hugged her leg and Calanele held her tight. Nakahodot, his face bloodied and beaten, looked at his wife and his tribe proudly. She held her fist in the air and exclaimed, "We *are* going to live here."

Sweat poured down Nakahodot's face and he breathed heavily as he clutched his bow in his fist. He announced to the tribe with confidence, "We have reached the end of our tribe's journey and ordeal. This will be marked as a day to remember. We will wander no more."

Chapter 7

After it was certain the battle was over, the tribal members helped one another and tended to the wounded. They were fortunate that no one had died but many were badly injured. Trapper and Nakahodot went to each person to evaluate the damage that had been done. Tuari was still impaled with an arrow just below his shoulder. Many had cuts and scrapes, and a few had broken bones, but Tuwa was in the worst shape. He was terribly wounded by a hatchet to his side. The men and women tried their best to stop the bleeding. They built a fire and tended to him for many hours until his wound was bandaged as best as they could. They let him sleep by the fire.

They gave Tuari some wood to bite on as several men came to hold him down while Nakahodot prepared to remove the arrow. "Forgive me, my friend," he said to Tuari. "Be strong." Without warning, Nakahodot yanked the arrow from Tuari's chest. He crunched the wood in two and wailed in agony. Blood poured from his chest as the arrow had been cleanly removed. Nakahodot looked at his stricken friend sympathetically. He couldn't imagine the pain he was feeling. He quickly directed some women to come to his aid. "Please look after him. Stop the bleeding." After they had patched his shoulder, they laid Tuari by the fire next to his son, Tuwa.

By mid-afternoon, the rest of the tribe began to wander around the open area, exploring their new homeland. Nakahodot walked with them as well, pointing out good places to construct their homes and choosing spots in which to plant gardens the following spring.

Calanele washed her face in the creek as Nakahodot came up behind her. As she noticed him approaching, she stood and said, "I still do not think this creek is suitable to bathe right here in front of the whole tribe. You will find me another place."

He nodded and said, "Come walk with me. I have something more to show you, my wife."

They walked together through the middle of their new village. Some of the tribe had already begun to place the poles in the ground that would be the frame of their beehive-shaped huts. Nakahodot was proud to see how hard they worked even though few of them had slept for days. After the many trials and unexpected battles to survive, the entire tribe was moving forward on adrenaline alone. Spirits were high after their triumphant victory.

"Do you think we will be attacked again, Naka?" she asked him as they walked.

"This war party had traveled far from their homeland and was desperate for food," he answered. "It was clear this was why we defeated them. Plus, we outnumbered them. I do not think their chief will send another party this way again. The markings on their faces were not ones I have seen among the Hasinai that live in this area. Father had told stories of our brothers near here."

This raised another question from Calanele. "You succeeded in bringing your parents here. What will you do now?"

"Before the tribe rests tonight, we will honor them in a new way. Father asked us to travel for three days and now that is done. We will give their spirits rest tonight." His wife remained understandably curious as to what that meant.

After about fifteen minutes of walking, they came to another area that Nakahodot wanted to show her. She was surprised to see another creek that was wider and appeared to be deeper than the other. She smiled appreciatively and said, "Now this is better, my husband."

"I would not lead our people to a bad place," he assured her. "Father knew of this land's beauty. It is why we are here and will continue to fight to stay here."

She put her hand to her chin and observed the flowing creek carefully. After a moment's thought, she finally said, "*Banita. Banita* only."

"*Banita* only?" he asked her curiously. "Are you sure?"

She repeated herself firmly once again. "This will be for the women only. It is away from the village and we will have the privacy we need. I have spoken my piece."

"I am the chief," he complained, "where will I bathe?"

She didn't hesitate, answering, "You can go to the other creek where the *lanana* will bathe. The young squaws, all the children will wash there. If you need to wash, take Kewanee with you. She needs a bath too."

Nakahodot was amused but also beside himself as he knew his wife was serious. "Me? With the *lanana*?"

"*Banita* here. *Lanana* over there," she insisted. "You and the men can go where you want as long as it is *not* here. You only come to protect our privacy. And only married men will do that."

He shook his head and laughed, saying, "The chief has spoken once more!"

That night, a fire was lit on the outskirts of the village in an open area. Nakahodot chanted softly to himself as he laid his parents bones beside one another on the ground. The newly-appointed medicine man, Atohi, slowly beat the drum in rhythm with the chants. Nakahodot took loose dirt he had removed from the Earth and covered the deceased with a carefully fashioned mound. Only Calanele knew that the bones of his mother also lay next to the chief. His voice raised, and his song was lifted to the heavens with the sacred smoke. He had given the tribe's former chief and his wife their final rest.

After the solemn ceremony, and after the last of the homes had been put together, the entire tribe sat together at the center fire. Trapper sat with them sharing a meal. "I am grateful for this bounty you have given me. It has been a long day."

Nakahodot commended him, saying, "You fought bravely today. We are in debt to you for your help and your warning. Tell me of this weapon you have. It was highly effective. How does it shine the way it does?"

"It is called steel. It is also used to make more efficient arrowheads. The weapon is called a Spanish sword."

Nakahodot was intrigued. "You know of the Spanish? Did they give you this weapon?"

"Yes," Trapper responded, "I have encountered them. After the French revolted against their commander, the others turned against his attackers. Only two survived and ran away. I remained alone in the forest until one day I came across a garrison of Spanish troops. They did not kill me when they learned I spoke the language of their enemy. They asked if I swore allegiance to the French, but I told them I followed no one. They let me go free but also gave me this as a sign of friendship." He produced the sword and removed it from its sheath and handed it Nakahodot.

The chief examined it closely with admiration. He carefully ran his finger across the razor-sharp edge. "Ah, a good Spanish sword, indeed. Quite sharp. It makes one man fight with the strength of two."

"Precisely. It can also make one enemy *into* two," he said coyly. A few of the men laughed at his comment.

Calanele frowned though and said, "Enough of this talk of battle in front of the children. They were frightened enough today as it was."

"You are right," Nakahodot concurred. He continued to speak with Trapper. "You must stay with us. A lodge can be built for you."

Trapper raised his hand and said, "No, there is no need. I live deep in the woods to the south. I hunt better alone. I will return there tomorrow. But if I may, I will honor the chief with a gift." He got up from the fire and came back with a large black bear pelt and handed it to Nakahodot. "It is for the little one, so she can rest comfortably tonight. The chief's daughter will grow to have her mother's courage."

"I am honored with this gift, Bear Trapper. You hunt well, indeed. Let us share a smoke by the fire." The two men spoke well into the night while the rest of the tribe wearily made their way to their homes for a well-deserved rest in their new homeland.

The next morning a light mist was falling just as it had been the day before when they arrived. People were out and busily working in their continued efforts to establish their village.

As Trapper gathered himself to set out for his home in the forest, he noticed Nakahodot approaching and said to him, "Greetings to you, Light Hair."

"You should not call me that," Nakahodot retorted. "I am surprised you are not out hunting. Do you not have some bear cubs to chase? I should have a name for you as well. Perhaps Bear *Cub* Trapper."

Trapper shook his head and chuckled. He liked their light-hearted joking with one another. "I have heard talk amongst your tribe. Your tribe should not remain nameless. Word will spread of your victory in the early morning *nuna dochito*. The local chieftains will want to know who it was that defeated the Wichita."

"I have been giving the matter some thought," Nakahodot replied. "The victory would not have been so one-sided if not for your bravery."

"And my sword," Trapper said with a wink. "To another day, great chief." He turned and headed south into the forest.

"To another day," Nakahodot said in reply.

Word did indeed spread to all four points in the territory of their arrival and the great victory over the war party. The elders knew that soon the tribal leaders in the area would come to honor them and the spirit of Chief Caddo. Concerns grew louder within the tribe and each norming Calanele would ask her husband, "Are we still nameless?"

His reply would always be the same, "I am thinking on the matter."

Calanele would emerge from their hut and the other squaws, Adsila, Awinita, and Keme would wait impatiently to broach the subject once more. "Are we still nameless?" they would ask.

"He is still thinking on the matter," was her same response and the squaws would walk away disappointed to report back to their families.

After another long day of work in preparation for winter, Nakahodot wandered alone searching for the right place to sit and take in the nightly sunsets. He had missed his evening custom and decided it was a good time as any to re-establish it. Near the eastern edge of the village, overlooking the *lanana* creek, stood a small hillside. Parts of the rolling terrain rose nearly a hundred feet and provided an unobscured and spectacular view westward. Being nimble and an expert climber, it took Nakahodot only a few minutes to reach one of the higher points among them. He found a good place to sit and take in the beauty of the evening sunset.

"Where is Naka?" Awinita asked Calanele.

She pointed toward the cliff and answered, "He has found a place for his evening solitude. That is a good sign. I feel we will no longer be without a name. Go and tell the others to gather at the village fire."

After the sun had set, Nakahodot came down from the hill and was inspired to see the entire tribe had gathered at the central fire. He was also happy to see that Tuari and Tuwa were healing from their injuries and present at the fire as well.

Nakahodot spoke to the tribe, "We will no longer be nameless. We have become our own tribe and worked hard to establish a new village in this land. I am proud of how we stood together on our trek, but also especially the morning of our arrival. None of you knew we would be challenged at the outset by the Wichita. But we defended our families and saved this tribe. Since we fought in the early morning mist and fog to claim our land, we will be known as the *Nakadochito*."

Chapter 8

1690 - Two Years Later

As the seasons passed, the Nakadochito established a solid foundation for their village in the pine forests. They grew crops of corn, beans and squash in the spring and summer months. They caught small fish in the nearby streams and even found rivers a few days walk in which to catch larger fish. The wild game was plentiful and many times the tribe would meet up with their nearby Hasinai neighbors for hunts. They created an alliance with descendants of the ancient Caddoan people that formed the Nabedache and Nasoni tribes. They also befriended the Hainai and Nadote people. Nakahodot and his men became highly respected for their skills in tracking and hunting and with farming.

The tribe continued to grow as well. Tuwa had come of age and married Keme and started a family.

A great celebration was had with dancing and chanting the night Calanele gave birth to her second child, a son. At the sacred fire, she and Nakahodot announced their son would be called, Nashuk, for he was born with the thunder. The children of his tribe continued to grow and learn the ways of the Nakadochito.

Nakahodot became friends with the local chieftains as well. Chief Nabe became one of his closest allies. He lived to the west in an area that was known throughout many parts of the territory. The Nabedache tribe presided over the sacred and ample hunting ground known as the Pine Springs. A natural spring flowed from the ground into a creek that was attractive to the wild animals as well as the people. Many time's the tribes gathered at the camping grounds in the warmer months for great hunts. During one such time, Nakahodot sat with Nabe after many days of hunting, smoking by the fire.

"You hunt well, Nakahodot," the chief said as he passed the pipe over to him. "If you are intent on going back to your village tomorrow, I will ride with you for a while. I want to show you another trail."

"You know of another way?" Nakahodot asked.

Nabe nodded his head. "Yes, there is an area that I think you will be interested in seeing."

Nakahodot and his men rode along with Nabe. They traversed northward of the other forest trail they had taken to reach the hunting grounds. As they rode, Nabe explained to them the significance of the northern trail. "This path was used by the ancients that came as far as the Great River to hunt here and in parts westward. The search for buffalo was great even then, but they had to travel incredible distances west to reach them. It is even said ancient white explorers called *conquistadors* used this trail to reach the desert lands to the south. It is the same trail where I first saw the white Frenchmen some years ago."

Nakahodot rode alongside him as he was quite interested in what he had to say. "You saw the one they called *LaSalle*?"

"It is the same man," Nabe answered.

"I saw him once on a hunting party with my father. I learned that he was slain by his own men. They traveled on this trail?" Nabe nodded again. "It is a known trail to the whites then. I have often wondered why we have not seen more of these explorers. It is said they are many in number and can travel across vast oceans."

"This is one of the reasons I have showed you this route," Nabe continued. "I fear the time is coming that the whites will travel this way again but in greater number." As they continued up the trail, they soon came into a wide-open space. The land was a beautiful rolling blanket of green and stretched all the way to the horizon. They stopped their horses and looked at it in awe. It was then Nakahodot realized where they were.

"These are the ancient and sacred burial grounds my father spoke of," he said. "This is the land he tried to show us but never did. It is more beautiful than I could have imagined."

"It is sacred to all the Caddoan tribes," Nabe added. He motioned to large Earthen mounds that dotted the outermost parts of the landscape. Just beyond the mounds on both sides of the miles-long expanse were the edges of the forest. "This was the center of the ancient culture from which we have descended. It was their ceremonial area and burial grounds. It is forbidden to set foot on the mounds themselves, lest we disturb their spirit. But we are free to roam the interior and hunt."

"My father spoke of buffalo on this land," Nakahodot told him. "Have you ever seen them here?"

Nabe shook his head, saying, "Only have I heard stories of the buffalo. It is a hunt I have always dreamed about." He pointed directly east and said, "Continue straight across the open prairie until it meets the forest. You will then find the trail that will lead you home." He then bid them farewell, saying, "Go in peace, Nakadochito."

Months later, Nakahodot sat in front of his hut with Nashuk on his lap, watching Kewanee play with the hens, while Calanele was hanging gourds for the swallows.

"I heard them singing overhead just this morning," he said, calling out to this wife.

"That is why I am standing the gourds up, husband. I could do it much faster if you would stop sitting and help."

Kewanee giggled as she chased the hens around the yard. Her father got to his feet with Nashuk in tow. "Kewanee, come hold Nashuk while I help mother. Do you know what the swallows eat?"

She grudgingly came and took her baby brother and answered, "I think they eat worms just like my chickens."

"No. They eat insects in the air. That is why they never have to come to the ground." Kewanee made a face at the thought of eating insects.

They finished lashing the gourds to the post and then he helped his wife stand it in the ground. "There," she said, "the purple swallows will have a home now to nest."

"I will ride this day along the creek toward the south," he told his wife. "I have not seen our country in that direction since last fall."

"Find a nice deer if you can," she suggested, "or at least some rabbits for dinner."

"We have chickens right here," Nakahodot complained.

Kewanee pouted and said, "But you cannot eat my pet hens, Father."

He laughed and patted her on the head, saying, "You and your hens. You are aptly named, little one. I will return before sundown."

That afternoon he rode southward along Lanana Creek until it met at the fork with Banita Creek. Then he continued farther south along the stream, catching rabbits and stirring up pheasants along the way. He rode slowly along until he decided to stop and let his horse drink from the stream. As he sat on his mount, he heard a sound coming from around the bend. He directed his horse a few steps more but stopped abruptly. He was surprised to see a white man standing near the edge of the creek, wearing only trousers and boots. Nakahodot could only remember one other time seeing a man dressed such a way, but this one wore no shirt and was much older. He watched curiously as the man appeared to be grooming his face while staring at a shiny object lodged in a tree branch.

The man took no notice of Nakahodot and appeared to be alone. He had just finished shaving and trimming his mustache. He stooped to wash his face in the water, when he noticed a rabbit nearby. The man quietly stepped in one direction, when suddenly he leapt towards the furry creature. The rabbit hopped just out of reach and the man thumped to the ground. He lunged once more at the rabbit with the same result. He repeated his efforts in vain, leaping all around the creek and the mud trying desperately to catch the nimble rabbit, but still he failed. In one last effort, he threw himself to the ground, but the rabbit dashed away, not giving him any more chances.

It was then the man noticed he had been watched the entire time in his futile efforts. Startled, he got to his feet and stared at Nakahodot on his horse. He said nothing as he looked him over. He noticed some rabbits dangling alongside Nakahodot's horse.

"I see you had better luck than I did," the man said in his own language. Nakahodot could not understand so he said nothing.

Nakahodot felt he should be alarmed at seeing the white man so close to their village, yet he was still curious about him. He decided to leave the man in peace, but to go tell the elders and braves of what he had seen. The man watched silently as Nakahodot rode slowly away on his horse and rounded the bend out of sight.

Just then, another white man came and stood alongside the older man. "Who was that, Governor?" he asked.

"I do not know, Manuel. He did not speak. But its obvious there are other natives in this area."

That night in the smoking hut, Nakahodot told the other men what he had seen.

"Why do you think the man was alone?" asked Atohi.

"Perhaps he is a soldier lost from his men," Pakwa wondered.

Tuari then spoke, "Naka said he saw no weapon with the man. Maybe he was exiled from his people."

"We should ride out at first light and scout the whole area near the creek fork," Tuari suggested. We'll take spears and bows and arrows."

"I did not sense the man to be hostile," Nakahodot interrupted him. "If there is a chance for dialogue with this man, then we must try that first. He was alone but there is a possibility there were others nearby. I will ride out with Pakwa at first light. Tuari, you will come too. We will see why this man is in our country."

The next morning, the two braves were already on their horses when Nakahodot came out to join them. He climbed on his horse, then said to them, "Let us go."

Less than half a league away from the Nakadochito village, Bear Trapper rode with the two white men. They emerged from a clump of trees and rounded the bend, when suddenly an arrow came zipping through the air and thumped into a tree near them.

Trapper held up his hand for them to stop. "Say nothing." He saw Nakahodot and his companions step out from under the trees and stood about a hundred feet away. "We must get down from our horses, so they do not think we are hostile." The two white men got off their mounts while Trapper retrieved the arrow. He called out to Nakahodot, "Greetings, Light Hair. I have brought two men who wish to meet the chief of the Nakadochito."

Nakahodot sat silently, frowning at Trapper's wisecrack, as he observed the men who were with him. Now there were two white men instead of just one. *Surely there would be more,* he thought to himself.

"Why does he not answer?" the governor asked. "Does he speak your language?"

"He speaks it," Trapper said dryly, "he is just trying to irritate me."

The governor stood flustered. "I do not understand."

"I will speak with him. Stay here." Trapper walked with the arrow in hand over to his friends.

"You should not call me that," Nakahodot griped as his old friend approached. "Who are these men?"

"They are Spanish officers from the fort at Coahuila. They come in peace. They wish to meet you."

Nakahodot was surprised and asked, "You have learned their language?" Trapper nodded with pride.

Nakahodot got down from his horse and said to Pakwa and Tuari, "I will go and talk to these men. You wait here." He walked with Trapper back to where the governor and the other man were waiting patiently. He examined their clothing as he slowly walked toward them. The man he recognized from the day before was dressed in white trousers and shirt with a dark blue coat with red trim. Gold buttons lined the center of his shirt and stood out in the bright sun. The other man was dressed more modestly, but still very unusual to Nakahodot. The man wore the same white shirt with gold buttons but with blue trousers that matched the color of his coat with red trim. Each man held a dark hat trimmed with red on the brim under their arms.

Trapper said to the governor, "This is Nakahodot, chief of the Nakadochito."

The governor answered in reply, "I am Governor Alonso DeLeon. This is my aid, Sergeant Manuel Cortez. We have traveled from our fort San Juan Bautista of Coahuila. I remember seeing you yesterday." Nakahodot answered but the governor did not understand. "What did he say?"

Trapper answered, "He said you hunt poorly."

DeLeon laughed at himself, saying, "Yes, I am sure that was a bit of a whimsical sight. The little rabbit caught me unprepared." Trapper continued to translate their conversation. "I must apologize for my informal appearance yesterday. I wanted to make a better impression meeting you properly. I am sure you are wondering why we are here. I would very much like to sit down with you so we may discuss it." He hesitated when Nakahodot made no response. "This…is beautiful countryside you have here. I am an old man, but I am thankful that the Lord is allowing me to see it before I die." He glanced at Pakwa and Tuari still sitting on their horses watching intently. "Your men back there, they look very impressive. I would very much like to meet them as well."

"He talks a lot," Nakahodot said to Trapper who cracked a wry smile. "Tell him I invite them to our village tonight. I will share a pipe with him."

As the foreigners entered the village on horseback behind Nakahodot and his men, everyone in the village stopped and stared at the strangers. It was the first time that most of them had seen white men before. They marveled at the colorful clothing they wore with long swords hanging at their side.

As they rode into the village, Nakahodot announced to his tribe, "These men are *te'chas*."

With that, everyone in the village began to greet the newcomers by calling out, '*Te'chas! Te'chas!*' DeLeon smiled with amusement as they proceeded just outside Nakahodot's personal smoking hut where he directed them to come inside.

DeLeon motioned to Cortez, saying, "You stay outside, Sergeant. I will be fine by myself." He followed Nakahodot into the hut before Trapper could catch up to them. As soon as Cortez dismounted, Pakwa and several braves crowded around him, studying his attire, hat and his sword. He said nothing but sweat formed on his head as he stood before them nervously. Pakwa glared at him menacingly, yet still observed him with curiosity.

"I am very impressed with your camp, Chief Nakahodot," DeLeon began. He didn't even bother to wait for his translator. "I must admit I am a bit surprised at the number of natives in this area. The more I travel, the more I see. I certainly appreciate the friendly welcome of you and your people." Nakahodot sat across from him with a blank expression. He stirred the fire and prepared tobacco in his calumet, waiting impatiently for Trapper. Finally, Trapper entered the hut and quickly took a seat next to the chief.

"Where have you been?" Nakahodot asked flustered. "He has not stopped talking."

"Trapper, tell me what it is the people were saying to us as we rode in," DeLeon said, speaking out of turn once again. "I have heard a similar greeting."

Trapper looked over at Nakahodot and said, "He wants to know about the tribe's greeting."

"Yes. Tell him."

Trapper explained, "It is the customary greeting of friendship of the Hasinai people. It is their wish to spread the spirit of *te'chas* throughout the territory and to have peace, not war."

"I see," DeLeon answered curiously. "I like that. I do not wish to make war either. I have seen enough of it. I like the idea of having a territory and customs based on friendship. *Te'jas*, did you say?"

"*Te'chas*," Trapper corrected him.

"Yes. Yes. *Te'chas*. I am happy to be in your *te'chas* territory." He cleared his throat. He was sweating profusely and produced a white handkerchief and wiped his forehead. "I heard this greeting from the Nabedache people. This is why I came to speak with you when we came across one another yesterday."

"You have seen the Nabedache?" Nakahodot asked curiously.

"Yes," DeLeon continued. "We have spent the last several weeks in the Nabedache village. I do not know how familiar you are of the happenings in this land in recent years, but we are not the only foreigners here. The French are a people we have been in opposition with before even my time. We are all explorers, but we try to stay out of one another's way. They have their areas of occupation and we have ours. It came to our attention that the French attempted an installation along the coast some years ago in our territory. We learned it was a failed mission when a few deserters were found captured by the Karankawas."

Nakahodot nodded in understanding and said, "I knew and saw these French men and heard of their uprising. So, you know of the Karankawa? I have heard stories of these people by the sea." He began to understand the reach of these explorers and how they had a much stronger influence than he had first thought. The more he learned the more distressed he became.

DeLeon continued, "Yes, we found this tribe and two Frenchmen living among them. After we liberated the men, we burned what was left of their dilapidated fort. The men told us of their expedition in this territory before they were captured and of the many tribes that were here. I am a curious man, but I know my days are numbered. My health is failing, and my years of duty have taken their toll on me. I wanted to make one more exploration into the wilderness while I was still able."

"Why were you with the Nabedache for many weeks?" Nakahodot asked. His curiosity was getting the best of him. It seemed unlike his friend the chief to welcome foreigners for such a long period of time.

"You are a direct man, great chief. I appreciate that in a leader, and I will answer you directly. It is the desire of my

94

people and His Majesty, King Charles II, to continue to spread the Christian Word throughout the new territory. I left a company of men and one of my friars with the Nabedache, where we constructed a chapel as their new mission."

"What do you mean by *chapel* and *mission* and the *Christian Word*? What is this word?"

DeLeon was more than happy to answer. "We Spaniards practice a religion called Catholicism. It is our duty to spread the Word of God the Father. It is my understanding that your people have faith in a higher power called the 'great spirit'. This spirit you speak of is one and the same with God the Father."

Nakahodot's eyebrows raised with intrigue. He was quite interested in the governor now that he learned of his knowledge of their religious customs. "This God the Father is the same as our 'great spirit' in the heavens?" DeLeon nodded with a smile. "You call our 'great spirit' the *father*. Who or what is he the father of?"

"The answer to that question is our purpose here. We have come to tell you about the Christ." He produced a small wooden crucifix. "This is an image, a replica if you will, of the one we call the Son of God. He walked as a man on the Earth centuries ago and is called the Christ, which means 'Anointed One'. The chapel was constructed as a place of worship, dedicated to Christ. We do this to continue what Christ called His *mission* or *church*."

He handed the crucifix to Nakahodot who studied it closely. He saw that the image of the man appeared to be asleep or perhaps deceased. "Why is the image of the man hanging from the cross?"

"That is the glory and mystery of this image. The Son of God was put to death by people who did not believe him to be the Messiah, or the Christ. But He conquered death and was raised back to the living after three days." Nakahodot was astounded at hearing this story. "He is called Jesus. After He rose from the dead, He ascended into the Heavens where He is seated next to the right hand of God the Father. He is our judge and compassionate teacher of forgiveness and conqueror of evil, or what is called *sin*."

"This is truly an interesting story, Governor. I see that there is more for you to say on this, but I must share what you have told me to my people first. Are your intentions the same as it was for the Nabedache?"

DeLeon coughed as he shifted on the ground. "I was unaware of the great number of villages here, so I was not prepared to establish more than one mission on this journey. But now that I see you are here along with many others from what Bear Trapper has told me, I would like to return here one day with other friars who can teach your people more about Jesus Christ. Please accept this crucifix as my gift to you."

"I accept your gift. Let us smoke now and enjoy the fire." Nakahodot took a few puffs from his pipe and then handed it to DeLeon, who did the same in turn. It was all the information Nakahodot could handle in one afternoon. He decided it was best if they exchanged simple pleasantries from then on and enjoyed the smoking pipe. He knew that one day he would meet and converse with a white man, but the topic of conversation was unlike he had ever imagined.

After more than an hour, the men emerged from the hut to an eagerly waiting tribe and a beleaguered Sergeant Cortez sitting next to a tree, surrounded by braves. He looked as if he had been hazed and intimidated endlessly by the curious braves. They never harmed him although he looked like a nervous wreck.

"Sergeant," DeLeon barked, "that is enough fooling around with those men. Enough rest, let us get back to our horses." His knees almost buckled as he stood with a frazzled expression.

"Yes, please, Governor. Let us go," he mumbled.

Chapter 9

After his meeting with Nakahodot, DeLeon had Bear Trapper take him to meet the chief of the nearest tribe, the Hainai. The chief didn't let them enter the village, however, and turned them away. Although discouraged, DeLeon held onto his hope of bearing fruit with his mission after the successful meeting with Nakahodot. Satisfied for the time being, he returned to the fort at San Juan Bautista.

Nakahodot sent riders in all directions to the Nasoni, Nadote and Hainai tribes to call a meeting of the chiefs and elders. Knowing that the Nabedache were now occupied by the Spanish, they gathered together to discuss how best to approach the situation there and DeLeon's intentions. They were also clearly alarmed by the religious aspects of DeLeon's message and what to make of it.

The chief of the Nasoni spoke first, "This man claims to come in peace but the Nabedache are under their control. How can we allow them to bring more Spaniards to our tribes? My people are anxious about this intrusion."

The chief of the Hainai responded, "The governor did not say they were there to overthrow the Nabedache but to establish a religious mission. Should we not keep his word of being peaceful?"

"We must find a way to speak with Nabe himself," the chief of the Nadote affirmed. "It is the only way to find out why they have allowed the Spaniards to live among them. But if we enter the village, we might be taken under their control as well."

Nakahodot stood and spoke before the gathering, saying, "I will take two good men and ride the trail to the Nabedache just short of their camp and see if we can scout the village and possibly speak to the chief in secret. When we return, I will send word to you on what we have seen. If the governor's words are true, we will make further decisions at that time. If I see that DeLeon has gone against his word, we will form a war party and liberate the Nabedache." All the men nodded in agreement. Then

Nakahodot reminded them of the other matter. He produced the crucifix that DeLeon had given him. "What do your people say about this image? What is your reaction to the story DeLeon has told about the 'great spirit' being the father of this Jesus who walked the Earth as a man?"

"My people are skeptical, as am I," the chief of the Nasoni answered. "How can one know personally the unseen spirit in which we believe, or that he has an equal that walked the Earth? If Jesus is his son, then the implication is that Jesus is equal to the 'great spirit'. How would one know this?"

The chief of the Hainai patted his shoulder and replied, "We were only told part of this story. There is obviously more to be told or the Nabedache would not have agreed to the chapel being built. We should learn more about this story to decide further. Or the people will grow more anxious."

"What do you think, Chief Nakahodot?" asked the chief of the Nadote.

"I was intrigued by his story," Nakahodot began. "A story about a holy man who walked the Earth is one thing, but to say that he died but then rose from the dead, this is considerably significant. I too am skeptical, but this is the one aspect of the story that troubles me. As you know, it is not our belief to speak of the dead, much less say they will rise again. If this Jesus was the son of the 'great spirit', then that is the only way I could believe it to be true. If the 'great spirit' *were* to have a son, not even death would overcome him."

Atohi had been sitting quietly listening to what all the chiefs were saying. As they continued murmuring amongst themselves, he posed the question to them, "If a man were to walk the Earth, he would have had a mother. Who would the mother be of this son of the 'great spirit'? And how can spirit conceive a son?"

The murmuring grew louder, and no one had clear answers to either question. Nakahodot spoke once more after the men settled, "These are key questions that we must get answers to. Otherwise our tribes will not be at rest. We will meet again after I return from the Nabedache."

The four leaders of the tribes were satisfied with their discussions on the matter and agreed to meet again after they received word from Nakahodot.

As fall slowly gave way to winter, the rain and cold was persistent and there were few days in which the weather was fair enough to make the journey to the Nabedache. While Nakahodot waited for the stormy weather to pass, the people in his village became more and more anxious. The women in particular, to his surprise, were the most anxious. There was one question that weighed heavy on their minds about the story of Jesus.

Every morning Calanele would rise before her husband and go and speak with the other squaws while they gathered water at the creek. She would wait for her husband to emerge from their home and would ask him each time, "What is his mother's name?"

Each day his answer would be the same. "I do not know this answer, my wife."

"The women want to know these answers, Naka. As do I. If these men are to return to live among us and start preaching about the holy man, the women will not listen if we do not learn more. I will not listen either. You must make this go away or give us a reason to believe." Nakahodot let out a heavy sigh. He didn't know how to answer his impatient wife. He tried to ignore her, but she persisted. "Their husbands are silent on the matter as you are as well. When will you go to see Nabe? Your hesitation cannot be because of the cold rain. Your friend deserves your attention. If you do not, the other chieftain's will take matters into their own hands." He tried to turn away from her, but she grabbed him by the arm and forced him to look at her. "Naka, *listen* to me. Are you believing this story? Why do you keep waiting?"

Nakahodot finally turned to his wife. She could see the look of worry and doubt on his face. "I have never been faced with something like this before," he began. "I do not know what to think about the man on the cross. All I know is the Spaniards *do* believe. To be able to travel such great distances as they do, without fear, and be able to explore foreign lands like ours, it must mean there are thousands more where they came from. That would mean thousands more believe in this man called Jesus. There must be a reason for this, my wife." He straightened himself and caressed the side of her face in a loving way. "I will put that aside for now. I assure you these answers will be revealed to us in their own way but for the present, we must focus on the Nabedache. Tell the women not to be anxious. We are still the Nakadochito." A look of pride overcame Calanele when she heard his words and saw his confidence. "I will ride today to see Nabe."

Nakahodot sat on his horse with Pakwa and Tuari on theirs. Calanele stood at his side to wish them well on their journey. "Take an extra fox pelt to keep you warm on the ride," she said as she handed him the pelt. "I still want to know his mother's name."

"You will know, my wife. We shall return."

The three men set out in the cold winter morning. They rode for two days down the ancient trail and across the prairie of the sacred burial grounds. The wind was blistering cold and they shielded their faces as best they could.

"The winter is harsh," Pakwa said as they rode. "It will only make the spring come in more severe."

"We have seen it before," Nakahodot added. He slowed his horse as he could see they were near the Nabedache village. He came to a complete stop and his did his companions. "We will go on foot the rest of the way."

They dismounted their horses and quietly made their way toward the village. It was late in the afternoon and the thick clouds brought the first signs of dusk in the dense forest. The leafless trees crackled in the frozen air and knocked against one another in the wind. When they caught sight of people in the village, they crouched low to the ground so not to be seen. They noticed right away the light of the fire in the center of the village. *That is a normal sign*, thought Nakahodot. The few people he could see appeared to be working and carrying on in their usual manner. One woman was carrying water skins while another combed the hair of two young girls wrapped in animal pelts.

Through the trees, he noticed a foreign structure set near the edge of the village. It was constructed with wood in a way he had never seen before. It wasn't round as their homes were, but straight walls of wood and stone and had angled corners instead of curved ones. The roof appeared to be lined with wood and covered with thatch. He could only surmise the structure was the chapel that the governor had spoken about.

Tuari leaned closer and whispered, "Nothing appears unusual to me. Let us go into the village."

Out of the corner of his eye, Nakahodot caught sight of more people. "Wait," he whispered back to Tuari. "Look." The three of them watched in awe as a long procession of white men and Indians slowly walked through the village toward the chapel. Some of the Spaniards were dressed in the same uniforms as DeLeon and Cortez were, and others were plainly dressed. At the head of the procession was a man dressed in a long black cloak. He had beads hanging from his belt with a small crucifix attached to the beads. On his head he wore a black, triangular cap and his outstretched arms he carried a staff that was topped with a larger crucifix. They paraded slowly across the village and finally reached the chapel where everyone in the procession entered.

"Why are there no drums or chanting?" asked Pakwa. "It is a strange sight."

"It must be one of their Christian customs," Nakahodot answered. "It is clear the people are following in this ritual."

"Should we go into the village?" Tuari asked.

Pakwa backed away and stood behind them next to a tree. A look of fear was in his eyes. "I will not go. This ritual looks eerie to me. Why are the people so quiet?"

Tuari got to his feet and retreated with Pakwa. "They could be under a spell. Their will looks taken from them."

Nakahodot stood and walked quietly over to his frightened companions. "These men do not cast spells. That is nonsense. Are we not solemn when one of our own has died? We do not know the reason behind this ritual we see. Do not rush to judgement. What I see is what DeLeon told us. It must be part of the teaching of the Christian Word. I see no need to disturb the chief during the ritual. We must go now and tell the others what we have seen."

The winter grew more harshly as the days wore on and it took them much longer to return to the village. It was several weeks before the chiefs from the other tribes could re-assemble to discuss the matter further. The day came when the leaders of the four tribes reconvened.

"The rumors are growing about our brothers at the Nabedache," the chief of the Nasoni said. "It is said they are under control of the whites."

"I am here to dispel these rumors," Nakahodot responded. "Nothing that I saw would suggest they were being controlled. The people walked freely amongst the whites."

"Did you speak directly with their chief?"

"We did not go into the village," Nakahodot answered. "The Christians were leading them in a procession."

The chief pushed him further though, saying, "You did not go into the village because your men were afraid of this procession. It is my opinion the whites have put the Nabedache under their control in their own village. We must *stop* this."

The meeting was going just as Nakahodot had feared. He had to think of something, or he knew the other tribes would form a war party and use force. He tried to diffuse the situation in saying, "I do not share that opinion. We saw squaws tending to children and doing routine tasks like you would see in any village. The ritual we witnessed must have been one that was part of the Christian faith. I did not see it as harmful to the people or their minds. I feel further attempts must be made to speak with Nabe. Entering the village is safe in my opinion."

The chief of the Hainai spoke, saying, "Spring will be here soon, and with it more of the Spaniards to build their chapels and to force us to do their rituals too."

"I do *not* think it is being forced on them," Nakahodot insisted.

102

"I agree," the chief of the Nadote said, ignoring Nakahodot, "when the winter has broken, we must act quickly to liberate our brothers." He turned and spoke directly to Nakahodot. "You will join the war party, or we will go without you."

The meeting was spiraling out of Nakahodot's control. Nothing he could say would change their minds, yet he tried in vain. "We must reconsider this, my brothers! More talk is needed with the tribe themselves. We must let them speak!" But the more he raised his voice in protest, the louder the gathering became in favor of war.

Later that night, Nakahodot sat alone in his smoking hut, staring helplessly at the crucifix DeLeon had given him. As he stared at the cross, he thought of the significance it must bear for the Spaniards. *To go through such extreme measures to spread this man's word, they must have exceptional faith in him,* he thought to himself.

Just then, Atohi entered the smoking hut. He saw Nakahodot examining the crucifix as he sat across from him. "You are still considering the man's story, are you?" he asked.

"Hello, my friend. Come share a smoke with me." He put the cross down and lifted the pipe and took a long draw from it. Then he handed it over to Atohi, saying, "Fresh tobacco."

Atohi took the pipe and smoked it. "Ah, that is a good smoke. Always helps after a gathering such as the one we just had."

"Yes, indeed."

"I understand your hesitation to go along with them. Their plans are hasty. They are only looking one way and not the other. Many of them, like myself, did not speak to this governor as you did."

Nakahodot nodded and said, "It was the first white man who had spoken to me directly. When we met LaSalle years ago, he only spoke with my father. The man I met here in this hut seemed very genuine to me. I did not sense any deception from him."

"A wise and trusted man knows when he is speaking to another," Atohi added.

Nakahodot picked up the crucifix once more and looked at it thoughtfully. "Atohi, what do you think it means when an entire culture, that we can see is very strong, puts its faith in a story like this one? That their entire way of life is based on this man's words?"

Atohi reached across to take the crucifix from Nakahodot and he examined it closely. After a few moments, the wise man answered by saying, "It means that this Jesus must have been an extraordinary man." He handed the cross back to him and added, "You will make the right decision for our people. I trust in you." He got to his feet and dusted himself off. He pulled the flap open, but before he left, he said, "That was a good smoke. And a good fire." Nakahodot nodded with a smile as he watched him leave.

He went back to staring at the wooden cross in a reverential manner and thought to himself, *Son of God, if you are the equal to our 'great spirit', then you already know the many ways to help us in this matter.* Then he spoke out loud, "Show us the way."

Chapter 10

With the dawning of spring came the drumbeats of war from the three camps of the Hainai, Nadote and Nasoni. Nakahodot had sent riders to see if there were any signs of a war party preparing to set out. When they returned, they informed the chief that plans were underway, and they would be setting out at first light. The entire tribe of the Nakadochito was on edge and awaiting word from their leader.

"What will you do, husband?" Calanele asked him. Pakwa was also anxiously awaiting what Nakahodot would decide.

Nakahodot turned to Pakwa and said, "I want you to stay here with the tribe. I leave you in my place while I am gone. Keep the people safe from any danger that you see."

"What will you *do*, husband?" Calanele frantically asked again.

"I will ride out to the Nabedache tonight. I must warn them before the warriors arrive. I owe that to my friend."

Pakwa grabbed him by the arm and insisted, "I will ride with you."

"No. I ride faster alone. I need you here to protect our people. Be prepared for any attack if they decide to turn on us." He hugged Calanele tightly and said, "Watch over our little ones. I will return."

She quickly grabbed a water skin and handed it to him as he leapt on his horse. "Go to our friends, Naka. Warn them!"

Nakahodot set out on the fastest horse in the village. He rode through the night by the light of the half moon. When he saw how much light the moon gave, he realized the war party might leave sooner as well, so he pushed his horse even harder. The wind howled through the trees as he raced through the woods. He rode for hours without stopping in the blistering wind. He reached the sacred lands and darted across the prairie bathed in moonlight. The swirling wind parted a path for him through the tall grass. The mighty horse dashed into the woods once again after crossing the prairie and soon he reached the outer edges of the village. As dawn approached, he pulled the tired, grunting animal to a stop and jumped off. He patted the horse and smiled at him gratefully. "You ran like the wind this night. Rest now."

He observed the village closely in the early morning mist. The wind continued to rage through the treetops. He could tell from the forming clouds overhead that a storm was coming. He walked closer to the village and saw no one about. There was no fire burning in the center, not even smoke from a smoldering one. As he drew nearer, he heard a person coughing from within one of the huts. The cough was one of severe illness. He fully expected to see many people outside at this time of morning but there was no one. *Where are all the people?* he thought to himself.

He entered the village and looked around curiously. It was though it had been nearly deserted. He found Nabe's smoking hut and headed toward it when suddenly a man grabbed him by the shoulder. Nakahodot was stunned to see Nabe, who appeared disheveled and gaunt.

"You have come too late, my friend," the chief said in a weak voice. He quickly led him away from the camp. "You must leave this place, or you will be stricken too. It is best if you stand clear of me as well."

Nakahodot was flummoxed. "Why? What has happened here? Where are the Spaniards?"

Nabe answered directly, "They have either died or fled to their post. People began to get sick. Months passed before the Spaniards sent relief to their own. When they came, they said the governor had died. When they saw the spread of disease, they said there was no more need for their mission."

"Why have the people become ill?" Nakahodot pressed him.

"They brought religion, but they brought disease with them too. Many of them were not clean and undisciplined unlike the friar. His people lost faith in him when they started becoming ill." He cleared his throat and tried his best not to cough. He continued, "Naka, there is nothing but death here now. My days

106

are numbered. I have already lost my beloved wife and my son. You must go for your own sake. Leave this place. It is only full of pestilence."

"Nabe, you must listen to me. Our brothers from the Hainai, Nadote and Nasoni are convinced you are being held against your will by the whites. They would not listen to me when I told them you knew the decisions you made were just for your people. They are coming with a war party. I came ahead of them to warn you."

Nabe shook his head and said, "There is nothing you can do here. If they come, they will put us out of our misery. Now go." He quickly turned and stumbled back toward the village.

Nakahodot was distraught and called out to him. "Nabe...*Nabe*." He became angry when his friend kept running away. "I will not let that happen! We will come for you. You have my word!"

With that he dashed out into the early morning fury toward his horse. The wind had become a raging storm when he leapt onto the stallion. He quickly headed back to the trail to try to head off the war party. Lightning flashed, and thunder roared as the rain began to fall. Soon the rain had become a torrent, yet Nakahodot continued to race toward the sacred plains. The rain slackened as the horse ran but the wind and thunder continued to slam against them. He reached the clearing and saw the fire light ahead of the charging war party. He heard the chants and yells of the warriors as they thundered across the prairie. Nakahodot yelled and screamed, waving his arms frantically to try to get them to see him and stop, but it was of no use. The war party continued its charge in the fierce wind.

In the raging fray, Nakahodot could hear the frightening sound of crackling, snapping wood behind him. The splintering roar was awesome yet terrifying. He turned to look over his shoulder to see what was happening. He was shocked to see the forest being shredded by the harrowing wind. Enormous trees were being snapped and swirled about like twigs. Within seconds it appeared as if the entire forest was being obliterated and thrashed about by the wrath of nature.

The charging warriors saw the flailing and screaming Nakahodot racing across the prairie when suddenly a giant swirling mass in the clouds ripped through the trees and pounded the open land with a fury. The tornado stunned the men and horses and all of them went scattering in every direction. Nakahodot leapt from his mount and the horse instinctively darted for cover on the outer edges of the sacred lands. Nakahodot fell to the ground face first and covered his head and ears. The sound was deafening, and the wind sliced through everything in its path. Both man and beast were swept into the incredible spinning, chaotic force and tossed like dolls thousands of feet across the sky.

As the tornado ripped its way eastward, a shocked and awestruck Nakahodot lifted his head and opened his eyes. The path of destruction was enormous and wide. Splintered trees and branches lay everywhere. He was stunned to see that none had fallen on him. His eyes followed the funnel cloud as it moved quickly away from him. "Calanele!" he yelped. He jumped to his feet and looked frantically for his horse. He stumbled over rain-soaked and fractured wood, still in shock from the sudden storm. He yelled out for any sign of life in the area. No one from the war party was seen anywhere. They had all been swept away.

He ran for hours following the wide path of tornadic destruction. The land was devastated, and he feared the worst when he would see his own village. Soon, to his surprise, he came across his faithful horse. The animal had settled and was no longer frightened. It even appeared to be happy to see Nakahodot when he approached.

"There you are, my brave friend," Nakahodot said with a smile. The horse neighed softly and nuzzled him gratefully. "You are courageous indeed, my trusted stallion. Come, let us find our home."

When he finally arrived home, he was shocked to see that the village remained untouched by the tornado. The wind had blown much of the thatch off their homes, but none had been destroyed. The people ran out to greet their chief when he rode to the center of the village.

"Naka, you are safe!" his wife cried out. She hugged him tightly as he jumped off his horse.

Pakwa immediately found him and said, "Naka, an angry cloud came down and nearly blew our homes away. It came near to the village but stopped before getting any closer. Did you see it?"

"Yes, I saw it," he assured him. "Much closer than I wanted to. There are many hearts on the ground though. The angry cloud struck the war party." The people stood in awe as they heard him tell the story. "I reached the Nabedache before the war party, but the Spaniards had left them. Many of the people were dying of illness. I do not even know if they survived the storm or not. But we must form a rescue party. They need food and care. Tell Atohi we will need his medicine and sacred smoke. We need to save as many as we can from the village and look for survivors of the war party. Come, we must act quickly."

Nakahodot set out with nearly everyone from the tribe, including women and children, who could help with the recovery and rescue. He sent a large contingent of people ahead to make the treacherous trek toward the Nabedache village to bring medicine and food. They had to traverse through a great field of debris, fallen trees and branches most of the way, so the trip there was slow.

They used their horses to move large trees out of the way, while others moved the smaller brush by hand. "We must clear the ancient path the entire way to the Nabedache," Nakahodot declared.

While they worked, others searched for survivors of the doomed war party. They did find some but were severely injured. They gave them aid and water and brought them along as they continued their search. They found many who were dead though, and all were gathered together for a sacred burial. They built a large fire and did dances while they chanted to the drums. They honored their fallen brothers and covered them with loosened Earth and formed one large mound.

Word had spread to the three tribes of how the Nakadochito honored their dead. When they had heard, the three chiefs sought them out to thank them and in doing so, joined in the process of clearing the trees and bringing more aid to the Nabedache. All the tribes had been affected by the terrible storm, so they came together as one to restore life to their country. The chiefs of the three tribes rescinded their intention to attack the Spaniards upon their future return and vowed to open a more thorough dialogue with them when the day would come.

When they reached the village of the Nabedache, they found the chapel had been badly damaged and the majority of the village destroyed by the storm. There were less than two dozen survivors, but the rescue party had been tending to their needs and they were no longer in danger of illness or starvation. Nakahodot was saddened to learn that his great friend, Chief Nabe, had died during the terrible storm. So, the entire gathering of the five tribes honored the fallen chief with a great burial ceremony that lasted three days. They processed with the chief's body deep into the forest to leave it to the 'great spirit' in accordance with his tribes wishes.

The Nabedache would live on in peace after the four tribes left them. Over time, life was renewed on the lands and new growth emerged from the scorched Earth. Nakahodot continued to visit the tribe and hunt with them by the Pine Springs.

Two years later, a small contingent of Spanish soldiers and friars came back to their chapel but only to burn what remained to the ground. With little or nothing to say, they returned to their fort in Coahuila and left the tribe in peace.

The mission that was called *San Francisco* had failed but Nakahodot and the other chieftains knew it would only be a matter of time before the Spanish would return and try again.

Chapter 11

In the spring of 1694, young Kewanee was seven years old and her younger brother Nashuk was four. When Kewanee learned that their mother was expecting a third child, she never left her mother's side.

"Your motherly instincts are coming alive in you, little one," Calanele said to her as Kewanee helped her to her feet. "Ah, but you are not so little anymore, are you? Perhaps one day you will be a mother too."

"I do not think so, Mother," Kewanee answered, squinting her face. "I do not care for any of these boys."

"Well, I did not care for too many of them at your age either, but you still have time. You never know when you may change your mind about a young brave someday."

"I hope you have another girl," she said excitedly. "I always wanted to have a younger sister. Please do not have another boy. Nashuk is so messy."

Calanele laughed as she walked outside and said, "I am afraid I do not have much choice in the matter. It is one or the other."

"Or maybe you will have one of each! Father is a twin. Maybe you will have twins too."

Calanele rolled her eyes and sighed heavily. "Please, child, for the sake and grace of the 'great spirit' and for mine, please let it only be *one*."

Nakahodot came walking up with Nashuk on his shoulders, who was carrying some small fish. "Mother, I caught fish!" Nashuk announced gleefully.

She smiled at them and said, "Ah, a tasty meal we will share then, yes? I hope you catch more because I am very hungry."

"We have to keep mother fed well," Nakahodot said as he set Nashuk down. "She is eating for two."

"I am hoping for three," Kewanee chimed in. Calanele playfully slapped her shoulder with her shawl.

"When will the baby come, Mother?" Nashuk asked.

"Not now and not while everyone is crowding around me," she barked. "Go and cook your fish. Kewanee, you go help." The children scampered off while she hung some pelts to air out.

"Here," Nakahodot said, "let me help you with those. You rest there on the stump." He hung the pelts on some tree branches while she sat and rested. "The time is drawing near, is it not?"

"Yes, I hope so," she responded, fanning herself. "I hope it is soon. The air is turning hot."

"I have been thinking," he continued, "once the baby has arrived, the tribe should go on a journey."

"A journey?" she asked curiously. "All of us? Where would we go?"

"I think its time we go and find our other families that are with my brother Natchitos. Many of us have missed them and it is my place to see that we visit our loved ones."

Calanele was overcome with joy. She pushed herself off the stump with one hand and ran over to her husband. "Oh yes, Naka. This is a wonderful idea. We must go see them."

He was glad to see his wife's enthusiasm and answered, "The weather is good. We could travel eastward and reach them in a week's time. I have arranged with the other tribes to look after our crops and let them use what they need while we are away. We could be back by the fall."

"Yes, this is a wonderful idea," she said again. She was very excited. "When will you tell the tribe?"

"I will tell them soon, my wife," he said chuckling at her.

In the coming weeks, White Owl stayed close to Calanele but knew in her old age she would not be able to attend her like she wanted to. "When the time comes, child, I will send for Mitena to help you."

"No, Mother," Calanele whined, "you have always helped all the women in the village. No one knows better than you."

112

"I am too old now," answered White Owl. "Mitena is well suited for this. I have sought Pakwa for his permission to let Mitena take my place when my time comes to cross over to the 'great spirit'. You will be in good hands with her. I will stay with you though."

"Good, good. As long as you are near." Calanele took her hand and smiled. "Do not say such things, Mother. You have years ahead of you."

One morning while Nakahodot took his ride along the creek, he heard in the distance the roar of an animal. He stopped on his horse and pulled his bow off his shoulder. He looked intently through the thick trees and brush, listening for the growl once more. The sound of the water trickled by and the wind blew softly through the tall pines. His horse became unsteady, sensing something nearby. He did his best to calm the stallion, but it remained restless. Then, from the corner of his eye, Nakahodot spotted three cubs tromping through the pine straw about fifty feet away on an incline. Following right behind the three cubs was their mother, slowly padding from side to side as she walked.

"Easy," he whispered to his startled mount. "We will stay quiet here for a moment and let them pass." As he watched the bears, he remembered the time when he was a young brave and his brother and Tooantuh played a trick on him with a sleeping bear. He smiled as he remembered being chased up a tree. As he waited on his patient horse, they quietly watched the mother bear and her three cubs disappear into the forest.

When he returned to the village, he saw Pakwa running from the fields toward his hut. "Where are you running to?" Nakahodot called out to him.

"It is your wife's time!" he yelled back. "I must get Mitena."

Nakahodot leapt off his horse and ran with him, asking, "Mitena? Why not White Owl?"

"White Owl has sent my wife in her place, although she will stay by Calanele's side. I have agreed to it."

Nakahodot shook his head and fretted, "The chief is the last to know. Go. Bring her as quickly as you can."

As the hours passed, he paced out in front of his home, watching his two younger ones play in the grass below the martin gourds. After what seemed like an eternity, an exhausted Mitena emerged from the hut.

"You may go in now," she told Nakahodot. Kewanee jumped to her feet, eager to go inside too. "But only your father," she instructed the frowning Kewanee.

Nakahodot entered the hut to find White Owl stirring the fire from a seated position. He saw that Calanele was asleep and the newborn was wrapped in pelts and lying on a bed near White Owl. "How is my wife?" he asked.

White Owl carefully lifted the child into her arms and said, "You have a second son. But your wife will need more rest. She had a difficult time. I must tell you that she may never bear any more children after this one."

His body trembled at hearing the unexpected news. White Owl handed him his son and he looked at him lovingly. His thoughts returned to Calanele though, and he asked worriedly, "Will she be alright?"

"She will, but you must give her time before returning to her side."

He understood and nodded. He thanked her as he handed the child back to her. "No one can replace you, great Onacona. I am glad you are here."

On the third day, another celebration was held for the newest arrival in the tribe. Nakahodot was worried that his wife would not be able to get out of bed but by the third day, she was able to come and join the celebration. He helped her to her feet and led her out to the fire where the entire tribe had gathered. Drums were played while others dressed in ceremonial headdress and colorful beads as they danced around the fire. They chanted and shouted and eagerly awaited the chief to announce the name of the newborn child.

After the dances had ended, Nakahodot stood and held his second son for all to see. "My Son," he began, "on the day you were born, I came across a growling bear protecting her three cubs. Therefore, you will be called Notaku."

Everyone yelled and chanted at hearing the name given and the dances commenced once more. Nakahodot sat with Notaku in his lap and Kewanee and Nashuk sat next to him.

"Did you really see a growling bear, Father?" Kewanee asked curiously as she watched by the firelight.

"Yes, I did," he answered her. "She had three cubs with her, just as your mother and I have now."

"I still wished she was going to have twins," she pouted. She looked over at her new baby brother and asked, "What is it like to be a twin, Father?"

He smiled at the question and answered, "Ah, it is a wonderful thing. You do the same things together and you even argue about the same things over and over. It is even said that twins know what the other is thinking and feeling."

Kewanee beamed at the notion. "Oh, I like that! I wish I had a twin sister so I could know what she was thinking. Now I have another little brother. I hope little Notaku is not as dirty as Nashuk."

"I am *not* dirty," Nashuk complained. "You are."

Kewanee ignored him though, saying, "I am not a twin, but I know all you think about is playing in the mud, Nashuk." She turned to Nakahodot and asked, "Father, do you know what your brother is thinking even though you have not seen him in a long time?"

"So many questions!" He adjusted Notaku in his arms and thought of an answer. After a moment he smiled at his other two children and said, "Perhaps I do know. I would say that he is thinking it is time our paths crossed again."

Two weeks later, the entire tribe of the Nakadochito marched with all their belongings eastward. Some rode on horses while others walked beside them. Calanele rode a horse with Notaku resting comfortably in a papoose against her breast. Spirits were high as they trekked toward the rising sun and the land they once called home.

When they reached the waters of the Sabine, they set out in canoes they had carried with them, chanting and singing the entire way across the river. Braves guided the horses across single-file through the water until they emerged on the other side. Then the journey continued onward slowly for several more days.

Rising high above the waters of the cane, sat Natchitos. He was quiet and contemplative as he watched the sun rise over the meandering river. For seven years he had presided over the Nashitosh in this fertile, yet humid land. He watched his tribe grow since the days they had lived by the Sabine River. They worked hard in their crops, fished the ample waters and hunted the dense forests nearby. Unlike his brother though, they had yet to encounter any white explorers in their new homeland.

After he was satisfied, he climbed down the hill that overlooked his village to start the new day. While he was still descending the hill, a rider came behind him from the west, cresting the hill and trotted down to the village.

"Chief!" he called out to Natchitos. "I have just come from the forest. A caravan of our brothers is approaching."

This perked Natchitos' curiosity greatly. "A caravan here? How many do they number?"

"Forty-five, maybe more," the brave answered.

"Alert Tooantuh and Sitting Crow," he ordered. "We will go out and meet these brothers." He quickly mounted a horse and rode up the hill and out toward the forest.

Within minutes Tooantuh and Sitting Crow came up alongside him. "Who do you think is coming?" they asked Natchitos.

Soon, they saw the band of people coming through the woods on foot and on horseback. Instantly all three of them recognized who it was. Natchitos' heart welled in his chest as his brother triumphantly walked up to him and stopped.

116

"Greetings, brother," Nakahodot called out. "The Nakadochito have come to visit your lands."

Natchitos smiled happily and hopped off his horse. He quickly ran to his brother and they locked arms in the traditional greeting. "Naka!" he cried. "It's *you*. And you have brought everyone."

"Yes, brother. It is a long journey to this land of yours. Much longer than three days."

"Greetings, Naka," Tooantuh said. "Glad to see you still have your light hair."

"Greetings, Tooantuh," he answered with a grin. "So am I."

Natchitos immediately pulled his brother to the side, eager to get caught up. He completely forgot about the tired mass of people waiting to proceed the last few minutes to the village. They waited patiently while the brothers talked.

"I see you still have my quiver of arrows," he joked.

"*Your* quiver?"

Natchitos laughed at himself. He was so full of joy seeing his brother and his tribe, he could barely contain himself. "Hang onto it for me for the time being. Tell me, Naka. What did you find after your three days of traveling westward?"

Nakahodot replied, "We found land with tall pine trees, rolling hills, and fresh water from two creeks. Our village sits between the two streams of water."

"*Streams*?" Natchitos asked astounded. "Sounds grim, brother. Do they ever run dry?"

"Grim?" he answered. "Perhaps one summer the waters were nearly dry. But we have always been blessed with more rains in the fall."

Finally, Natchitos noticed how the tribe was waiting patiently on them. "Look at me going on. We will have plenty of time to talk in the village. Your people are tired and need rest. Come, let me show all of you something wonderous."

As they reached the crest of the hill, the tribe was astonished to see the vibrant village set alongside the lazy river. The river ran as far as the eye could see in both directions north and south. Nakahodot shook his head, staring at it in bewilderment. He patted Natchitos on the shoulder and said, "An excellent choice indeed, brother."

The Nakadochito settled in along with the Nashitosh and a great feast was prepared that same night to celebrate their arrival.

Taima sat with Calanele who was holding her newborn Notaku on her lap while they watched the dancing at the fire. "Notaku is a beautiful baby, Calanele. I know the journey must have been hard with such a little one."

"Thank you," she answered. "The journey was long, but I am so happy to be here with you again. I love the river you have chosen. How many children do you have now?"

She motioned to one of the young braves sitting with the other boys. "We still just have little Anoki. He and Tokala are good friends. They are always hunting together."

"I cannot believe how much they have *grown*," Calanele exclaimed.

"Yes, they have." Then she looked back at Calanele, saying, "You are so blessed to have three already. How wonderful that must be." A dour look came upon Calanele's face when she said this. "What is the matter?"

"My mother said to me that Notaku may be my last," she answered sadly. "She told me I was close to death." Tears began to stream down her cheeks.

Taima did her best to comfort her. "Do not lose hope. There is still time. I have prayed much for another, but the years keep passing for me as well. I do wish very much so to give Natchitos another son, or even a sweet daughter like your Kewanee."

Calanele wiped her tears and said, "Forgive me for being selfish. Of course, you will. The 'great spirit' will bless you again I am certain. You are still very young."

The next night when the village had settled after all the celebrating, Natchitos invited his brother into the smoking hut. They sat across the fire from one another and Nakahodot watched him unroll a leather pouch containing a calumet. Then he produced a pouch of fresh tobacco and slowly prepared the pipe to smoke.

"You have done well here, brother," Nakahodot began. "Your crops look better than I have ever seen. And the river is quite suitable."

"Not quite the same as our home on the Sabine, but the waters of the cane still are quite nice."

"There is cane by the waters?" Nakahodot asked curiously.

"Yes," Natchitos replied. "I will show you tomorrow. I will have Tooantuh cut some bagasse for us."

Nakahodot smiled at the thought. "It has been years since I have chewed some good bagasse. I look forward to that." Then his tone became more serious. "Tell me, brother, have you come across the whites in this territory?"

"Do you remember the white French man, LaSalle, when we were boys?" Natchitos asked. Nakahodot nodded to him. "He was the first and last white man I have ever seen. I have heard stories of them to the south of here and to the west, but none have I seen here thus far." He could tell from the question that his brother may have encountered more since their meeting with LaSalle. "Have you?"

"Yes, I have."

Natchitos was curious. "More Frenchmen?"

"No," Nakahodot answered, shaking his head. "These men were Spaniards. And they came spreading the word of a holy man from hundreds of years ago whose image they carried on a cross. Have you heard the story of the man called Jesus?"

"No, I have not."

"The story was told to me by the Spanish governor DeLeon. He claimed to have come from lands far south of where we are.

119

He spoke of the Karankawa by the sea. I only met him and another soldier along with Bear Trapper."

"You have seen Bear Trapper?" Natchitos asked surprised.

Nakahodot nodded, saying, "Yes, he lives alone with bears and the deer. He trades with these white men and works for them as a translator. He even knows the Spanish words. But the governor told me he started a religious chapel among the Nabedache called a 'mission' and that he intended to build more at our village and other nearby Hasinai villages. He never returned though. We soon learned that he had died and given up on the chapel at the Nabedache. We then learned that the white men had brought disease to their tribe. Our brothers wanted to make war on the Spanish, but they had already left."

"I do not know of this Spaniard you speak of," Natchitos said in return, "but I have heard stories around many campfires of this war party. The story is an intriguing one," he said with a smile.

"What is this story?" Nakahodot asked curiously.

"The story is of a great light-haired warrior who rode his horse across a prairie alongside an angry cloud from the sky. The warrior thrust the angry cloud upon the war party and swept them away." Natchitos took a long draw on the smoking pipe and asked wryly, "What do you know of this story?"

Nakahodot's face turned red and he smiled sheepishly. "Well, the story I know is that the light-haired warrior jumped to the ground as fast as he could while his horse ran off scared into the woods. The warrior escaped the angry cloud, but he ended up chasing his horse for miles!"

Both men laughed heartily, and their laughter echoed across the village and the river. Calanele smiled over at Taima as she combed Kewanee's hair. "The boys are telling their stories again. It is so good to be back and hearing their laughter."

As the months passed, the two tribes enjoyed being as one once again. Even the younger children who did not know each other before the tribe separated, began to get acquainted with one another. One day, Tokala noticed a young girl wading in the river and humming to herself. She was about his age and he knew that she was the daughter of the chief of the Nakadochito. He was intrigued by her but still was afraid to speak to her. He also didn't want the other braves to tease him if they found out.

He watched her from the reeds while she splashed her feet in the water, humming to herself. She waded over to the water's edge and found some white wildflowers and picked them one by one. With a handful of flowers, she began to toss them into the water one at a time. The petals would flutter away like butterflies before splashing into the water and she would giggle each time she let one go.

After she tossed the last flower, she looked over her shoulder directly at Tokala and asked, "Are you going to come into the water or are you just going to stare all day?"

His face turned red as he quickly emerged from the reeds and said shyly, "I was not staring. I just noticed the butterflies diving into the water. It made me curious."

"They are not butterflies, silly," Kewanee retorted. "They are flowers."

Just then, Anoki and some other young braves came running down to the river. "Tokala, are you coming? Our fathers are preparing for a hunt. What are you doing playing with flowers?" The others laughed out loud at him.

Tokala stumbled as he turned to face his friends and Kewanee laughed too. His face became redder as he stammered, "I am ready for the hunt. I was just filling my water skin." He clumsily patted his sides, hoping and praying he had remembered to bring it with him. "Which I left at home." The boys erupted again with laughter as did Kewanee.

"Come on," Anoki repeated. "We have plenty of water skins. Now stop playing with that girl and come with us."

Tokala shook his head and gave Anoki a shove as they walked back to the village. "I am not playing with a girl."

Kewanee laughed as the boys jogged away and then went back to picking more wildflowers.

Nakahodot came out of his hut and noticed his brother sitting on the hill overlooking the river. He observed the other braves getting their weapons ready for the hunt. When he realized that task was already done, he saw they were mainly waiting for Natchitos to come down.

After the sun had fully risen, Natchitos came down from the hill and found his brother. Nakahodot shook his head and said, "Why do you waste the early morning sitting on that hill while the others wait? There is much work to be done. The deer will not wait, I can assure you."

Natchitos found nothing wrong with his routine and replied, "That is how I start every morning. You know this."

"You should bid farewell to the sun like I do in the evenings. Mornings are for work."

Natchitos scoffed at him. "Ah, I have better things to do in the evening. Like having a good smoke."

Taima overheard their bickering and she approached them and scolded, "Some things never change. Quit arguing and go hunt. The men are waiting for you."

All the men and several young braves gathered around Natchitos, Ayashe and Tooantuh, who were leading the hunt. Natchitos smiled at all his old friends, including Pakwa and Tuwa. He looked over at Nakahodot and said, "It is good to be together again with all our brothers. We will do what we do best. Tooantuh will lead our track. Today we will hunt deer. In the early morning, the woods will be full of them. Enough to last us through the winter."

Everyone smiled at the notion. They were all eager and ready to go. Just as they were setting out, Nashuk came running up to Nakahodot, crying out, "Take me with you, Father. I want to go too!"

"No, Nashuk," Nakahodot said, holding up his hand. "You are still too young. One must be very quiet in hunting deer. Go back and mind your mother." Nashuk kept whining until his father finally persuaded him to go back to the village.

The men set out into the woods and hunted all morning. The deer were plentiful as expected and they were able to stealthily hunt dozens of them. Even the younger braves were able to make some nice kills that made their fathers proud. As the sun grew hotter and the deer scarce, they decided they had all they could handle in dragging back to the village.

It was a joyous summer for all with having the two tribes back together again, but one morning tragedy struck the village when Atohi found that his beloved wife, White Owl, had passed away during the night. The cherished midwife of the tribe was greatly mourned, but none more than by her daughter Calanele. Not even Nakahodot could console his grief-stricken wife.

Natchitos continued the old tradition of the solemn procession with the body deep into the woods. Atohi led the procession of only a few select braves, including Natchitos and Nakahodot, and his daughter Calanele. She would cry and beat her breast the entire procession. The village would mourn for three days with a ceremonial fire of sacred smoke that was kept going day and night. Calanele and her father kept a silent vigil with fasting by the fire for all three days. Only then was Nakahodot able to get them to eat again.

When summer began to give way to fall, Natchitos knew the time had come that his brother would return to their home by the two creeks. The last night before they were to return, Nakahodot found his brother in his smoking hut.

"Come in, brother," Natchitos said. "I was just preparing the calumet for a smoke." Nakahodot sat across from him and waited patiently for the pipe. "Did you bid farewell to the sun?"

"I did."

Natchitos took a long puff on the pipe and let out a grateful sigh. "A nice way to end the day." He handed it over to his brother who did the same. "Calanele is no longer mourning?"

"She will be fine," Nakahodot assured him. "Onacona will be greatly missed."

Natchitos straightened himself. There was a topic he had been wanting to discuss, but he was never sure how to approach the subject. "Brother, when you led your tribe westward after our father died, you took him with you, did you not?" Nakahodot nodded as he was suspecting the question would be asked sooner or later. "I know we should not speak of the dead, but I would like to know what ceremony you chose for our father. I know how the solemn procession that we practice has always disturbed you."

"I have been expecting this question, brother. I honored them as the ancients did. On the night of our arrival at the Lanana Creek, I covered them with Earth and fashioned a mound over them."

"*Them?*" Natchitos asked incredulously.

"I took our mother alongside our father and reunited them in the sacred burial."

Natchitos became incensed and nearly got to his feet. He stopped himself and instead put the pipe down. Nakahodot waited for his response, knowing that he would be angry. Finally, Natchitos spoke, "You did what our elders had warned us to never do. You disturbed the bones of a sacred burial site?"

"I did not feel it right to leave our mother in this way. I decided a change was needed, just as our father had asked us."

"Father asked us to honor *him* in another way, not our mother," Natchitos protested.

Nakahodot raised his voice and said, "Are you not one with your wife? I have great respect for our traditions but once a man is joined to his wife, they become one. It is right that they always be one in life and in death. This is how I see it with myself and Calanele and for you and Taima. Father was heartbroken without his wife. I felt it was my duty to reunite them after his passing."

Natchitos sat quietly across from his brother for many minutes. Soon, he picked up the pipe once more and lit some fresh tobacco. He handed the pipe over to his brother and said, "I will think on this matter. Let us smoke now."

The next morning, tears of sadness were all around but also grateful smiles for the tribe's long reunion during the summer.

"I am grateful for the Nakadochito coming to stay with us," Natchitos told his brother. They clasped their arms together to say goodbye to one another. "The Nashitosh will repay this honor with a visit to your village someday. You have my word."

Nakahodot smiled and said, "It will be a great celebration beside the Lanana. Until our paths cross again, I say farewell, brother."

Chapter 12

It was early spring, six years later in 1700. Winter had been especially harsh, and it was all the Nakadochito could do to survive the dry and blistering cold. The rains stopped in the early winter and remained dry from then on. Both creeks had frozen over for a long period of time and when they thawed, very little water trickled in them. Gathering water was a delicate matter and the lack of rain was a great concern. Many nights they would do ceremonial dances in hopes that rain would soon return.

Finally, the spring rains came with the southerly wind, warming their lands once again. Soon, the fields began to come alive in color from the wildflowers. There were giant swaths of bluebonnets mixed in with orange paintbrush as well as light pink buttercups and deep red ones too. It was Kewanee's favorite time of the year as she loved to dance among the myriad of wildflowers.

Nakahodot had brought his entire family out to see the beautiful patches of flowers. He sat with Calanele as they watched their children play. Kewanee was now thirteen years of age and Nashuk and Notaku were ten and six respectively.

Nakahodot's face had become rough and leathery in the cold, harsh winters and the long hot summers. Small wrinkles had formed under his eyes and his light hair had shades of gray in it.

Nakahodot kept a lookout each year for the return of the Spanish, but each year there was no sign of them. The thought of their return weighed heavy on his mind but as the seasons came and went, even the chieftains from the other villages agreed there would be no such return and the events with the Nabedache years before were long behind them.

"It will be time to ready the crops soon," Nakahodot told his wife. "All three children will help this time. Notaku is ready to learn."

"It is time he learned to hunt as well, my husband," Calanele added. "You will take him this time."

He laughed and smiled back at her. "The chief's wife has spoken!" He watched his daughter dancing in the flowers and asked his wife, "What will you decide on our daughter?"

"Decide on what?" she asked innocently as if she didn't know what he was referring to.

"She will be of age soon," he said matter-of-factly. "Is there anyone she has shown an interest in? What are the people saying?"

Calanele slapped his leg and answered, "No one is saying anything. She still has plenty of time to decide on such matters. She is only thirteen. Let her be a girl for now."

As they were sitting in the sun, Pakwa came up on his horse and announced, "Naka, I think I see your brother coming."

Nakahodot jumped to his feet and ran back to the village. Calanele got up and called the children, "Come. Come! The Nashitosh have arrived!"

Natchitos was leading his tribe from his horse. The entire tribe followed behind him on foot and on horses. When he saw his brother running toward the village, he leapt from his horse and briskly walked after him.

"Naka!" he called out. "It is I, Natchitos! Where are you running to?"

Seconds later, the entire Nakadochito tribe came out to greet them by the side of Lanana Creek. Nakahodot came bounding up behind them with a big smile on his face. "I had to alert the others in the village. Welcome to our home, brother." The two men clasped their arms together in the traditional way. He glanced over Natchitos' shoulder and raised one eyebrow. "I see some new faces with you." Natchitos smiled proudly at him.

Calanele came rushing with her children and she noticed the two smaller children sitting with Taima on a horse, a girl and a boy. "Taima!" she shouted. "Are these *your* little ones?"

Natchitos helped them off the horse and said, "Yes, these are two of the newest members of the Nashitosh, Talulah and Nito." Nashuk and Notaku ran to the little girl and boy to greet them.

"You have been busy, brother," Nakahodot joked. "This is good to see. We will celebrate them as well as your arrival." Then he saw Tooantuh and clasped arms with him. A young man came and stood beside him. "Greetings, Tooantuh. And who is this young warrior I see? How you have grown, Tokala. You look as fierce and brave as your father."

"Greetings, Chief Nakahodot," Tokala answered politely.

Kewanee briefly smiled at Tokala as she walked away with two small children in tow. He took notice and smiled back at her.

Nakahodot was filled with joy at seeing his brother's tribe once more. "Come. We will help you with your huts and find good places for you."

Natchitos walked with him toward the village. "Where are the two creeks you told me about?"

"We were standing by one of them when you arrived," Nakahodot explained. "The other is a walk farther to the west."

Natchitos stopped and looked back at the trickling, narrow creek. "*That* is one of them? Seems quite narrow, brother."

Nakahodot nodded in agreement, saying "Yes, it appears that way for now. Luckily, we had some rain not long ago or it might have been completely dry. The Banita has water still, it just makes it harder to fill the water skins. I fear we are in for a longer drought."

"I have seen this as well at our village," Natchitos concurred. "This is why we arrived at the beginning of spring. The planting is useless until we get more rain. The soil is too dry. We hoped to find ample game in your forests instead."

"What of the fish in your river?" his brother asked.

Natchitos shook his head and answered, "Even the fish are hard to find when there is no rain. We have been able to manage thus far, but we must get more rain soon."

"It will come, brother. All in good time."

The two tribes were reunited once again, and a great ceremony and feast were created at the center fire. They asked

Ayita, wife of Tooantuh, to honor the gathering with a dance to start the celebration, for her name meant, 'first to dance'.

The next morning, Nakahodot came out searching for his brother. Soon, he found him sitting on a large boulder, watching the sunrise. He shook his head and smiled. He called out to him as he approached, "There you are, wasting the best time of the morning. Is that the best place you could find?"

"It is not the same as my hill," Natchitos said without turning away from his view, "but it will do for now." Nakahodot climbed onto the boulder and sat next to him. Without looking over, Natchitos continued, "Good morning, brother. Were you surprised to see us coming yesterday?"

"No. I had been looking for you every year now. I was glad that you came. How did you find the terrain after you left the Sabine?"

"You had to traverse some high and difficult hills to get to this land, brother. I can see that now. You have done well in settling here. I have heard of the great respect you have earned from the nearby Hasinai."

"Have you encountered the whites?" Nakahodot asked curiously.

"No," his brother answered. "There is word of them near the Yatasi, but we have still not seen them at our village. Have the Spaniards returned here as they said they would?"

Nakahodot shook his head. "We have seen nothing. It is my wish that they do not come again. It only brought confusion and fear."

"I understand, Naka. But we cannot wish that they will merely pass us by and take no notice of us. One day they will come, and we must be strong leaders for our people." The two men jumped down from the large rock after the sun had risen. "Can you show me the sacred mound you formed for our father and mother?"

"I will take you there, but we must not alert the others of its whereabouts. I keep a personal watch over the area, so it is not disturbed." He took his brother by the arm and led him away from the village. As they walked, he pointed toward the western horizon. "Just beyond those trees is the Banita. My men can escort your squaws there to bathe. Calanele has declared it to be for women only."

"Smart choice," Natchitos laughed. "That would explain the names you have given the creeks."

"It was not me. *She* was the one who came up with the names." Natchitos laughed even louder. Soon, they came upon a secluded area amongst some large oak and pecan trees. Under the large trees was a small, grass-covered mound with some tribal relics left in certain places on the mound itself to mark it. The two men stopped at the foot of the mound and Nakahodot said, "This is where our father and mother rest."

Natchitos stood and observed the mound carefully and reverentially. He tried to understand his brother's objections to their traditional practices and why they would lead him to take up the ancient ways instead. He thought of the journey they had taken to arrive at this new land and how difficult it must have been to carry the remains with them.

"You had a long, hard journey to get them here, did you not?" he finally asked.

"It was," Nakahodot replied, "but that was long ago. The hard part was fighting against the Wichita to secure this land. That was unexpected, I must admit."

Natchitos looked at him inquisitively. "You have not told me of this battle. You had to defeat another tribe?"

"It was a war party that caught us by surprise." He shook his head trying to forget the days from long ago. "All that matters, is we are here now. This is our land and we will fight again to protect it if we must."

"As you should," he answered in understanding. Natchitos looked at the mound once more and then said, "I will think on this matter of the burial site no more, brother. Nor do I condemn what you did for our mother. This place is indeed sacred and has my blessing."

Taima and Calanele sat outside under the martin gourds, watching their children play with one another in the courtyard. "I am so pleased you have been blessed with more children, Taima," Calanele cooed. "They are such a joy to see."

"I am pleased as well," Taima answered. "I love my boys, but I always did want to have a girl. I cannot lie about that. Talulah brings me joy that I always envied when I saw you with Kewanee. Speaking of which, she has grown into a lovely young squaw, has she not?" Calanele nodded proudly. "Has she found favor in one of the braves?"

"Kewanee is beautiful but also highly outspoken," Calanele responded. "Many of the braves lack the courage to approach her." Taima chuckled at the thought. "She keeps her thoughts close to her on such matters. Her father is impatient with this, but I know she still has time before she comes of age."

Tooantuh and his son, Tokala, were putting the final touches on their family hut with a few more pieces of thatch. Climbing down from the side, Tooantuh said to his son, "Now that we are done here, I want you to water the horses."

"But Father," Tokala answered, "there is barely any water in the Lanana."

"The chief has told us of another creek to the west. Take them there and make sure they are watered well."

Tokala gathered the horses and slowly walked them toward the other creek. He noticed the colorful wildflowers in the open fields surrounding the crops and found them very pleasing. When he finally reached the other creek, he led the animals to the waters edge to let them drink. He found a nearby tree with a low-hanging branch in which to sit on and rest in the shade.

While the horses gathered in the shade by the water's edge, Tokala stared at the blue sky above. A hawk flew overhead, and its screech echoed across the colorful landscape. The sky was dotted with enormous white, puffy clouds. He drew in a heavy breath of air and exhaled tiredly. His feet ached after the long journey from their village.

As he sat and relaxed with his eyes closed, he soon heard a familiar humming. His eyes opened at hearing the sweet sound of a girl humming songs to herself off in the distance. He instinctively jumped from the branch and hid behind the tree. Out in the middle of the wildflowers was Kewanee. She was walking and skipping along as she hummed to herself, occasionally dropping to her knees to smell the fresh scent of the flowers. Tokala watched her curiously and admired her beauty from afar.

He was enjoying the pleasant view of her before she skipped farther out into the field. He glanced over at the horses to check on them and saw they were huddled together and resting by the water. He took in a deep breath and walked out from behind the tree. Kewanee was still humming and skipping while he began to gather some of the wildflowers. He picked several of each color until he had a rich bouquet of purple, blue, pink and orange. When he straightened himself, he looked to find Kewanee once more out in the field, but she was gone. He panicked as he darted all around looking for her until he finally caught the sound of her humming over by the water. He followed the sound of her sweet voice until he saw her standing on the waters edge out in the bright sunshine.

Her back was turned, but he couldn't take his eyes away from the lovely feminine shape of her shoulders and hips. His heart began to pound in his chest as he nervously approached her with the flowers. He licked his lips as they felt parched.

He cleared his throat to speak to her, but she spoke before he could, saying, "You know this creek is only for squaws."

"I," he stammered, "I did not know. I...I only came to water the horses." He felt foolish already, but he had come this far, he wanted to speak with her some more. He took another deep breath and said, "And I wanted to bring you these." He extended the bouquet of flowers and offered them to her.

She glanced over her shoulder and saw the beautiful flowers in his hand. A slight smile formed on her mouth and she tried to hide the blush of her cheeks. It was the first time any brave had offered her flowers, much less have the courage to approach her.

She kicked the water with her toes and shook her head, saying, "You cannot give me those flowers."

Tokala's heart sank and his face went sullen. "I cannot?" he asked sadly.

She turned all the way around to face him and plainly stated, "No, those flowers are poisonous."

He recoiled in fright and tossed the bouquet across the creek as far as he could. He immediately dropped to the ground, feverishly washing his hands in the water. Kewanee couldn't contain herself any longer and began to laugh heartily.

Tokala stared at her crazily while he continued washing his hands as best as he could. "Why are you laughing? I could have *poison* on my hands."

She couldn't stop laughing and finally admitted, "Stop washing yourself, silly. The flowers are not *really* poisonous."

His face turned beet red as he continued kneeling in the mud. He put his hands on his hips, trying to hide his embarrassment. Soon, he started to laugh just as hard as she was. "You tricked me. You are very clever."

"And now my flowers are on the other side of the creek."

He got to his feet, now feeling embarrassed that he had tossed them away. "I will go and retrieve them."

"No, let them be," she insisted. "I will always remember them though. No one has ever offered me flowers before. It is good to see that I am not the only one who appreciates their beauty."

He gathered more courage and said in response to her, "Not even the flowers could match your own beauty."

She stopped laughing and stared at him nervously. It was also the first time a boy had complimented her in such a manner. She was lost for words. She was clearly flustered and finally said to him, "I must go now. My mother will wonder where I am. Tend to your horses."

Every morning after that, Tokala would wait near Nakahodot's hut waiting for Kewanee to come out. Each morning he would nervously ask her to go walk with him by the creek and each time she would respond, "I cannot walk with you today."

He never gave up though. He would rise early every morning and wait for her to emerge so he could ask her, "Will you walk with me this morning?" But each time, he received the same reply, "I cannot walk with you today."

One morning, after many failed attempts, he decided to approach her in another way. He waited patiently for her to come out. As always, his heart leapt in his chest at the sight of her. She noticed him right away but quickly walked past carrying some empty water skins. "Will you walk with me this morning?" he asked. "I will help you fill the water skins."

She was about to give him her usual response when suddenly she stopped. She extended the water skins toward him and said, "Take these."

Surprised, he stumbled over a rock before taking the skins from her. She immediately started walking briskly toward the creek and he hurried to catch up with her. From the corner of her eye, Ayita watched as her son went off with Kewanee to fetch some water.

As they walked together to the creek, Tokala searched for something to say. "It is a beautiful morning today."

Kewanee ignored him though and got straight to the point, asking, "Why do you wait for me each morning?"

"I just want to talk with you more, that is all."

She stopped abruptly, and he skidded to a stop as well. "So, you are not wanting to help me with the water?"

"Yes," he said clumsily, "and to help you with the water." She gave him a suspicious smirk and studied him for a moment. She looked back at the village to make sure no one was watching them. "I can help you every morning if you like." She nodded shyly and decided to continue. He smiled and walked alongside her feeling triumphant. "I am Tokala."

"Yes, I know who you are," she answered astutely. "And do you know who I am?"

"Yes, you are Kewanee. It is a very pretty name. It means 'Little Hen'."

They stopped at the edge of the creek and she yanked one of the water skins from him. "Fill the other ones," she ordered. As they worked, she said, "And do you know who 'Little Hen's' father is?"

"Everyone knows that. You are the chief's daughter."

"Exactly. Do you not know there are many eyes on us every time you ask me to walk with you each morning? The chief's daughter just cannot go off walking with a *boy*. I am glad you finally got some sense in your head and offered to do something useful."

Tokala smiled as he filled another water skin and said, "You are glad, are you?" He got to his feet holding three heavy water skins, smiling at her from ear to ear.

"Yes," she finally admitted. "Here, carry this one too." She handed him the fourth water skin and he grunted under the weight. She walked slowly empty-handed as he trudged along behind her laboring with the water. He was incredibly strained from all the weight, but he was still happy as he could be in finally finding a way to spend time with her.

From then on, it became routine for Tokala to help Kewanee each morning with the water. They were able to get to know each other better and became closer as they did. Even if it were raining, he would wait for her to emerge from her home each morning to fetch fresh water. He loved every minute he was able to spend with her.

On the morning of another hunt, the braves and elders prepared their horses and weapons. Ayita stood next to Tooantuh holding his water skin, waiting for him to mount his horse. He glanced around looking for his son. "Where is Tokala?" he asked. Just then he spotted Tokala walking back from the creek with Kewanee, both carrying a load of filled water skins. He called out to him, saying, "Tokala, let us get ready for the hunt. The chief is waiting." He found it curious to see his son helping with the water duties. He looked over at his wife and asked, "Why is he doing that and not getting his horse ready?"

"Are you blind, husband?" Ayita asked with a laugh. "Do you not see our son has eyes for a squaw."

Tooantuh hopped on his horse and took the water skin from her. "Which squaw?"

Ayita rolled her eyes and answered, "Come now, Tooantuh. The boy is falling for Kewanee."

"The chief's daughter? Has there been any talk about this?"

"No," Ayita admitted, "but a mother does have eyes. I see how he follows her each morning. No one will say anything, husband. People would like the match."

Tooantuh dismissed it though, saying, "This is not our village. We will be returning soon. Besides, our visits with the Nakadochito are infrequent."

"Well, I think they should be more frequent," she blurted, and turned to walk away.

Tokala came riding alongside Tooantuh and said, "I am here, Father."

He gave a stern look at his son but said nothing about Kewanee. She walked past them with the water skins, but she never made eye contact. Tooantuh observed his son curiously as she walked by and then looked her over once more. Tokala sat still trying not to give his emotions away. With a nod of his head, Tooantuh motioned to his son and said, "Let us go hunt."

The summer grew hot and the rains were scarce. Lanana Creek had nearly run dry and the Banita was getting lower each day. Natchitos informed his brother that the tribe would be returning to their village soon and he urged his brother to come with them where the river would provide more water. Nakahodot declined however, saying they needed to stay and save as much of their vegetable crops as they could from the heat.

Tokala and Kewanee continued to find more and more creative ways to spend time together as not to rouse too much suspicion. Many times, she would go with him to help water the

136

fields. When they returned to the Banita to retrieve more water, they would sneak into the shade of the large trees that stood by the creek.

Kewanee knelt to fill another water skin but Tokala snuck behind her and grabbed her by the hand, pulling her behind an oak tree to kiss her. "The people will see," she moaned in between kisses. She pulled away for a moment and fretted. "Your tribe is leaving soon. What will we do?" He lightly kissed her forehead, her cheeks and her fingertips, before she pulled him close again for a long romantic kiss. They couldn't help themselves as they were deeply in love. "What will we do, Tokala?"

He looked at her lovingly and assured her, "It is you that I wish to be my wife."

"Yes," she whispered as she looked deeply into his eyes. Then it dawned on her of what must be done before they could marry. "How do we do this? Your father must give you permission to speak to mine. We will not be of age for another *two* years." She began to panic at the thought. Tears began to well up in her eyes in thinking of the long wait and the great obstacles to overcome with the distance between them.

"Listen," he said, "we must keep the word in our parent's ears of our intentions. That we must reunite the tribes when the time comes."

"It seems so impossible, though. Why would they do that just for us? The last time we saw each other, we were just children. That was years ago."

Tokala tried to think as fast as he could. He knew they should be returning with more water for the crops soon. "We do not have much time. We must get back." He panicked even more, trying to think of a solution. "What...what if I ask to speak to your father now? For you to come with us. Come live with us, with our chief and his wife as your guardians. Then we would not have to be apart."

She began to cry profusely and trembled in his arms. "I cannot, Tokala. I could not bring such sadness to my mother and father. Please, we must do this the right way. We must wait and let the 'great spirit' be our guide. I will convince my father to return in two years-time. Will you wait for me? Will you?"

He knew she was right. He knew there was no other way but to wait. He pulled her in close and declared to her, "You know I will wait for you. I will wait forever if I must." He kissed her softly on her forehead and looked deep into her eyes. "There is only one Kewanee. You are the only flower for me." With that he kissed her deeply once more before they returned with the water.

Chapter 13

1702 - Two Years Later

The Nakadochito were faced with yet another hot year by the drying up Lanana and Banita creeks. Rain was still scarce after many seasons had passed with no relief in sight. Nakahodot called a meeting of the elders in his hut to discuss the matter.

"Our crops do not have enough water to fully mature," Nakahodot began. "The years of drought have made the soil too hard. There is nothing but dust. Soon, we will not have enough for ourselves to drink or water the horses. We must find a solution for our people."

Pakwa spoke up and said, "I was thinking of a dance with a sacred fire. We should send sacred smoke to the sky, so the 'great spirit' will send rain."

"A dance with sacred fire and prayer is a good thing, but we must search for water that is already on the ground."

"What of our old lands by the Sabine?" asked Tuari. Many of the men nodded in agreement with him.

Atohi, in his old age, wished to impart his wisdom to them and nodded to Nakahodot for attention. His voice was soft and hard to hear, so Nakahodot raised his hand for complete silence. "We will let Atohi speak."

Everyone looked to Atohi as he spoke. "The winds that bring the dry air came many moons ago and our people were faced with the same problem as we are today. The rains will come, but we must not wait here any longer. The old lands near the river are a good choice, but we must respect the Nadaco who may have taken control of them. They will be experiencing the drought like the rest of us are, so it may be difficult to strike a treaty with them to share the river." Everyone listened to him intently. "If we must leave, I will go where the tribe goes. But a second plan should be made ready if the first one fails. That is all I have to say."

Unbeknownst to the men, Calanele was sitting outside their home, listening to the meeting with Kewanee at her side. She looked at her daughter sympathetically, knowing what she wanted to do. "I will do what I can to sway your father's mind," she whispered to Kewanee. "There are two reasons to visit the waters of the cane again."

"Yes, Mother. Thank you," she answered gratefully.

Inside the hut, Nakahodot told the gathering, "I will think on this matter more. In two days, I will tell my decision. Be ready to break the camp for departure."

The next morning after the children had left the hut, Calanele waited behind to speak to her husband. "What will your decision be?" she asked.

"I am still thinking on the matter, wife," he casually replied.

"You have to come up with your second plan, do you?"

He looked at her agitated and asked, "Must you listen in on our meetings?"

"I want to know what is said just as anyone else does. This is something we have never faced before." She thought carefully of what to say next. "Going back to the old Caddo lands should be your second plan, not the first."

"Why do you say this?" he asked perplexed. "What would you have as the first?"

Calanele straightened herself and answered, "For Kewanee's sake, we should return to the waters of the cane where your brother lives. They have a nice wide river there, enough for all of us."

"For Kewanee?" he asked again. "Why would we go there for her sake? The journey is much farther than the Sabine. We have many elderly to look after as well. What would the reason be?"

"Come now, Naka," she replied anxiously. "Do you not see how she has spoken of nothing but Tokala since they left here? She has eyes for him, Naka, and has been waiting patiently for her day to come where she will be of age. Have you not seen this?"

140

Nakahodot tried to side-step the issue in saying, "Tokala is not among our tribe. He is with the Nashitosh. How would you know this? There are braves in our tribe that surely she must hold favor, does she not?"

"Naka, can the chief of our people be so blind to not even see what is happening with his own daughter? She holds no favor for anyone here. Her heart is set on a path to Tokala. Each time we visited one another they were inseparable. Did you not see?" She knelt down next to her husband and pleaded with him, "Think of what this means to her. She has been waiting bravely and patiently for this moment and now the opportunity has come. It is meant to be for her and Tokala, but you are the one who must let them have that chance."

He shook his head though, and said, "It is not *all* up to me, my wife. You know this. Tokala must seek his father's permission first before he comes to me. And, where is he? The distance would not be an issue if that much were at stake for a young brave seeking his wife."

"How do we know that the Nashitosh do not have the same problems with the drought as we do?" she continued to plead. "Maybe they are unable to come back here. Or else I am certain Tokala *would* come for Kewanee. The most logical choice is to go to them while we still can." She got to her feet and then said, "The Caddo lands should be your *second* plan." She left Nakahodot sitting alone on the bed.

Later that day, Nakahodot announced to the tribe that they would prepare the village and travel eastward at first light. "We will make for the Nashitosh village by the waters of the cane. But we will do this in two stages to give rest to our elders. We will stop for three days at the Sabine and find the Nadaco to establish trade with them. Then we will continue onward to the Nashitosh."

After he had spoken, the tribe began to work quickly and efficiently to gather everything for the long journey. Kewanee found her mother and hugged her tightly after hearing her father's words.

The wind blew hot and the sun beat down on the tribe as they slowly moved eastward over the rolling hills and through the forest. Brittle limbs cracked and popped under the scorching sun. Wherever they could find water, they would stop and fill as much as they could in their water skins. Nakahodot made the rounds to see everyone each hour to make sure all were well. By night, they slept under the stars and moonlight, welcoming any kind of coolness in the breeze.

After four arduous days, they reached the Sabine, and all rejoiced in seeing the flowing river. The water level was much lower than any of them could remember, even the elders, but there was still plenty to quench their thirst.

"We will rest here for three days," Nakahodot said to them. Then he summoned Pakwa and Tuari. "Come with me to see Lahote. We should tell him we are here."

When they returned that evening, Nakahodot looked dejected as he walked past the campfire where his family was resting. Instead of stopping to rest with them, he walked over to the river for a drink alone. After he had satisfied his thirst, he leaned against a rotted tree stump and watched the sunset over his exhausted tribe.

Atohi noticed his son-in-law's behavior and wondered what had happened with the Nadaco. Calanele noticed him too but looked to her father for guidance. "I should go to him," she said.

But Atohi raised his hand and said, "Let me go. I will speak with him." Kewanee rushed over to help him get to his feet. He patted her on the head with a smile. "Thank you, Little Hen."

Atohi hobbled slowly over to the river where Nakahodot was sitting. "Is there a place by that stump for an old man?" he asked.

"Yes, Atohi," Nakahodot answered. "Come. Please sit with me." He helped Atohi get to the ground to sit next to him. "You remain strong through the hot journey. The strength of all the Caddo!"

Atohi chuckled at him and said, "I have my fathers to thank for that. You lead us well, my son. These days are hard ones." He sighed heavily as he took in the awesome spectacle in the sky.

"Even in the hottest days, we are still blessed with remarkable colors at the days end."

"That we are," Nakahodot agreed.

"Did you find trouble with the Nadaco?"

Nakahodot shook his head in frustration. "The Nadaco suffer as we do, but the hot sun has set fire to Lahote's mind. He could not be reasoned with. I sense he has had more troubles than we know about. He claimed there were no animals here and the fishing is scarce. He insisted that we keep moving." He looked over his shoulder at the flowing river. "Where else would the animals go for water? It would be here."

Atohi nodded and said, "The sun can make anyone go mad. Lahote has a difficult disposition as it is, just as his father did. I would let them be. I do understand your decision to carry on to the Nashitosh, though."

"You do?" Nakahodot asked.

"Yes," Atohi answered. "I would do the same if it were my daughter." Nakahodot smiled and nodded, knowing that everyone in the tribe must know the reasoning behind his decision. "Do not forget, Naka, we are the same tribe despite the distance. It is right to bring her to Tokala." The old man got to his feet without any help. He tapped Nakahodot on the knee before leaving and said, "The strength of the Caddo." Nakahodot watched with pride as Atohi meandered back to the campfire to retire for the evening.

On the third day of rest, the tribe was rejuvenated. They filled as many water skins as they could carry. They would set out again across the river at daybreak.

As the early morning sun still glowed beyond the horizon, Calanele lay next to her husband, waiting for the sun to rise.

"You are awake, my wife?" he asked her.

"Yes."

"Why are you so restless?"

She rolled over to face her husband and said, "I have been thinking of what you said before we left. It troubles me."

Nakahodot propped up on his elbow to listen to her. "What did I say?"

"You were right about Tokala. He *would* have come for her."

"What are you thinking, my lovely wife?" He could see the concern in her eyes and how she had been thinking of this for a long time. Then he realized what she was saying. "You think they have trouble?" Calanele nodded nervously. He put his hand in hers to console her. "Let us not alarm Kewanee with this."

It was too late though. Kewanee was lying awake as well and heard them whispering to each other. Her hands shook as she held them close to her heart.

When the sun finally rose, all the tribe was ready with their canoes. The expression on Kewanee's face was palpable. She was eager to get across the river.

They set out in their canoes with a string of horses following alongside. The morning breeze across the water was refreshing and even caused some yells of joy from the braves leading the stallions. Nakahodot called out as well to join in their enthusiasm. Soon, everyone in the tribe was calling out and their chants echoed across the water. Everyone except Kewanee. She was more anxious than she could ever imagine.

Two more days they traveled as they neared the Nashitosh village. Both Nakahodot and Calanele kept a watchful eye on their worried daughter, sensing her nervousness. Soon, they crested a familiar hill, knowing they were close. Nakahodot called over to Pakwa and asked him, "We are only a short ride away, are we not?" Pakwa nodded to him. "Go and find the fastest horse we have." Pakwa immediately went over to the line of horses and brought a magnificent white and brown mare. He walked it to Nakahodot who then said, "Help Kewanee mount the horse."

He didn't need to though. Kewanee already knew what her father intended. With one stride, she jumped and threw herself onto the back of the mighty horse. The animal neighed anxiously but before she could settle, Kewanee yelled out, "*Hyah!*" With that the horse ran like the wind toward the village.

"Go!" Calanele called out. "Find him!" They watched as a trail of dust kicked up behind the speeding horse as it disappeared over the next ridge.

"We will catch up to her in a short while," Nakahodot said.

Kewanee sped across the open prairie and back into another forest. Soon, the racing horse popped out from the cover of trees and sped over another rolling hill. Finally, she reached the small ridge that overlooked the Cane River. She stopped the horse momentarily as she looked down upon the village anxiously. Her mouth fell open at what she saw. She kicked the horse once more to get a closer look and galloped down the slope to the remnants of the Nashitosh village.

There were no sign of the huts or people anywhere. "Tokala!" she called out frantically. She leapt off the horse and ran everywhere. She checked all the areas where the homes once stood, but she found nothing. She ran down the river as hard as she could, calling out his name over and over. To her shock, she came across a structure she had never seen before. A large barn rose high above the water, fashioned with mud and finely cut wood. The foreign sight puzzled her even more and tears streamed down her face. "Where is *Tokala*?" she cried. "*Where are all the people?*" She looked all around the area but saw nothing but the odd building. She grew angry and looked hastily on the ground for a rock. She splashed in the mud and water and finally found one and threw it as hard as she could at the structure, screaming as she did. The rock bounced off the wall of the trading post and the impact echoed across the river. She fell to her knees and sobbed uncontrollably.

Soon, the rest of the tribe came down the hill toward the river. Everyone was shocked to find the village had been deserted. Calanele shook her head when her deepest fears were confirmed. Nakahodot stood by the river, looking dumbstruck. He was lost for words as the members of the tribe walked around aimlessly in tears.

Calanele walked up to him and asked, "What could have happened? Could they have come looking for us?"

He observed the low water in the river and the dusty ground. As he slowly walked the waters edge, he then saw dried up animal carcasses and dried corn stalks as well. "They would have come across us. Look how low the water is," he said. "The drought has been even worse here."

"We must find Kewanee," Calanele said through her tears.

Pakwa came running up to them and exclaimed, "Naka, you must come see this."

He hurried along with Pakwa and soon came upon his weeping daughter next to the river. Tears of sympathy welled in his eyes, knowing how grief-stricken she was. He knelt beside her to comfort her. It was then he noticed the trading post. The structure was similar to the one he had seen years before at the Nabedache village. The entire building was made of wood and fashioned with mud. It was showing signs of neglect as some of the wood had fallen away leaving gaping holes in the sides. He shook his head in confusion, trying to understand what had become of his brother and his tribe.

"It is the work of the whites," Pakwa stated. Kewanee sobbed even harder at hearing this.

Nakahodot helped her to her feet. "Come, my child. Let us return to your mother."

Kewanee was inconsolable after their shocking discovery. She hugged her mother, shaking and sobbing uncontrollably, before falling to the ground where she sat silently alone for hours just staring at the water.

The rest of the tribe spread out in search of signs or clues of what may have happened to the Nashitosh. All they found were dried up crops and a river that had dwindled to less than half the size of what they had remembered. They tried catching fish, but none were to be found other than tiny minnows and a few small sunfish. They set up camp for one night, but it was quickly decided to head back the way they had come. The eastern banks of the Sabine would be their destination in hopes they could find territory to stay in temporarily to wait out the long hot summer.

Nakahodot sat by the fire that night with Pakwa and Tuari. Kewanee sat staring into the flames in a trance. No one objected to her being there and no one dared to say anything of the chief's daughter being present during their discussions. Nakahodot kept a watchful eye on her as he saw that she was not eating any food nor drinking any water.

"What do you think happened with the whites here?" Tuari asked him. "The wooden structure by the creek is very troubling. My fear is the whites have killed all the Nashitosh."

Nakahodot shook his head. He was at a loss just as much as everyone else was. "I do not know what to think about the strange hut they have built. Natchitos must have made an agreement with these men, perhaps for trade or maybe for the Christian religion. But if they abandoned their village, where did they go? I know my brother, he would have never let his people be overrun by the white men. He must have trusted them. My instincts tell me they may have followed them somewhere when the animals and fish disappeared, and the crops dried to dust." He thought for a moment more as he stirred the fire. "One thing that I know is certain, to agree to such a hut being built on their lands, he must have trusted them enough to strike a treaty with them. We have found no signs of violence here. We have found no hearts on the ground. I do not think the tribe met their demise as you say. No, the Nashitosh are alive. The question to be answered is 'Where are they'?"

Pakwa looked dejected as he listened to him speak. "Everyone is being displaced in our country. When will the rains return?"

"When will Tokala return?" Kewanee finally asked in a weak and sad voice.

"Daughter," Nakahodot said, "you must eat something." She didn't answer him though and stood and retreated from the fire.

Three days later, the tribe arrived once more on the eastern banks of the Sabine. Nakahodot sent scouts in search of any tribesmen in the area but they found none. As a precaution, they still didn't setup their huts by the river until they could be certain they were not encroaching on someone else's territory.

The tribe gathered around the fire that night and asked Atohi to bless the smoke as it rose to the sky in hopes the rain would return. As the solemn drumbeat echoed across the river, the people were surprised to see three braves emerge from the darkness at their campfire.

The drums stopped as did Atohi's chanting. Nakahodot and Pakwa stood to greet the men. They noticed how they were dressed only in loin cloths and wearing single-feather headbands. The braves stood with spears at their side not appearing threatening, but curious.

"I am Nakahodot, chief of the Nakadochito," he said in greeting.

The brave in the center answered, "I am Coahoma, chief of the Choctaw."

Nakahodot could tell the men were curious as to why so many were by the river. He quickly tried to explain themselves. "We are a wandering tribe, scattered by the hot sun, waiting for the rains to return to our land. We came in search for our brothers, but we found them gone. Now we grieve for we do not know what has happened to them. May we share your river and hunt with you while we wait for the rains?" The three men approached him and set down their spears. "Will you sit with us at our fire?"

Quietly, the men sat with the tribe at the fire. Coahoma, which means Red Panther, sat next to Nakahodot. Finally, he spoke, saying, "The hot winds have scattered many in our country. Many hearts have traveled to the 'great spirit' for lack of food. We suffer as you do. You may stay along the river to find what you can. Tell me of the brothers you came to find."

"We are grateful, Chief Coahoma," Nakahodot answered. "We came in search of the Nashitosh, but found their village deserted and a hut built by the whites. What do you know of the whites in this area?"

148

"The French white men are in these lands," Coahoma stated plainly. Nakahodot listened to him intently yet could see the weariness on his face as he spoke. "We have traded with them in the past, but it has been many moons since we last saw them. I have heard talk of them among the Yatasi and the Nashitosh. But I do not know why you found their village deserted."

"They may have gone where the white men came from," Nakahodot replied, "when their crops dried up. But I cannot know this for certain. My people are tired though. We only wish to go back to our village as soon as the rains return."

"You may dwell here until the rain returns," Coahoma answered. "The river still has fish. You will find this to be the best way to gather food for your people."

The Choctaw left them in peace beside the Sabine River. The rest of the fall remained dry and they resorted to fishing for the majority of their food. Occasionally they would find small game to hunt but the fish became their main diet for the time being.

The rains would finally return as winter arrived late that year. Spirits rose when it was decided during the middle of winter that they would return to their village by the Lanana and Banita Creeks. The elders had decided they would take as much fish as they could and return to prepare their lands for the upcoming spring. All were happy that their ordeal was near the end, all except for Kewanee. She would never be the same again, not knowing what had become of her beloved Tokala.

Chapter 14

Recovery from the drought was slow, but with time the tribe was able to re-establish their crops, although they were much smaller than before. The parched land sprouted with new green growth and soon the creeks were filled once again. The tribe was happy to be at their home once more between the two creeks. The wildlife returned, and hunting parties resumed their annual trips to the Pine Springs to hunt larger game.

Each year, Nakahodot would return to the Nashitosh village with a small company of braves to see if his brother and his people had returned. Kewanee would bravely travel with them, keeping her hopes alive for Tokala as well. But each year they would only find disappointment and sadness when seeing no one had returned.

Kewanee remained faithful to her word that she would wait for Tokala. She held closely to her heart the promise she made and kept hope and faith in that someday she would see him again. She grew weary however, of the constant questions and gossip around the village about her not taking up with another brave. Talk grew louder as she found no favor in anyone else. She stubbornly held on to her belief that one day she would reunite with Tokala and would not listen to any suggestions otherwise. Although she showed great courage in her steadfast vigil, the continued gossip wore on her greatly.

As each year passed, many nights she would retreat to her family's hut in tears after another day of snickering and belittling from the other squaws. Her mother sympathized with how she was being treated and sought out her husband to put an end to the talk.

"Our daughter continues to cry," she told Nakahodot as he entered the hut.

"Why does she continue to cry?" he asked. "She has seen for herself that the Nashitosh do not return. How long will she grieve for Tokala?"

"Her grief for Tokala, she holds in her heart. What makes her cry is all the talk amongst the squaws on why she continues to stand alone past her time of age."

Nakahodot looked at Kewanee as she wept on her bed and said, "Daughter, do you not find favor in any of the braves here? Why do you submit yourself to this talk?"

She wiped the tears from her cheeks and sat up to answer. "There is only one brave for me. That is why I travel with you each year to the Nashitosh and I will continue to do so. I will stand alone until Tokala returns. The others can talk all they want, whether you do anything about it or not. But I will *never* resign to them just to please their chatter. There is only one Tokala and I will stand alone until I see him again." She stared at him defiantly and then laid back down.

Her mother looked on proudly and gave Nakahodot a look with an obvious gesture that he should speak for their daughter. "If you do not, husband, then I will."

"Very well," Nakahodot said. He left the hut and had his wife gather all the squaws by the village fire. When she had done so, he said to the gathering, "Anyone who has talk of why my daughter still stands alone after her time of age will answer to me. That is all I have to say." From that day on, no one said hurtful things to or about the chief's daughter ever again.

As time went on, Kewanee entered her twentieth year and made the best of her self-imposed single life in ways she had not imagined when she was a young girl. Along with her normal duties, she became the charge of many of the young braves and squaws while their parents worked in the fields and hunted. When her tribal duties were done for the day, she began to train herself in the arts that were normally reserved for the braves. She practiced every day with the bow and arrow and even throwing spears, using trees for targets, while the children watched. She soon became an excellent markswoman with incredible accuracy. Many of the people of the tribe noticed her training but no one dared to question it. Soon, she began to ask her father for permission to join the braves on the hunts, but each time her father would turn down her request. She complained bitterly that even her younger brothers could go on the hunts, but she couldn't.

One day, Kewanee and Keme took the group of children far up Lanana Creek to play and to bathe in a secluded area. The skies were covered with white puffy clouds and the sun peaked in and around the edges throughout the morning. Kewanee carried her bow and quiver full of arrows across her back and the children giggled and called her *hehewuti,* which means 'warrior mother'.

"Do not say such silly things," Keme scolded them. "What if a snake jumped out to scare you? Who would frighten the snake away?"

"Hehewuti!" the children yelled in delight.

Keme rolled her eyes and berated them once more, "Enough of this silliness, children. Come, let us wash in the waters now." They all moaned in protest. "Come. Come. Or I may find a brown snake to frighten you good myself."

"I do not mind them being silly," Kewanee said, amused. "They are good little braves and squaws." She poured some water on one of the girl's head, saying, "Are you not?" The little girl giggled happily. "They like to watch me practice."

As soon as she mentioned the word, all the children began to beckon her simultaneously, "Practice! Practice!"

Keme put her hands on her hips and groaned, "I wish you would not."

"Oh, it is nothing," Kewanee answered. "It will give us something to pass the time. I will just aim at trees."

"Trees! Trees!" the children all squealed.

"I never can understand your interest in shooting the arrows and throwing the spears," Keme argued. "I know the braves enjoy learning but what does this teach the little squaws?"

"What does it teach them?" Kewanee asked, surprised as she lifted one of the little girls out to dry her off. "It teaches them to fend for themselves and be great hunters if they need to be."

"The braves hunt, Kewanee. We prepare the meals. That is how it has always been."

Kewanee winked at the little girl and answered Keme, "Who says it *always* has to be that way?" The little girl laughed as Kewanee wrung her hair out. "There, now you will be cool in the afternoon air."

"Your father would say, I can assure you of that," Keme said in reply. "Alright children, out of the water. We will sit and dry off in the shade."

"While I practice with some arrows," Kewanee announced to the delight of the children. Keme frowned and shook her head.

As the afternoon wore on, the clouds grew thicker and darker and soon, thunder was heard in the distance. "We should find our way back to the village," Kewanee announced to the moans of the children. "The rain is coming. We have already dried out once today."

They had ventured far from the village though, and the rain began to fall as they walked the water's edge. "Come, stay together," Keme told them. "If we keep moving, we will be home soon."

The rain fell harder, and it was not long before the creek began to swell with water rushing faster downstream. Lightning lit up the sky and thunder boomed all around them. The children would jump and shriek each time the sky would flash and rumble overhead. The ground became treacherous to navigate as it was a mass of mud and water and debris. The troop sloshed their way slowly down the edge of the ever-widening creek.

In a matter of minutes, the creek had become a raging river over twenty feet across. "Careful where you step!" Keme yelled out over the thunder and rain. "We will get to higher ground and find another way!"

The children trudged nervously up the muddy banks, following Keme with Kewanee bringing up the rear. As she and the last child climbed to higher ground, the mud suddenly gave way under their feet and they both slid toward the sloshing creek. Instinctively, Kewanee reached out for a nearby tree root and grabbed hold of it, stopping her slide, but the little girl went tumbling helplessly into the churning water.

"*Meli!*" Kewanee cried out. The little girl shrieked as she hit the water and sailed down the chaotic river.

Kewanee slipped and stumbled but finally got to her feet and went dashing through the mud toward the screaming Meli in the driving rain. The others heard the screaming and turned to see her flowing away. Keme, realizing they were near the village, directed the rest of the children toward home and yelled for more help. Soon, men and women came dashing out into the rain, hearing her cries.

Kewanee kept running down the mud-soaked banks of the creek while she kept a sharp eye on the child. She scanned downstream, looking for anything the little girl could grab onto. She saw up ahead that the wind had blown some tree branches into the water. "Grab the branches, Meli!" she called out. Meli flowed around a curve, slowing her speed as chunks of wood and debris flowed around her. "Grab onto anything!" Kewanee yelled again. Meli flailed her arms about but was too shocked and dazed to focus on the branches. Kewanee thought of jumping in after her, but the current was too swift. She would never catch up to her unless little Meli could stop her momentum somehow.

A few braves who saw what was happening, came dashing down to the creek. One jumped into the fury as Meli went sailing past and the other ran farther downstream to get ahead of her and scoop her out.

Then Kewanee spotted a tree way downstream. A large branch had fallen across the creek and water was lashing all around it. "The tree ahead!" she yelled. "Reach for the tree, Meli!"

Meli heard her and spotted the tree far ahead. She then saw a young brave tossing about in the water several yards behind her. As she quickly approached the fallen tree, she reached with both hands and closed her eyes, knowing she would slam right into the wet soggy wood. Her hand grasped onto the first outlying branch she ran into and the she held on for dear life.

"*Yes*," Kewanee shrieked. "Hold on! They are coming!"

Just then the brave came slamming into the tree branch with a thud, several feet from Meli. She cried out at the frightening impact and the large branch began to move in the driving current. Temporarily stunned, the young man maneuvered around to try to get a good grip and swim toward Meli. As soon as he gained his footing, he was stunned to see a soaked bobcat clutching to the top side of the large branch. The animal snarled and whined loudly, scratching at the young brave's hands. The cat lunged at his face and the boy immediately ducked under the water. The momentum of the current washed him under, and he popped out on the other side. He helplessly yelled as he flowed away from the terrified Meli.

Kewanee's eyes widened in terror at seeing the bobcat trying to attack the little girl. She ran as hard as she could through the mud and rain to find a good vantage point.

Meli heard the bobcat's snarl as the frightened animal inched toward her next. She shrieked even louder as she came face to face with the angry wildcat. It snapped and swiped its paws at her hands. She yelped and slid farther and farther down the narrow branch. The bobcat dug its claws into the soaking log and growled again. The force of the current pulled Meli perilously closer on the bending branch toward the log once more. A few more seconds and she would either be swept under the tree or be pounced upon by the enraged bobcat. Meli cried out just as the bobcat lunged at her face.

In the fury of the rain and thunder, Meli heard an arrow slicing through the air. In a flash, the arrow thumped directly into the bobcat and sent the stunned, flailing animal over the tree and into the churning water. Meli held on tightly in stunned shock. Seconds later a brave came splashing into the water and plucked her from the tree branch and pulled her to safety on the banks of the muddy creek.

Meli rolled over in his arms and was happy to see it was Nakahodot. "Now you are safe, little one," he said to her. He got to his feet and picked her up in his arms. They both looked up stream to see Kewanee standing confidently with her bow. Nakahodot smiled proudly back at her.

The other braves emerged from the water farther downstream and came back to the village to find Meli safe and back with her family. One of them was carrying the arrow with the bobcat still dangling lifelessly at the end. He brought it to Nakahodot, saying, "The wildcat nearly reached the girl, but someone aimed a precise shot."

Nakahodot observed the dead bobcat and graciously nodded. "I saw it with my own eyes. Kewanee is the one with the sharp aim."

Chapter 15

The Nashitosh Village - 1714

Seven Years Later

It was spring, and life had returned to the small village that rested on the banks of the Cane River. Upon their triumphant return from the shores of Lake Pontchartrain and the bayous near Fort St. Jean, the Nashitosh were happy to be back in their homeland. They wasted no time in rebuilding their homes along the Cane.

They had also returned with a small group of French explorers and settlers led by their close friend and ally, Louis Juchereau de St. Denis. The lieutenant was accompanied by his associate, Andre Pénicaut as well as Pierre and Robert Talon. The latter were brothers who had served in LaSalle's doomed final expedition but were rescued years later from a Spanish garrison near the site of LaSalle's failed establishment along the Gulf Coast. The rest of the French numbered about twenty-five men tasked with the job of rebuilding the dilapidated trading post that had been abandoned twelve years earlier before the area was devastated by drought.

Natchitos assigned many of his braves to assist in the rebuilding of the fort, but also set aside his best hunters, including Tooantuh and his son Tokala.

Knowing that he had not seen his brother, nor his tribe for over a decade weighed heavy on his mind, for he knew they had been searching for them, not knowing where they had gone. As soon as he saw fit, he aimed to set out to reunite with the Nakadochito, but first he had to re-establish order in his own land.

"The land is no longer dust," Tooantuh said to Natchitos. "We must hunt the forests and see what bounty has returned to them."

Natchitos observed the healing wound on Tooantuh's shoulder and asked, "You feel your arm is ready to pull back a bow again?"

Tooantuh shrugged him off though, saying, "As ready as I was when confronted by LaRouche."

Natchitos laughed and said, "Yes, how soon I forget. Your arm is ready. We will return to the hunt today."

Just then, St. Denis approached them carrying a musket and asked, "I think the men are doing just fine without me, Chief. Mind if I come along with you on the hunt?"

"Come with us, Lieutenant," Natchitos answered. "But do not bring the musket. If we see deer, it will frighten them away and then we will only have one kill."

"Fair enough," St. Denis answered. "But what if we come across a bear?" he asked with a smile.

Natchitos thought for a moment, then said, "You are right. Bring the musket."

The men set out into the forest and hunted all morning. They were delighted in finding many deer and rabbits alike. The animals were so plentiful, there would be enough for everyone in the village for a week from just one day of hunting.

They stopped to rest after hours of hunting and built a fire in an open area to share some of their catches. As Tokala cooked two rabbits over the fire, St. Denis relaxed with his smoking pipe.

Natchitos admired the smooth wooden finish of the black pipe and said, "Good pipe."

"Yes," St. Denis smiled, "you should come try it with me." The men traded puffs on the pipe and rested against a tree. "It is good to be back in your land, is it not?"

"It is very good," Natchitos replied. "I am thankful to the 'great spirit' for delivering us to our land once more."

"So am I."

"How long will you stay this time?" Natchitos asked abruptly. "Your trading post will be done soon. Then what will you do?"

St. Denis nodded as he puffed some more on his pipe. "I am glad you asked that question. To be quite frank, I would like to stay and live here." Natchitos looked at him surprised. "I have explored many lands, my friend, but none have I found as beautiful as this. Yes, I have been asked to establish a trading post here and I will continue to serve my duties. But I have asked my superiors to remain here as a settler and oversee the trading. What do you think of that?"

"You are wise, Lieutenant," Natchitos said to him. "I know for certain you have proved yourself quite useful in the field of battle. And I know your intentions here with my people are sincere, or you would not have stood with us against the Acolapissa. I think it is a fine idea." He took the pipe once more from him and took a long draw from it. "But one thing troubles me. One should not walk alone as you have. You should find a wife."

St. Denis laughed out loud and asked, "So that is what bothers you, is it? I will get right on that." He kept laughing and Natchitos just shook his head. "In all seriousness, I have not thought about that too much. I quite enjoy what I do. I am always thirsty to learn and see more."

"Ah, knowledge is always a good thing," Natchitos agreed, "but so is a good wife."

Tokala had finished cooking the rabbit and handed pieces to all the men around the fire. St. Denis sat up and put away his pipe and devoured the leg of rabbit. "You cook good rabbit, Tokala," he said. All the men agreed in satisfied silence. After he was done, he turned to Natchitos once more. "My superiors have agreed to let me stay in this land with you, but it is not without conditions."

"Go on," Natchitos said.

"They want me to continue my explorations using the fort as my home base. We have come to an understanding with the Spanish that it is better to establish trade and exploration rather than make war with one another." Natchitos nodded. "So, they are asking me to establish a trading route westward and eventually on down to Mexico. That is why I have brought the Talon brothers with me. Before they were taken prisoner by the Spanish many years ago, they lived among an indigenous tribe along the sea. They learned the language that is common in that area. It will be useful to have them along while I make my way to Mexico. They know where the Spanish fort is located, the one called San Juan Bautista."

"You seem to have all this planned out already," Natchitos commented.

"Well, I still need to work out some details, gather provisions. But the fort needs to be completed first. Once we have established the post, then I will think on when to start this new expedition."

Natchitos got to his feet and looked over at St. Denis curiously and then over at Tokala. St. Denis could tell something was on his mind. "You say you plan to head westward on this trail?"

"Yes. What are you thinking?" he asked curiously.

"When you do decide to leave, I will come with you and show you this trail. I know the way you must go." Then he motioned to Tooantuh and his son. "They will come to." Tokala looked over at his father and cracked a smile.

St. Denis got to his feet looking intrigued. "How is it that you know the trail westward?"

"I have a brother that I must visit," Natchitos answered without hesitation. "A visit that is long overdue."

They spent the rest of the year putting down roots once again on the banks of the Cane River. The post was completed, and trade soon began. Later that winter, another garrison of troops arrived with Sieur Charles Claude Dutisné and built a larger fort alongside the trading post. Governor Cadillac arrived in the spring and commemorated the fort, naming it Fort St. Jean-Baptiste. It's prime location along the Cane River and its proximity to the Red River, gave the French a vital stronghold for their future goals. The governor congratulated St. Denis in a job well done and then gave him permission to begin his newest assignment.

When the dignitaries left, and things had settled down in the village after the commemoration, St. Denis approached Natchitos and asked, "Well, my friend. What do you say we go find your brother, shall we?"

Natchitos smiled back at him and answered, "We will go."

Chapter 16

The long hard winter slowly began to give way to springtime in the piney woods near Lanana Creek. The Nakadochito that had once been a small, close-knit tribe, was now a much larger one with children grown and starting families too. Nakahodot saw their two sons, Nashuk and Notaku grow into fine young braves who had taken wives of their own. They too had begun raising children as Nakahodot and Calanele, the proud grandparents, watched over all of them happily. All the while Kewanee remained a steadfast guardian over the children in the tribe, including her beloved nieces and nephews.

Not all was happy in the tribe as the years went by. There were great losses among the elders who had lived long and honored lives. The tribe, along with Calanele, mourned the death of Atohi three years before. And a year prior to that tragic event, the well-respected Tuari had passed away as well.

Yet life continued in the village between the two creeks and with spring came the vivid wildflowers and more importantly, the great hunts. Just as every spring, the hunting party made its way to the Pine Springs hunting grounds near the Nabedache village. They hunted for days and reveled in the crisp, warming air. Kewanee proudly rode along with her father and brothers with the rest of the hunters and everyone knew her as one of the most accomplished archers of them all.

After many days of hunting alongside the Nabedache, the hunters started to make their way home. Their tally of game was plentiful, and it was more than they could carry. As they neared the open prairie of the ancient burial grounds, Kewanee slowed the pace of her horse. Nashuk noticed she was slowing down and asked her curiously, "What is the matter?"

Kewanee eventually stopped all together with a profound expression on her face. Nashuk alerted Pakwa at the head of the party and they all stopped. Nakahodot, who had been resting his eyes as they slowly rode, awakened and asked, "Why have we stopped?"

"It is Kewanee," Notaku replied.

The rest of the party turned around and trotted to where Kewanee had stopped and looked at her inquisitively. "What is it, Kewanee?" Nakahodot asked. "Something troubles you?"

"*Shh*," she hissed. "I can hear something." Nakahodot looked at her confused and surprised that she snitched at him. "Feel the ground. Something is coming."

The group of braves looked all around the prairie and into the tall trees lining the edges, but they saw nothing. All except her father. "Yes, I sense it too," he finally admitted.

Across the prairie near the horizon there began a low rumble. There were no clouds in the sunny blue sky, yet they could all hear the low, sustained tremble of thunder.

All of a sudden Kewanee gasped in awe when the source of the thunder appeared on the crest of a slope hundreds of yards in front of them. Every brave looked on in shock and amazement.

Nakahodot, his eyes wide with wonder, uttered quietly to himself, "*Buffalo...*"

The incredible sight roared across the prairie in a magnificent display. The herd numbered in the hundreds and they ran majestically together westward across the lengthy prairie, swaying one direction and another, up and over rolling hills and shallow valleys. The sheer width of the herd was astonishing, and it carved a path clear to the horizon and beyond. No one knew where they had come from, but no one dared to step in the way of the furious stampede.

As the animals quickly drew closer, some of the braves raised their spears and called out with a hunting yell. Before they could pursue the buffalo, Nakahodot raised his arms and stepped in their way. "No!" he cried. "Let us not disturb the buffalo." Clearly disappointed, the men relented and returned to their places. "They have chosen to grace this sacred ground with their majestic run, and we will let them pass. We have enough food to carry anyway. This day will always be remembered though. The day the buffalo herd crossed our path."

The hunters stood and watched the great herd roar across the prairie, a display that lasted many minutes longer. Kewanee sat proudly as she watched the magnificent sight before her but also gazed upon her father with respect and admiration. It was a day that all of them would never forget.

Later that afternoon, the hunting party neared the village as they crossed over Banita Creek. As they drew closer, it was clear there was excitement coming from the village. The column of horses stopped when they heard the noise from the camp.

"Something is happening in the village," Pakwa said to Nakahodot.

The chief strained his aging eyes to see what he could make of the commotion when suddenly he felt a lump in his throat and his heart quickened in his chest. He knew it could only be one thing.

Kewanee galloped alongside him and stopped, asking, "What is it, Father?"

Nakahodot smiled at her and said frankly, "It seems the surprises come in twos today, Kewanee. We have an extra greeting waiting for our arrival."

"*What?*" she gasped as she felt her heart leap from her chest. She nearly fainted until her father steadied her. "*Who* is greeting us?"

"Go, child. *Go.*" She dug her heals into her mount and the horse neighed loudly and bolted for the village. Nakahodot looked at the rest of his smiling companions and said, "We will celebrate this night. Our brothers and sisters of the Nashitosh have returned." The men yelled and called out with delight and continued their final leg home carrying their bounty with them.

The village was abuzz with activity as the hunting party returned but also from the astonishing arrival of Natchitos and his tribe. Celebratory yells and chants were heard all around as loved ones greeted one another once more after fourteen long years of separation. In the middle of all the celebrating were St. Denis and his companions Pénicaut, Pierre and Robert Talon, and his trusted friend and translator Buffalo Tamer. Members of the tribe greeted Natchitos' foreign friends with the familiar chant, *"Te'chas! Te'chas!"*

Nakahodot got down from his horse and made his way through the crowd to greet his brother. Finally, he found him, and the men clasped their arms together in the traditional manner. "I see you still have your hair, brother," Nakahodot said with a beaming smile.

Natchitos smiled and said in return, "I see you still have yours, brother. Only a little more gray than light this time."

"Greetings, brother. It is pleasing to see the Nashitosh once again. We had searched your village many times over the years in hopes of your return."

"I know, brother. I will explain our unexpected absence all in good time." He turned to find St. Denis amongst the throng of curious onlookers. "I have brought some men to meet you."

Nakahodot was intrigued, asking, "It is said you arrived riding with white men. Is this true?"

"It is," he answered. Just then St. Denis made his way over to them. "This is one of the men that rode with us. He is the leader of the French explorers. This is Lieutenant St. Denis." He looked over at St. Denis and said, "This is my brother, Nakahodot. Chief of the Nakadochito."

St. Denis was immediately impressed with Nakahodot as he looked him over. The aging leader was a true likeness of his brother Natchitos in every manner with one exception; his hair. He could tell he was a man of great stature amongst his people. St. Denis took a liking to him right away.

"I am very pleased to meet you, Chief Nakahodot," St. Denis said in their language. "Thank you for welcoming us into your village."

Nakahodot raised an eyebrow of surprise and unexpected respect. "You speak the words of the Caddo?"

"Yes," St. Denis answered proudly. "With the help of your brother, I have learned your language. I may have even taught Natchitos a little French. Have I not, Chief?"

"*Oui,*" Natchitos replied. He tried holding back a smile as Nakahodot looked at him oddly.

"And now you ride with the Nashitosh?" Nakahodot kept prodding. He was understandably curious at the incredible turn of events. He wanted to know as much as possible and as soon as possible.

"Yes, I am happy to say," St. Denis continued. "We have cultivated a friendly and working relationship with the Nashitosh. And we hope to do the same with you and your tribe."

"We have much to discuss, brother," Natchitos said.

Nakahodot nodded and said, "I will have men help you get settled. Tonight, we will have a great celebration for our reunion. I invite the lieutenant and his men." Then he noticed Buffalo Tamer standing behind Natchitos. "It is pleasing to see you as well, my friend."

"Greetings, great chief," Buffalo Tamer answered. "They do not need my services any longer, but I came along for the ride. I am glad to be back in your country."

Tokala wandered through the crowd breathlessly. Everywhere he turned people were there to greet him and welcome him back. He returned everyone with a gracious smile, but he was still anxious as he had not found who he really wanted to see. Finally, he caught sight of Calanele. She approached him slowly and smiled. "Welcome, Tokala. What a handsome brave you have become."

"Thank you," he said cordially.

"I know that you still stand alone. Ayita has told me this. The years of separation have been cruel to your heart. I know you are looking for her. Waste no time in your search. She will be down by the Banita." He ran toward the creek as fast as he could.

Nakahodot watched closely as Tokala ran out of the village toward Banita Creek. Tooantuh and Ayita came and stood alongside him. "My heart is warmed by your return. I look forward to hearing all about your adventures. But for now, let us give our children what they longingly deserve. There is no need for Tokala to come and speak with me. I know his heart has been true to Kewanee in choosing to stand alone as she did all this time. My permission to Tokala is granted."

Kewanee nervously walked along the edge of the creek, her cheeks streaked with dried tears. She tried to remember the day they once shared an embrace and a kiss beside the same creek and under the same tree. The years had faded her memory and she found it difficult to even picture Tokala's face. All that she could remember was how she felt about him and how those feelings had never left her. As brave and courageous as she had become, she now could not find the courage to finally face him at last. Everything she had kept alive in her heart in hopes this day would finally come, was now springing forth in an avalanche of emotion. Her hands trembled, and her knees shook. As the water slowly trickled by in the babbling brook, she heard light footsteps approaching. Her heart began to pound in her chest as fresh tears streamed down from her eyes.

"I brought you these," she heard him say. "These beautiful flowers are for you, even though they could never match your own beauty."

Her lips quivered as she slowly turned around to see Tokala standing there, holding a freshly-picked bouquet of wildflowers. She fell to her knees and could no longer hold back her emotions. She cried uncontrollably and soon he rushed to her side on his knees and embraced her. She wrapped her arms around him but still could not stop crying. He held her tightly as they swayed together on their knees.

She finally regained control of herself and whispered through her cries and tears, "*Please, do not let me go. Please, do not let me go.*"

Tokala couldn't hold back his tears either. The joy and euphoria of seeing her again was overwhelming. "You have my word," he assured her. "I will never let you go again. I promise you. From this day forth, we will never be apart."

She finally pulled away and sat face to face in one another's arms. She continued trembling, still not believing she was with him once more. She glanced down at the crumpled flowers that had been pressed between them and her sobs turned to laughter. "We are not kind to these wonderful flowers, are we?"

Tokala began to laugh as well and answered, "We have plenty more, I can assure you of that."

"Forget the flowers and kiss me," she said passionately, and they embraced with a deep and loving kiss. The fire and passion overwhelmed them as the love for one another came forth once more like an eternal spring surging from the core of the Earth. The birds in the trees sang happily and the sun reflected off the trickling waters of the Banita like sparkling diamonds lapping at the surface. All the while two lover's hearts became as one under the shade of the guardian oak.

Chapter 17

The two tribes were reunited once more, and they gathered around the tribal fire as one. St. Denis sat quietly and respectfully with his companions as they watched the incredible celebration unfold. The dancers danced in cadence with the rhythmic drumbeat and they chanted songs of thanks as they circled the fire. Squaws danced alone and then many joined in as a group, with each dance having its own significance. They danced for joy in being with their families once more, they danced for rain and for thanksgiving. They danced for the harvest that was soon to come and for the great bounty they had brought home from the hunt. And lastly, they danced to welcome the new friends that had arrived with the Nashitosh.

After the dancing concluded, Nakahodot stood and spoke. "Today as we returned from the hunt, we were greeted with a new sign at the sacred prairie of our forefathers. With the coming of the buffalo that crossed our way, I saw it as a sign of new things to come. The 'great spirit' has brought our brothers and sisters back to us from lands unknown. And with them, they bring us strangers that the Nashitosh say are not strangers but friends. To this I say, the friends of the Nashitosh are friends of the Nakadochito. To these I say '*te'chas'* to our new arrivals."

The entire gathering did likewise, and everyone repeated the greeting in saying, "*Te'chas! Te'chas!*" St. Denis nodded and smiled respectfully to the chief and to all the tribe.

"Let us share in a great feast!" Nakahodot declared.

There was food and drink for everyone, and the celebration went on joyously throughout the night. The entire tribe never retired for the evening and even the children stayed awake for the fun and revelry. The party became even more festive when word quickly spread that Nakahodot and Tooantuh formally agreed to the marriage of Tokala and Kewanee. Calanele and Ayita rejoiced in seeing their children together once more. Calanele was especially pleased to see the broad and happy smile on Kewanee's face as she sat lovingly next to her betrothed.

As the night wore on, Nakahodot summoned his brother and St. Denis to come and join him in his smoking hut. He produced his calumet as the three men sat around the fire.

"I can see why you men enjoy these smoking rooms," St. Denis admired. "I think they are a splendid idea."

"We will share a smoke," Nakahodot said, handing him the pipe. "You speak our language well, Lieutenant."

"Thank you," St. Denis answered. "I feel communication is the best way to progress through life. If we can communicate better with the many different people in foreign lands, the fewer enemies we would have. That is what I always say."

"A wise approach."

St. Denis handed the pipe over to Natchitos and said, "I must thank you for such an extravagant welcoming to your tribe this evening. Watching your ceremonial dances and being able to witness them is remarkable."

Nakahodot went straight to the point once they had all shared the pipe. "Tell me, brother, of how you came across these men. We saw that your village was ruined by the drought. Is this what caused you to desert it?"

Natchitos cleared his throat and said, "The lieutenant came to our village a year before the rains stopped. He arrived with Buffalo Tamer from the Yatasi."

"So," Nakahodot countered, raising his eyes with interest, "you are the explorer that visited the Yatasi." St. Denis nodded.

Natchitos continued, "They came in peace and asked to live among us. They proposed a treaty to make trade with one another and asked permission to build a trading post near our village. But all the lieutenant asked for himself was to learn our words. After the post was finished, they returned to their fort to bring back supplies. They never returned though, so I felt he must have come into trouble. Then the rains stopped not long after that."

St. Denis interrupted, saying, "I must say that I did fully intend to return, but an explorer's life is not his own. I had many superiors to answer to and the usual political bureaucracy stood in the way of our return." He looked over at Natchitos with admiration and added, "Your brother is quite loyal though, and a true friend. I was unaware of their hardships in the village, but I was not surprised to see them when they arrived at the fort. I did all that I could to accommodate them for I was quite moved by his gesture."

Nakahodot looked over at his brother and asked, "So, you lived among the French at this fort?"

"The French gave us land beside a great lake, and we lived alongside the Acolapissa. I became friends with Chief Red Hawk. That is where we remained until now."

"Life must have been good by this lake," Nakahodot said. "Why then did you return?"

St. Denis stepped in to answer the question and said, "A very foolish man under my command stole a pistol from Chief Red Hawk that had been a gift from the Nashitosh. Then the man very deviously made it appear that Tooantuh had committed the crime. As you can imagine, this did not sit well with Red Hawk, so they attacked the Nashitosh."

"I would not be sitting here if it were not for the help of the lieutenant and his men," Natchitos admitted.

Nakahodot became even more interested at hearing their story. He looked over at St. Denis and asked curiously, "Are you saying you stood with my brother in a battle against the Acolapissa?"

"I am," St. Denis confirmed. "I was ashamed of the actions of one of my men. I knew that Red Hawk would retaliate swiftly. We fought side by side with the Nashitosh. I am proud that I did so. Your brother is a fine warrior."

Nakahodot looked upon St. Denis with extreme admiration and at his brother with equal pride. "Let us smoke again to honor this great victory."

After they enjoyed the pipe once more, St. Denis continued. "My superiors had given me a new assignment just prior to this incident. They had ordered me to return to the Nashitosh village with the tribe to re-establish the trading post there. After the skirmish with Red Hawk, we had all the more reason to come back."

"It was how the 'great spirit' meant things to happen," Natchitos said.

"Yes," St. Denis agreed. "You were always meant to live in your homeland. Now it is my wish to live the remainder of my years there as well."

"You have rebuilt this post then?" Nakahodot asked. "And you wish to remain with the Nashitosh?"

"Yes, the fort has already taken shape and trading has begun. We are calling it Fort St. Jean-Baptiste. After I complete this journey, I will return with your brother to live there." He laughed at himself and said, "Somebody has to run the post. It may as well be me."

"What journey do you speak of?"

Natchitos stepped in and answered, "He wishes to follow the ancient trail all the way to his enemies." Nakahodot found the answer confusing, yet he was still intrigued.

St. Denis shook his head and said, "No, my friend. I do not see the Spaniards as my enemy. We are no longer at war with them. I see them as an ally in exploration and partner in which to trade. If we can connect these posts with the ancient road, it could be an important corridor for trade in this region. My commanders have seen this, and I agree it is worth pursuing."

"I feel it is a dangerous journey you wish to go on," Natchitos replied. "You trust your former enemy too quickly."

"He is right," Nakahodot added. "You must use caution in your approach. I have come across the Spanish and found they do not keep to their word. They too said they would return to these lands, but we have never seen them since." St. Denis took in his words wisely. "Where is the Spanish fort? I was told of one many moons ago by a man named DeLeon. Is it the same fort?"

St. Denis nodded, recalling the names of Spanish leaders from long ago. "I recognize this name, yes. He was a commander at the Spanish fort. And you actually met him? *Amazing.* Yes, this is the same fort. It is south of the river called Rio Grande in an area called Coahuila. I will be mapping the trail as I make my way down there."

"I know stories of this river," Nakahodot replied. "But I still implore you to use caution on this journey."

St. Denis thought for a moment, contemplating how he would prepare before moving onward toward Coahuila. "With your permission, I would like to stay with your tribe for a few weeks while my men and I prepare to make this trek south to the fort. And if I may be so bold, how would you both like to make the journey with me? You know part of the trail from what Natchitos has told me, and I could use the company as well. The men are hard workers, but they are too quiet for my taste."

The two brothers looked at each other with surprise, but curiosity too. Nakahodot could tell from Natchitos' expression that he was interested. "You are indeed an explorer, Lieutenant," he answered him. "Once the tribes have settled in for the summer, we will make this ride with you. But first, my duties as chief and a father require me to be here for the time being. I have a wedding to officiate."

"Another fine idea for a celebration," St. Denis concurred. "I am delighted with your decision and I look forward to your daughter's ceremony."

A week later, Tooantuh was in their hut helping his son prepare for the wedding ceremony. Ayita had made moccasins just for the occasion for him to wear. Tokala frowned at them as he rarely wore anything on his feet.

"Do I have to wear these?" he protested.

Ayita didn't bat an eye. "Kewanee will have very nice moccasins on too."

"Stand up straight," Tooantuh told him. "Let me look at you." He nodded with approval. "This is a day we have waited on far too long. I am angry at myself for letting our tribe keep you away from your true love."

"It is no one's fault, Father," Tokala quickly answered.

"It has always bothered me," Tooantuh continued. "Your mate for life is not just your spouse, she is your purpose. And many years of this purpose were taken from both of you. But I commend you in staying true to your heart and to your beloved. You stood alone as she did with honor. There is no shame in it. Your paths have been leading you to this day and as your mother and father, we are both pleased." He clasped his arms with his son and smiled at him proudly.

In the home of the chief, Kewanee sat in front of her mother who combed her long, shimmering black hair. "Did you ever believe this day would come for you?" Calanele asked her as she worked.

Kewanee reflected on the answer, contemplating everything that had transpired in the past week. "It is strange, Mother," she began. "I somehow felt I knew it was coming, but I never actually believed it. I had resigned myself to be the old caretaker of the tribe and the odd one who enjoyed the hunt."

"It was your father who set your mind in doing the things the braves do. He passed down his skills with the bow and arrow and spear to you. But still you look after the children with honor."

"I do not mind those things; you know how I love the children. But I also love the wind in my hair, riding my horse as we chase down the next catch in the hunt." Kewanee sat quietly for a moment more. "When I saw the buffalo and how majestic and regal they were, I knew right away I would not shoot my arrows at them before Father gave the order not to. It was a sign for me. The buffalo thundered across the plain to speak to me, to tell me Tokala was speeding his way back. One would not dare try to extinguish such a sign. Not I." Then she realized something and leapt to her feet.

"What is it, child?" Calanele asked worriedly. "I have not yet given you the moccasins."

"I will be leaving with him, will I not?" she asked with tears in her eyes. "I gain one but lose another, is that it? I cannot leave you and Father! And Nashuk and Notaku and their families. I cannot leave the children behind!"

Just then Nakahodot entered the hut to see Kewanee fretting terribly. "What is the matter, my daughter?"

She rushed over to him and pleaded, "Will I be made to leave my family and live with the Nashitosh? The thought just aches my heart."

"You will not be leaving your family, Kewanee," Calanele insisted. "You will be going with your husband."

"But I will not see you for months or years at a time. I cannot *do* that."

Nakahodot tried to calm her. "You have always been unique. That is what makes you Kewanee, the most courageous and loving squaw in our tribe. This union with Tokala will be a turning point for both the tribes. The distance between them will no longer be as it was. It is this union that will bring us back together. Change is upon us, Kewanee. The coming of the whites will not cease. Trade will continue to increase and caravans from the east will be more frequent. Tokala knows the sacrifice you are making. I know in his heart he will do the same for you, but you must give it time. I know in my heart you will live once again with the Nakadochito. You must have faith." She embraced him and tried her best to dry her tears. "You will never lose your family, child. With Tokala, our family only grows larger and stronger. This day is a happy day for all of us."

At the center tribal fire, the chants were low and steady with the drums as their rhythm. Nakahodot stood at the head of the gathering, wearing the ceremonial headdress of the chief. Tokala stood off to the side with Tooantuh and Ayita standing behind him. Buffalo Tamer, St. Denis and his men stood on the edges of the crowd looking on with respect and curiosity.

Tokala strained to get a look at his betrothed as she came forth from her home, but he could not see over all the heads of the crowd. Kewanee emerged to the stunned gasp of the gathering. She was dressed in soft white skins from head to toe with the fringes of her clothes dyed in dark blue. She wore

175

moccasins that matched her attire. Her hair was carefully braided and hung down the length of her back. Around her neck she wore colorful beads only worn by the bride on her wedding day. They were the same beads her mother had worn and her grandmother before her.

Tokala finally caught sight of her as she slowly walked to the rhythm of the drumbeat with Calanele following close behind. His heart swelled in his chest and his love for her grew with each step she took toward him.

When they were finally standing together, the drumbeat and chanting stopped. A hush fell over the gathering. Tokala smiled briefly at Kewanee, who customarily looked at the ground in front of her. She knew he was smiling at her and she tried desperately not to break character and smile back at him. A slight hint of a smile appeared on her lips as she kept her composure.

"I see we are nervous at this moment," Nakahodot said with a smile. "Let the fresh, cool morning air wash over both of you and let it soothe you. This is a day of great joy. As chief I am honored to see that this day has come. Many moons ago, the Caddo were displaced and went separately in opposite directions. With this marriage, the 'great spirit' brings the Caddo back as one. We are the Nashitosh and the Nakadochito and as such it will always be, but for this day, we are the Caddo once more. A long and heartbreaking road it has been for both of you. But hearts will heal from this day forward. No longer will you be apart." Tokala and Kewanee both took a deep breath as they continued looking down, trying as hard as the could not to look at one another until they were told to.

"Tokala," Nakahodot continued, "I have granted my blessing for you to take my daughter, Kewanee, into your home. You will make her your wife and you will honor and protect her all your days." On cue, Tokala looked up and nodded to Nakahodot. Nakahodot then motioned for him to finally look upon his bride. Kewanee lifted her eyes to him, and a single tear trickled down her cheek. He put his hand in hers and the gathering rejoiced.

The two tribes celebrated the rest of the day and into the night once again. It would be a day everyone in the Caddo would remember.

Chapter 18

A week later, St. Denis was ready to continue his journey to the Spanish fort, San Juan Bautista. Word had spread that the two chiefs would join his men along with Buffalo Tamer. Both the tribes gathered to give them a great send-off.

Tuwa, who was now the holy medicine man of the tribe, blessed them on their departure. "May your journey be swift and free of danger. And may the lieutenant's efforts bear fruit with the Spaniards. Return to us soon."

"Thank you, most kindly," St. Denis said.

Nakahodot and Natchitos left Tooantuh and Pakwa as guardians of the tribes in their absence. Nakahodot climbed on his horse and found Kewanee in the crowd looking on proudly. He winked at her and said, "Keep an eye on everyone."

"I will!" she called out with Tokala at her side.

The six men rode together down the ancient trail toward the sacred prairie. As they rode along, Natchitos noticed the bow and arrows his brother was carrying. "I see you are still using my quiver."

"*Your* quiver?" Nakahodot blurted.

"I think you have had it long enough," Natchitos continued to kid him. "I will most likely take it back with me when we return to our village."

"You can try," Nakahodot retorted. He looked over at his brother and at his horse. "Are you sure you can make such a long ride now? You are getting quite old."

Natchitos face turned red and shot back, "I can go as far as any man on this horse. You just keep an eye on my quiver and try not to fall asleep on your horse."

St. Denis chuckled and shook his head as they continued riding, saying, "You two are brothers, no doubt."

As the sun began to set, they came across the sacred prairie. The Frenchmen marveled at its beauty as the setting sky blanketed the rolling sea of green with an ebbing, radiant light.

Pénicaut was taken with the great land and asked, "Is this where you saw the buffalo? I can see the path left behind them. It must have been incredible."

"Fascinating," St. Denis concurred.

They made camp after they crossed the vast prairie and rested after the long ride. They shared a meal by the fire and St. Denis produced his smoking pipe after he had finished. Nakahodot took notice immediately of the unique looking pipe.

"I have never seen a pipe that small," he commented. "And one that is black and shines in the moonlight."

"I would be happy to share a smoke with you, great chief," St. Denis said. "It is fashioned from clay and finely polished by craftsmen in my country. Here. Have a look at it and try it." He handed it to Nakahodot who studied it closely with admiration.

"Good pipe," he said.

"Natchitos said the same thing. It's definitely a fine thing to do after a good meal, I always say."

"You have many times," Natchitos added.

Pierre and his brother had been sitting quietly, finishing their meal. They had been mostly silent during the ride. Nakahodot noticed how they did not say much of anything except to one another.

"Do the brothers there not have anything to say?" Nakahodot asked.

"Oh, I apologize," St. Denis answered. "They only know French and a little Spanish. They also picked up some of the language of the Karankawa, but I am afraid that's a dialect much different from your own."

Robert realized they were talking about them and finally spoke up, asking, "Lieutenant, when will we reach the village tomorrow?"

Pierre added, "How do we know they will not be hostile?"

"What was said?" Nakahodot asked.

"They want to know when we will reach the Nabedache village tomorrow and they seem to be worried they will be hostile," St. Denis answered.

Nakahodot waved the question off and said, "They are trusted friends for many moons. We will reach them in the morning. They are not far from here. I will introduce you to their chief. They will insist on sharing a meal with us, but then we will continue. The chief can direct us to the trail that you seek that heads southward. But once we leave the Nabedache, we will rely on your direction to the Spanish fort."

"I trust my instincts," St. Denis said confidently. "We will find the fort."

The next morning, the riders approached the Nabedache village where they were greeted with chants of welcome. Nakahodot was pleased to see that his friends were thriving once more.

A fierce-looking brave approached the men and held up his hand for them to halt. "Greetings to you, Nakahodot," he said.

"Greetings, Lion Paw."

"Who are the whites riding with you?" he asked sternly. "Why have they come here?"

"Have no fear of them," Nakahodot assured him. "They are allies from the east who trade with the Nashitosh. We only wish to pass through your land with the chief's permission. We are riding with them to the Spanish fort."

Lion Paw seemed perplexed and incredulous. "Why would you travel to such a place where there is death and disease?" St. Denis was confused by the question, but he remained silent.

"We know of your past sufferings but is not agreed that all of the white Spaniards bring disease, or these men would not wish to trade with them. May we speak with your chief?"

Lion Paw relented and motioned for them to follow. St. Denis said to Pénicaut and the Talon brothers, "Stay here. I will see if I can request an audience with the chief."

Nakahodot asked Lion Paw, "May we introduce the leader of these white men to the chief?"

"Wait here," Lion Paw answered and ducked inside the chief's hut. Moments later he reemerged and told them, "Enter."

Nakahodot and Natchitos entered the hut with St. Denis. Sitting on the far side of a small fire was the aging chief of the Nabedache. His face was like leather and his wrinkled hands were scarred. He sat cross-legged, poking the fire with a long stick. He was old but wise in appearance. When he noticed the men entering, he smiled and motioned for them to sit.

"Come. Come," the old man said in a raspy voice.

"Greetings, great chief," Nakahodot said respectfully. "I am glad to see you are well. I bring you my brother, Natchitos, chief of the Nashitosh. And this is Lieutenant St. Denis from the trading post at the Nashitosh village. He and his men come in peace."

"*Te'chas,*" he said to St. Denis. "I am Chief Aneway, brother to Nabe."

"Good morning, Chief Aneway," St. Denis said cordially. "It is an honor to meet you."

Aneway looked at him curiously and asked, "You speak our words?" St. Denis nodded. "Very impressive. What is it that you seek?"

"We are traveling southward to the Spanish fort in Coahuila," St. Denis stated. "We only wish to pass through your land with your permission. I have been asked by my superiors to establish a trade route from the Nashitosh post to the Spanish fort, San Juan Bautista. I do not know if I will succeed but it seems favorable to strike a treaty with them."

"And if you do succeed, you will trade along this route you are traveling?"

"That is our wish for the future," St. Denis answered. "This trip is primarily to establish a relationship first. If we can agree on trade, then that will come later. But it brings the possibility of bigger prosperity to this land, where tools and food can be brought, farmers who can help with cultivation, craftsmen for building and doctors who practice medicine."

The gravity of his words profoundly affected Nakahodot and Aneway. Natchitos knew already of the change in which St. Denis was describing. It was something all the chiefs knew was inevitable as time wore on.

St. Denis continued, "All of this does not happen overnight, but I have seen what good relations can do if common ground is found between one another. I am an explorer, Chief Aneway, and a believer in building strong relationships with everyone I encounter. My aim is not to overthrow but to work with the natives of these lands. I point to the relationship I have with Chief Natchitos and his people. We have worked together and have been friends for many years now."

"I appreciate your words," Aneway answered, "and I know they are sincere. The change that you describe will be a matter for my sons and theirs that follow. You are right that good dialogue and fruitful relationships will be needed when this time comes. But I must share with you our own trepidation when it comes to the Spaniards. Although their efforts were honorable, the Nabedache suffered due to their neglect and unwillingness to sustain the relationship. I only say this as a warning to you. Many moons have passed, and I am aware that new leaders are now present at the fort." He adjusted his position on the pelts he was sitting and continued stirring the fire before speaking again. "I give you permission to pass through. Lion Paw will show you the ancient trail that leads southward. You may come across Bear Trapper on the trail. He is in this area this time of year and knows the Spanish fort well and their words. Look for his smoke on the horizon."

St. Denis produced a cloth pouch and unrolled it. Inside was a smooth, black pipe just like the one he had used the night before. "I am very grateful, Chief Aneway. Let me honor you with a gift. It is a smoking pipe made in France across the sea. It has never been used." Natchitos smiled and shook his head. Remembering the flint-lock pistol, he could see that his friend truly was a wonder in dealing with people.

Aneway looked at the shiny pipe with respect and admired it greatly. "I accept your gift. We should share a smoke on our agreement."

"With pleasure," St. Denis answered happily. "If I may, I will prepare it for us." Aneway handed it back to him and he stuffed it with tobacco before lighting it.

After the four men smoked together, Aneway arranged to have a meal to share with all the travelers out by the village fire.

As they ate, Nakahodot said to Buffalo Tamer, "We will look for your brother on the trail to the fort. It is said he knows the Spanish words. He will be of great use."

Buffalo Tamer nodded proudly and said, "If he is here, he will serve with honor." He looked at the top of his head and chided, "Just do not expect him to keep quiet about your hair."

After they left the Nabedache village, they found the trail as Lion Paw had directed them. They continued past the Pine Springs hunting grounds and into lands none had ever explored. After two days of riding, they came across a line of smoke rising high above the trees in the distance.

"It is Bear Trapper," Buffalo Tamer said. "I am certain of it." They continued riding closer when an arrow zipped through the air and sunk into a tree in front of them. Buffalo Tamer retrieved the arrow as he rode past and said, "I will ride ahead. It is indeed him." Nakahodot and the rest stopped their horses and waited. Moments later, Buffalo Tamer signaled for them to approach.

The men dismounted their horses and approached the fire where they found Trapper cooking some squirrel. He didn't seem surprised to see his brother, even though it had been decades since they last saw one another. He also wasn't surprised to see him riding with white explorers. He was intrigued however, at seeing Nakahodot and Natchitos once more.

"Greetings, Chief Natchitos," he said, still turning his meal on the spit. "It has been many moons." Then he cracked a wise smile when looking over at Nakahodot, saying, "Greetings to you as well, Light Hair. You are far from the hunting grounds."

Nakahodot walked over with a perturbed expression and plopped next to him by the fire. "You should not call me that. We are not hunting. We are traveling with these men to the Spanish fort."

Trapper observed them cautiously and said, "They are not dressed like the Spanish."

"They are from the French trading post established at my brother's village east of the Sabine. They wish to establish a trade route."

Trapper looked surprised and asked, "On the ancient trail? And you want to bring Frenchmen to a Spanish fort? Are you sure that is wise?"

St. Denis grew impatient and decided to introduce himself. "My name is Lieutenant St. Denis. These are my men. Your brother tells me you know the way to the fort, and you know the Spanish language."

"You speak the Hasinai words well," Trapper commended him. "Why do you go to the fort when you know they do not want you there?"

"It's just as the chief has said, we want to establish trade with the Spaniards. The war was started in the old country, but in this country, it is my belief that cooperation is needed instead of aggression. These men behind me, Robert and Pierre, know some of the Spanish language. That is why they are here, but if you came along with us, I think our chances of success in dialogue would be much greater."

"He talks a lot," Trapper whispered to Nakahodot. He looked over at the Talon brothers and nodded. "I have seen them before." He switched to speaking Spanish and said to them, "You lived among the Karankawa, did you not?"

"*Si*," they both answered.

"The Spaniards liberated you. Why are you now with these men?"

Robert looked over at his brother and Pierre spoke up, saying, "When our commanders found us at the old site of LaSalle with the Spaniards, they asked where our allegiance lay. We asked to be re-patriated for we wanted to return to our families. So, the Spaniards agreed to let us go. We think our presence and knowledge of the fort at Coahuila will be helpful to the lieutenant's goals."

"That we will see," Trapper said again in his own language.

St. Denis understood him and said, "So, you will travel with us then?"

"Perhaps it was meant to be that you found me here," Trapper answered. "You would not get past the gate without me."

Chapter 19

As they made their way farther south, the terrain began to change. The rolling majestic hills gave way to flatter, less dense countryside. They saw different kinds of trees that were never found near their villages, and even cactus as the climate was much hotter and drier. After four more days of riding, they came upon a river.

"The Rio Grande," Trapper exclaimed. The group of riders looked on the sight with wonder. The river stretched as far as the eye could see in either direction. "The fort will be just beyond the slopes across the river."

In the distance they could see a range of mountains as the backdrop to the picturesque scene. "That is an incredible view," St. Denis said out loud.

The horses wandered down to the river and the men let them drink before going the rest of the way to the post. The river was not wide, and they easily rode across to the other side. Trapper lead them up the slope and as they crested the top, they were able to see their destination.

The presidio stood like a guardian overlooking the river valley. It was flanked by the mountains that dotted the horizon. As they neared, they could see a few guards standing outside a small gate that opened to the compound. Stone and mud walls ran on either side of the gate until they cornered toward the back. Nakahodot was clearly astonished at seeing the size of the fort. It was the largest community he had ever seen. Natchitos had already seen Fort St. Jean but he was impressed with this one as well. Rising above the walls was a structure with a triangular roof. It was the highest building to be seen inside the fort. At the top corner of the roof was a cross. Nakahodot recognized the symbol immediately, recalling his encounter so long ago with DeLeon.

Trapper approached the guards and got off his horse. St. Denis watched intently as Trapper spoke to the guards in

Spanish. After a moment, one of the guards went inside the gate while the other waited with Trapper.

It seemed like an eternity as they waited before finally the gate opened and a smartly dressed officer came out with the guard. He was dressed the same as DeLeon had when Nakahodot met him.

The officer looked at Trapper suspiciously but said nothing. Then he walked over quietly and observed the three Indians and four Frenchmen on horseback. He noticed the muskets stowed on the side of all four of the Frenchmen's horses. After looking them over carefully he went back to the guards and ordered, "Escort them inside."

St. Denis felt a sense of relief as they entered the presidio. Once they were inside there were people all around. Some working in gardens, tending to animals, washing clothes and other tasks. Nakahodot sat quietly observing all the activity and the strange attire the people wore. Then he noticed a group of men all dressed in long brown garments and their hair was trimmed in a peculiar way. Their hair circled the sides, but the crests of their heads were bald. Then he noticed one of them had beads hanging at his side with a cross dangling at the end of the strand. He could only assume they were holy men as he had witnessed in the Nabedache village.

They dismounted their horses and the captain approached them. "I am Domingo Ramon, commander of the guards at this outpost. I serve alongside my brother, Diego. The fort is under the command of our father, Captain Diego Ramon. He oversees everything else you see in this place. Tell me, why have you come here?"

Trapper began to answer, "They have come..."

"I would like to hear these men speak," Domingo interrupted him, referring to the four Frenchmen. "What is your purpose here?"

"It is a diplomatic mission we have come on," Pierre said in Spanish."

Domingo nodded suspiciously and said, "Yes, you do know my language. I remember you and the one standing next to you. You were saved from those natives on the shore, but then we showed you mercy and let you go free, back to your countrymen." He stepped closer to the four men and smiled. "And now you have come *back* carrying weapons."

St. Denis could hold his tongue no longer. In broken Spanish, he tried to defend them, saying, "These are my men. They are with me on a mission in hopes to establish trade with you, not quarrel with you."

Domingo stepped in front of him and asked, "And who are you?"

"I am Louis Juchereau de St. Denis. I am an explorer, not a man of war." He motioned to Trapper and asked, "If I may speak to you through Bear Trapper. He is fluent in your language as we are not. I can understand his words."

Domingo agreed to have Bear Trapper interpret for them. "Well, Louis," he said connivingly, "what am I to make of this? I come to my gate to see four Frenchmen carrying muskets, riding with four aging natives."

"They are my friends. They have come from the tribes in lands north of here. We have established trade with them at an outpost east of the Sabine River and now we would like to establish a trade route between here and our outpost."

"And what is it do you wish to trade? We are not a military garrison here. This is a village of religious peasants spreading the Gospel. They only have us here for their protection. When I see Frenchmen carrying weapons into my outpost, I must not take this lightly."

"I understand," St. Denis answered worriedly, "but we do not wish to trade weapons here. We merely..."

"Perhaps you wish to trade them elsewhere, is that it?" Domingo persisted. "Some other hostile faction inside my country?"

St. Denis became flustered and said, "No, that is not it at all!"

188

"You had best come with me," Domingo said abruptly. He motioned for his guard. "Take him into custody. Hold these other Frenchmen for questioning."

St. Denis was stunned as the guards tied his hands behind his back and led him away.

Nakahodot and Natchitos stood looking on bewildered. "Where are they taking him?" Natchitos asked Trapper.

"He is being arrested," Trapper answered frankly. "It appears the commander suspects him of smuggling weapons." He shook his head and added, "I had a feeling this journey was unwise."

The guards led Pénicaut, Pierre and Robert away but did not tie their hands. The incident stirred the attention of several onlookers in the compound, but once the men disappeared inside the military command, the people continued with their daily tasks.

Nakahodot could sense many eyes gazing at them curiously and with suspicion. He had an uncomfortable feeling and wished that they could leave the fort, but he was also unsettled in how their companions were led away.

"How long will they be held in there?" he asked Trapper.

Trapper shook his head, answering, "I do not know. They will question them further, I am certain. It takes much time to earn the trust of the Spanish white men. They are very distrustful of outsiders. And it appears they make no exception particularly with former enemies."

Natchitos nodded in understanding. "Very difficult to sit down with an enemy. But I know the lieutenant, he will talk to these men in a just way."

"I do not think so," Trapper countered. "His command of their language is poor. Unless they allow him to speak through the two brothers."

"You go and speak for him," Natchitos insisted.

"I am certain they will not let me enter. At least not today." He looked toward the sky and saw that the sun was setting. "I have a place where we can make camp outside these walls. We will return at first light to see if we can help your lieutenant."

Nakahodot was grateful to hear him say this and added, "Outside these walls will be good."

The four men setup camp alongside the river and built a fire. Nakahodot wasted no time in catching some fish, while Buffalo Tamer prepared some rabbit they had carried with them.

They were all tired and hungry and Natchitos waited impatiently while Nakahodot cleaned his catch. Exasperated, he finally said, "You are taking too much time with the fish."

Nakahodot shook his head and ignored him. He looked over at Buffalo Tamer, who was still roasting the rabbit, and commented, "Better make his meat soft. He does not have any teeth." Buffalo Tamer smiled slightly, but stayed quiet, avoiding their bickering. Natchitos glared at his brother with contempt.

"The chief is right, Light Hair," Trapper joked, "you are taking too long."

"You should not call me that," Nakahodot shot back as he lowered the fish over the flames. "The fish will be ready when they are done." He handed the fish to his brother and added, "You cook. I will watch the sun." He walked over away from the fire and sat on the ground to watch the brilliant sunset fade over the horizon.

Natchitos eagerly took the fish and continued cooking them. "We will eat sooner this way for certain."

Trapper glanced over at Nakahodot with a confused expression. "It is very odd that Light Hair sits to watch the sun in the west."

"I agree," Natchitos said. "Now is the time to eat and have a good smoke."

Nakahodot wasn't concerned about their opinions though and said, "It is right to take time to give thanks at the day's end. It is not any different from my brother facing east in the morning when there is work to be done. You will see." He took in a long breath of fresh air and sighed heavily as he watched the sun disappear. "And stop calling me that."

"The sun is gone," Natchitos said. "Come eat."

The next morning, the men awoke to find Natchitos sitting on the ground facing eastward awaiting the sunrise.

"I told you," Nakahodot said to Buffalo Tamer and Trapper. "There he sits and with much work to be done."

Natchitos paid his brother no attention though and stated, "We must ensure they release the lieutenant today. And his men. They must allow Bear Trapper to speak for him."

"We will not get anywhere if you keep sitting there," Nakahodot quipped. "The sun will rise, I assure you." Just as he spoke, the brilliant rays of the sun spilled over the horizon and sparkled on the waters of the Rio Grande. "See?" he laughed.

Natchitos nodded satisfyingly and said, "Yes. We will go."

Trapper had no problem gaining re-entry for the four of them back inside the fort. They walked slowly amongst the stares and curious looks from the local people who were milling about.

One of the men dressed in a long brown cloak was walking past alone with his head bowed in a prayerful, meditative pose. His curiosity got the best of him when he noticed the four natives passing by. He skidded to a stop and his face lit up. The curious man trotted toward them and greeted them with a cheerful smile.

"Good morning!" the little man said cheerfully in Spanish.

"Good morning," Trapper answered for them.

"I am terribly sorry for interrupting you, but I could not help myself." He studied Nakahodot and Natchitos with great interest. "You are the one they call Bear Trapper, yes?" Trapper nodded. "Yes, I remember you. And I am guessing this man is related to you in some way," referring to Buffalo Tamer. Then he turned his curious gaze back to Nakahodot and Natchitos. "But I must say, these two remind me greatly of the natives Father Damian described in his journals. Yes! These are the *Tejas* people, are they not?" The man was so excited he could barely contain himself. "These are members of the tribal areas where Father

Damian established a mission so many years ago! I studied all about this mission."

Trapper did his best to interject, saying, "*Te'chas.*"

Nakahodot and Natchitos then both greeted in unison, "*Te'chas.*"

"Yes. Yes!" the friar exclaimed. "*Tejas* indeed."

"Te'*chas*," Trapper annunciated slowly, trying to correct him. But his efforts were of little use, the little man was too excited. He continued, "Yes. They have come from the wooded areas north of here. We travel with the lieutenant and his men."

"Yes, I heard about the incident yesterday evening. Very unfortunate," the man said as he continued to study them carefully as if they were statues. "Truly magnificent, they are. Just as Father Damian had described. They both look so regal and wise." He put his finger to his chin and thought considerately. "And dare I say these two men are brothers as well. The resemblance is amazing."

"They are," Trapper continued to answer him in Spanish.

"What are their names?"

Trapper motioned to his brother and said, "He is Buffalo Tamer." Then he pointed to Nakahodot, saying, "This is Chief Light Hair." Buffalo Tamer nearly laughed out loud but contained himself.

Nakahodot looked at Trapper curiously and asked, "What did you say to him?"

Trapper ignored him and continued, "And this is his brother, Chief Natchitos."

"Light Hair?" the little man asked inquisitively. "What a becoming name that you have, Chief Light Hair. It suits you quite well. And it is a pleasure to meet you too, Chief Natchitos and Buffalo Tamer." Nakahodot gave him and Trapper both a contemptuous look in return, even though he didn't know what they were saying. He had a feeling he did though, at seeing Buffalo Tamer's reaction. "You must forgive my rudeness. I have not introduced myself. I am Father Antonio Margil. I am one of the many Franciscan friars here at the monastery. Forgive me if I am rattling on. We at the monastery are enjoined to silence for much of the year. When I saw you with these men, I just knew they were from the same areas as Father Damian had been. I am most interested in the *Tejas* territory that he wrote about." He motioned to all of them, saying, "Welcome to you all, to our little outpost."

"We are wishing to see the lieutenant and his men that were taken last night," Natchitos said to Trapper to translate.

Father Margil nodded with a concerned expression. "Yes, I understand. I have prayed for their release as soon as possible. Very unfortunate when a Frenchman is not taken at his word during a time of peace. The Captain is a good man, he will be fair and just. I am sure they are only following procedures in such an unusual circumstance. I am certain it is all a great misunderstanding. I will try to help but I am afraid we do not hold much sway in military inquiries, or political ones for that matter." He could see that the men were growing impatient with him. "Well, let me say again how pleased I am to have met all of you. I pray for your success in securing your friend's release. I sincerely hope we can speak again in the future. Good day to you." They watched as the peculiar, but friendly Father Margil continued on his way to the chapel.

Nakahodot kept glaring at Trapper and said, "You did not introduce me properly, did you?"

"I thought I did," Trapper chuckled. "Come. Let us go to where the lieutenant is being held."

Chapter 20

The four men stood outside the makeshift prison. The structure amounted to little more than a barn built for a few milking cows and a courtyard scattered with chickens. A guard was assigned to stand outside the only door that led to the rooms where the Frenchmen were being held.

"We wish to see our companions," Trapper said to the guard in Spanish.

"Only the Captain can give you permission," the guard answered. "You must wait here."

Just then the leader of the fort, Captain Diego Ramon, came striding up behind them along with his aide. "Ah, I should have known what early-risers you natives are. Hello again, Bear Trapper. No doubt you are waiting to see Señor Juchereau." Trapper nodded to him. The Captain looked over the other men carefully and then added, "I only need you. We will get through this much quicker with your help to translate. The rest of you must wait outside."

When Natchitos understood what he was saying, he protested, "We must see him. I am the best choice you have to attest for this man." However, the Captain would not hear any of it. Again, he insisted that all wait outside except for Trapper.

Nakahodot put his hand on his shoulder and said, "We will wait here, brother. The lieutenant can speak well with these men." Natchitos reluctantly stood aside as Trapper followed Captain Ramon through the door. He walked across the path dejected and sat in the shade of the building opposite the prison. Buffalo Tamer and Nakahodot sat alongside him.

Inside a large, open air room, sat St. Denis. He sat on a wooden bench near a small window waiting patiently for his interrogation. The barn room, that was normally used for the cows, had a loft for hay and a single window that overlooked the courtyard. He sat staring out at the early morning scene of clucking chickens and proudly-strutting roosters. Soon, he heard the door being unlatched from the other side. He looked on wearily as the Captain and Bear Trapper entered. He was surprised to see someone else besides Domingo.

"Good morning, Lieutenant," Captain Ramon said. "I trust they are looking after you since last night?" Trapper translated for them.

"Yes," St. Denis answered. "Where are my men? Are they being looked after?"

"Yes," the Captain answered casually. "In fact, they have been released. I have no need of them here."

"Then you must not have any need of me here either," St. Denis snapped. "I have done nothing just as they have. Who are you, anyway?" St. Denis fumed as he glared at the older gentlemen with contempt.

"My apologies," he answered. "I am Captain Ramon. I am commander of this outpost."

"Then you must know as a seasoned military man, that those muskets are of little use in any kind of battle. The only use they have is for pheasants and rabbits. They are not war-musket caliber at all."

"Yes, I know this."

"You *know*?" St. Denis asked with apoplectic dismay. "Then why is this Domingo holding me here? This is an outrage."

Captain Ramon approached and tried to calm him. "Domingo is my son. He and my other son, Diego, have command of the guard and security here. I must apologize for his sudden temperament. He is quick to judge at times. But in his defense, our superiors give us explicit orders when it comes to matters that deal with the French. I am sure you have the same precautions when it comes to Spaniards as well." St. Denis knew he was correct in his assessment, but he was still quite upset about being held prisoner. "I personally would be happy to entertain your proposal of trade, but it is not up to me now."

"What do you mean?" St. Denis asked perplexed.

"I am afraid that word has spread rapidly of your arrest, albeit it was done quite hastily by my over-zealous son. But nevertheless, I have already received word overnight from riders at our nearest outpost. I am to hold you here indefinitely until I receive official word from the viceroy."

"*Indefinitely?*" St. Denis was now beside himself with rage. He nodded furiously, already knowing what the reason was. "You have a French officer in custody and your superiors are overjoyed. Yes, I see what this is. *Thank you* for your consideration and trust." He paced around the dirt floor back and forth fuming. "And just how long will it be before we get this *word?*"

"I do not know," he ashamedly admitted. He walked over to St. Denis and placed his hand on his shoulder. "Louis, if I may call you that, I am an old man, I am not your enemy any longer. I sympathize with your unfortunate situation. I do not agree with this and I apologize for my son's actions. I will do what I can to speed this along. I will see to it that you are treated fairly and get what you need. I only hope you will not hold this matter against me."

St. Denis calmed a bit and could see that the Captain was being sincere. "I appreciate your position, Captain, and your candor." He thought for a moment and then asked, "I must tell my men and the Indians that I traveled with what has transpired. I brought them here as representatives of their people in hopes good relations could be established with you. What should I tell them? This news will not go over well with them."

"I will speak to them myself and will assure them you will be treated fairly. I will also do my best to assure these natives that a good relationship can be salvaged here. It will just take time and patience. But I am under strict orders to not allow you visitation at this time. Again, I sincerely apologize."

St. Denis shook his head disappointedly, and said, "I guess there is nothing more I can say to persuade you then. Please send them my apologies and that I will be out soon."

"I will." With that, Captain Ramon and Trapper left him. He sat by the window and sighed heavily as he stared at the chickens.

Outside the walls of the fort stood the four Indians and the three Frenchmen. Natchitos was the most apoplectic of them all. He could not believe things had gone from bad to worse.

"So, they are using the lieutenant as an example, then?" Natchitos asked bewildered.

Trapper answered, shaking his head, "That is the way it seems. You heard what the Captain explained to all of you, it is in the hands of the Viceroy now."

"Where is this man?"

"I do not know," Trapper admitted.

Robert Talon understood what Natchitos was asking and said, "I am certain this leader is in a place called Mexico City. It is very far from here."

Natchitos shook his head angrily and responded, "These white men are far more difficult than what I have encountered. These decisions have no honor."

"Will you still have trade with these men as the Captain has proposed?" Nakahodot asked. "Should we take his word after hearing they will hold the lieutenant indefinitely? I agree, there is no honor in this."

"This trail is not needed in my opinion," Natchitos flatly stated. "I will wait until the lieutenant is released. But then my people will only trade with the French white men."

"We are not waiting," Pierre declared fervently.

Trapper's eyebrows raised and responded, asking, "You will abandon your lieutenant here?"

Pierre shook his head and replied, "We are not abandoning him. But we know it could be months, if not longer, before he is set free. They will most likely force him to see the viceroy personally in Mexico City. But we cannot stay here. Not again. These are not our people."

Pénicaut spoke up as well, saying, "The governor must know that Louis is being held here. That is why we must return to Fort St. Jean for help. That is the only way to speed this along."

"Then you will be enemies once more," Buffalo Tamer concluded. "What you suggest will surely cause war to break out. You must hope that the lieutenant will be set free before this happens. I cannot join you in this journey. I will stay with the Hasinai."

"So be it. We will find our own way back," Robert snapped. "Somebody has to do something." Pénicaut and the two Talon brothers mounted their horses and headed north across the river.

Nakahodot looked over at the remaining three and asked, "Shall we remain here as well? We cannot rely on those men to send word to the tribe about our situation."

"I do not wish to leave here knowing the lieutenant is in the prison," Natchitos said. "But there is little game here to hunt. And I do not care to ask the Spanish for help. We must find a place to survive."

Nakahodot came up with a plan and stated, "We know how many days ride it is up the trail. Let us go back to the Nakadochito and inform them of what has taken place. Bear Trapper can inform the lieutenant of our plans if they will not allow us to speak to him. Then we will return with provisions and stay here by the river as long as we have to." They all agreed and decided to set out on their horses after Bear Trapper sent word to St. Denis.

St. Denis sat in his spacious barn prison cell, watching the chickens scamper around the yard and the birds fluttering in a lone, nearby mesquite tree. "Very different terrain they have here," he muttered to himself. "Such strange trees. I guess I will have to get used to this view."

He heard the latch of the door at the far side of the barn open. In walked a beautiful Spanish woman, carrying a wooden tray of food for him. She had long, flowing, silky black hair and wore a red, yet slightly faded, dress with a tattered brown apron about her waist. She looked to be no more than twenty-five years of age and St. Denis sat with his mouth agape, admiring her stunning beauty.

"Some food for you, *Señor*," she said shyly.

St. Denis nearly fell off his stool in trying to remember how to thank her in Spanish. "*Gracias, Señora*," he finally stammered.

As soon as he did, she quickly left the room, but not before she stopped abruptly with her back turned and answered quietly, "*Señorita*." St. Denis smiled broadly as she slowly closed the door.

Chapter 21

The next morning, St. Denis was in an unusually good mood as he eagerly awaited his next meal. He had great hopes he would see the beautiful woman in red once more. He checked his attire to make sure he looked presentable and did his best to mat down his hair.

"If only I had a looking glass," he mumbled to himself. "No telling how dreadful I look after being in this barn for so many days."

Finally, his excitement grew as he heard the latch of the door. He couldn't help but smile as he waited patiently for the door to be opened. He wasn't disappointed when the same beautiful woman entered the room with a tray of corn tortillas and fruit. After seeing how desolate the landscape was in the area, he wondered where she had come by such fruit. It didn't matter. His heart quickened in his chest as he watched her every delicate move.

"Be still my heart," he whispered in French. "'Tis truly the best part of my day."

"Some food for you, *Señor,*" she said as she had the day before. Quickly she headed for the door to leave.

"*Señorita,*" he called out. "If I may." He crossed the floor over to the table where she had laid the tray. "I apologize," he said, "my Spanish is not good."

He was clamoring to speak Spanish as best he could. He had spent most of his time alone in the cell the last few days desperately trying to remember his school lessons in Spanish when he was a boy. His parents in France had insisted on him learning both languages as times even then were tense with neighboring Spain. His father made the point fervently that it was best to learn the language of one's enemies so good communication could be established. "If you do this," his father would say, "then soon they will no longer be your enemy." Ever since, St. Denis made it a point of order to learn as many languages as he saw fit in order to succeed in his explorations. It had been many years since he practiced Spanish but now his memory of it was slowly returning to him.

"I do not get to see many people," he continued. "I would be honored if you would sit with me." His command of the language was indeed sporadic, but she understood what he was saying. He motioned for her to join him at the table. His heart pounded in his chest as he awaited her response.

She looked over her shoulder at the closed door and then back at him. She enjoyed the warm smile he had as he gazed at her. She thought he was quite handsome as well. She knew she would be scolded if anyone knew, but she answered sheepishly, "*Sí.*"

His face beamed when she accepted his invitation. "Please," he said as he pulled out a chair for her. "Allow me."

"Thank you," she said sweetly. "I will only stay a minute."

He nodded and clumsily took a seat opposite of her. "Of course. I do not want to keep you from your duties. I thank you for sitting with me." He soon realized he was mixing French words with Spanish words. It made sense to him, but he knew she must be confused. He continued to stammer, "You are kind to bring this food to me. I would gladly share it with you."

She smiled slightly as she looked at the table, she couldn't bring herself to make eye contact with him.

"Why are you smiling?" he asked gentlemanly. "Did I say something wrong?"

"You are right," she answered. "Your Spanish is not good."

He laughed at himself and said, "I know. You must forgive me. Please, let me introduce myself. My name is Louis." She finally lifted her eyes to look at him. She blushed as she knew he couldn't take his eyes off her. She had never received such attention from a foreign man. She did love his smile though. "And you are?" he asked.

"Manuela," she replied as she quickly turned her gaze away once more. She could feel the warm blush of her cheeks and felt embarrassed.

"Manuela," he echoed with a pleasant sigh. "Such a beautiful name."

She suddenly got to her feet and announced, "I must go."

St. Denis rose immediately and fretted, but he understood. "Of course. But I hope to see you again." He hesitated a moment as she turned for the door. "I will see you again, will I not?" She nodded with a prudent smile. "It was a pleasure meeting you, Señorita Manuela."

She opened the door but before she closed it, she stuck her head around the edge and whispered, "Work on your Spanish."

He smiled happily at her and said, " *Sí, Señorita.*"

The days turned to weeks and St. Denis saw no positive news or changes to his incarceration. He would receive cursory visits from the Captain but only to see if he was being well looked after. His jailor never gave him any inclination as to what would happen next with his case.

But as the days went by, St. Denis was pleasantly distracted by the presence of Manuela. He looked forward to her visits twice a day and, even though their encounters were brief, he took every moment to practice her language and get to know her better. Soon, she became more comfortable with him and it was obvious she enjoyed his company as much as he enjoyed hers.

As the summer turned to fall, he could sense the change in the air from his only window. He sat gazing outside when he heard the familiar unlatching of his cell door. He leapt to his feet and eagerly awaited her entrance. She rounded the large barn door with a broad smile on her face, carrying his tray of breakfast.

"Good morning, Manuela," he said cheerfully.

"Good morning, *Señor.*"

He walked over to her eagerly and helped her place the tray down. For the first time he quickly noticed she had scented herself with a pleasing perfume. He was instantly taken by the romantic fragrance. He wondered immediately what she had done to create such an intoxicating aroma. Whatever it was, she knew he was pleased with it.

"Please," he said, "I insist you call me Louis."

She looked at him more confidently than she ever had before and responded, "As you wish. Good morning, Louis."

He clamored for something more to say. Her delightful scent had caught him off guard completely. "You are looking lovely today, Manuela."

"Thank you."

He motioned to the window and commented, "I...I was noticing how fresh the air is this morning. Autumn is arriving now, thankfully."

"Yes, it is," she answered sweetly.

"It would be a splendid idea if I could escort you for a walk in the courtyard." He looked glumly at the window. "If only there were a door."

She walked over to the window and slid the bench away from the wall to reveal a wooden latch that was just below the window. "You do have a door," she said matter-of-factly. "They have concealed it very stubbornly."

"Well, I would have never..." he muttered. He pulled the latch and discovered the window was part of a small entryway that opened to the courtyard. Immediately the chickens made a beeline for the open door, but Manuela quickly shut it.

"You must be sure to keep them out, though."

"So, I can go out there and walk around?"

She shrugged her shoulders and answered, "I would if I were you. You will not get any farther than the walls though, so I do not see why you cannot."

He held out his arm to her and asked, "Will you join me for a stroll with the chickens, then?"

She backed away and said, "I cannot." His face fell. He was overjoyed at the discovery of the door, but he wanted to share his new extension of freedom with her. His spirits lifted however, when she said, "I can ask for permission, though."

"I see. I understand completely." He sighed gratefully at the revelation of the door latch and exclaimed, "Thank you very much for showing me this. I am very pleased."

"I knew you would be. I must go now."

The next day, St. Denis had made his way into the courtyard and was wandering around the small throng of chickens and roosters and taking in the fresh air. He was overjoyed with his newfound freedom to wander around and stretch his legs more suitably. He heard the latch from within the cell and heard Manuela call out to him.

"I am out here!" he answered her. "I will be right there. One moment, please." He scurried over to the door and the chickens scattered. He slowly opened the door and used his foot to keep away the curious birds. "Back away, now," he panted as he quickly re-entered his barn cell.

When he entered, he was surprised to see Manuela standing with two older women behind her. "Good morning," he said to all of them. "What a pleasant surprise. I am Louis Juchereau."

Manuela turned to the ladies and introduced them. First, she motioned to the oldest woman and said, "This is my *abuela*. And this is my mother, Mariana Sanchez-Ramon."

"Ramon?" he asked out loud. The name surprised and flustered him, yet he kept his composure. "It is a pleasure to meet you, ladies. Very kind of you to come."

Her mother leaned over and whispered to Manuela, saying, "His Spanish is not too bad."

"I have been helping him," she whispered back.

St. Denis nodded and said, "Yes, your daughter is a fine teacher. I am very grateful." He understood now why she had brought her mother and grandmother along with her. "It is a lovely day this morning. Would you ladies care to join me in the courtyard for a stroll?" They all agreed with a smile. "Manuela, if you can help me with the door, I can manage the chickens."

"Certainly." They worked together to open the latch and then he quickly trotted outside to keep the birds away. The three ladies emerged, and Manuela closed the door behind them.

He walked side-by-side with Manuela through the courtyard that was partially shaded by the large mesquite tree just on the other side of the wall. The ladies slowly walked closely behind them. He should have known that such an invitation would require chaperones, but he didn't mind. He was happy to be enjoying the morning air with her outside of his cell finally. He was, however, very curious about her last name.

"You said your mother's name was Sanchez-Ramon. Is it the same Ramon as the Captain and his sons?"

"It is," she admitted. "I am sorry for not telling you. Captain Ramon is my grandfather. Diego is my father and Domingo my uncle."

"No need to apologize," he answered respectfully. "I know they are only carrying out their duty. Besides, if they had not, I would have never met you. Trust me, there is no need to worry." He looked over his shoulder and said, "I enjoy their company as well. It gives me great satisfaction in seeing they do not think badly of me. I admire that very much. I only hope I can be just as persuasive with your father and grandfather."

"My father keeps me away from his business. I have only been told to bring you food, but I can say this; I think something is happening. I have seen my father speaking with the Captain more often these past few days."

"No need to betray their confidence," he assured her. "They will tell me when the time comes. There is no reason for them to hold me here much longer I feel. I have done nothing wrong. But I am afraid I am being held on political grounds, rather than criminal. My superiors operate in a similar way. It is never productive."

They continued walking through the courtyard together as the chickens scurried here and there. In the shade of the tree they came across a single flower that had poked up from the dry soil. He reached down and picked the white flower and admired it.

She smiled at the pretty flower too. "Will you permit me?" he asked. She flashed her long eye lashes yes and blushed as he placed the flower behind her left ear. The white flower stood out beautifully in her silky black hair. "*Muy bonita*," he said softly. She blushed even more as she quickly glanced over at her mother and grandmother who were waiting patiently.

She swallowed hard, staring into his eyes, knowing that she was falling for him. And she knew that he was falling for her too. Would a relationship with a Frenchmen be permitted? What kind of life would they have if they really were to be together? Her mind raced as he stared lovingly into her eyes. She knew he must be having similar thoughts as she was, or he would not be pining for her each day. They kept their feelings to themselves for the time being, but she couldn't help her romantic thoughts of him. She imagined what it would be like for him to hold her hand, to caress her face and to kiss her. She shook her head and snapped back into reality. Flustered, she said, "We should go back in now."

He again kept the birds at bay while she opened the door for her mother and grandmother. He came in closely behind them and shut the door. This time, he was surprised to see her father, Diego, waiting just inside the cell door. He looked very much like his brother, Domingo. The three ladies stood off to the side and waited quietly for him to speak.

"I trust you had a pleasant walk?" he asked smartly.

"We did indeed," answered St. Denis.

Diego motioned to the three ladies and said, "I will speak with him alone." They all quickly left the barn cell.

"A lovely family you have, sir," St. Denis said respectfully.

Diego ignored him though and responded, "Word has come from the Viceroy. You will plead your case with him."

"Very well. And where is the Viceroy?"

Diego sat at the table and put down his cap. "It is several days ride from here. The Viceroy is headquartered in Mexico City." St. Denis looked dismayed, knowing that he would have to travel even farther away from his friends and that they would not know where he was going. "But there is someone else that will accompany you on this ride." He turned to the door and called out, "Send him in!"

St. Denis was curious to see a friar walk in. He was unaware, but it was the same friar that had spoken to Nakahodot before they left the fort. "This religious man is going with us?" he inquired.

Father Margil couldn't help himself and interjected, "I must introduce myself, if I may. I am Father Antonio Margil. I have been requesting to visit you in your lonely incarceration but to this point have not been given permission."

"I can hardly say he was lonely," Diego quipped.

"I appreciate your gesture, Father Margil," answered St. Denis. "I am Louis Juchereau. But for what reason will you accompany us on the ride to the Viceroy?"

"It seems the Viceroy has some ideas about this *Tejas* territory and wishes to see you and my brother, Domingo, about it," Diego affirmed.

"You mean the Hasinai people? What ideas?"

Diego sat confidently at the table and casually asked, "You said you wish to establish trade, did you not? Well, now is your chance to prove that statement."

"Prove it? How?" He was understandably curious.

Father Margil interjected once more, saying, "Oh, its most exciting. I have been eager to take up where my predecessor left off and try once more in spreading the Word of God to these *Tejas* people and hopefully convert them to Catholicism."

St. Denis was intrigued but still was puzzled. "You want to convert them? What does this have to do with me?"

Diego continued. "The wooded areas that you came from. You said you have established a fort amongst the natives there. And this trail you have taken, you know these areas well?"

"Better than most. But it is the Hasinai who know it best."

"The areas that the Viceroy are interested in are where the natives are located west of the Sabine. Not where you have established your fort. We will respect the territory you have already explored, unlike your predecessor LaSalle afforded us."

St. Denis bristled at the mention of his late cohort's name. "LaSalle was a renegade, but he was a pioneer and forthright and just man. He was also a mentor. He was only doing what he was commanded to do. His only mistake was thinking the fort he erected was near the mouth of the Colbert River."

"Yes, and we burned his fort to the ground," Diego boasted. "It seems he made more than one mistake though, or he would not have been slain by his own men."

"I think you have said enough."

"Regardless," Diego said, trying to defuse St. Denis' obvious growing anger, "this is what the Viceroy wishes to speak to you about and perhaps if you say what he wants to hear, you may win your freedom."

"I understand."

Diego said to Father Margil, "Leave us now, Father, if you will. I have more to say to Louis in private." Father Margil nodded and left the room. Diego looked back at St. Denis and asked, "You do not like me, do you?"

St. Denis sat at the table opposite him and commented, "I would not say that, sir. Perhaps I just do not know you very well. What can I say to a man whose brother made a snap judgement over me and put me in a prison?"

"You would have made the same snap decision if you were in his shoes."

"Would I?"

"Come now, Louis," Diego prodded, "We are Spaniards, and you are French. Our countries have been at odds since our grandfather's father's time."

St. Denis corrected him quickly, saying, "We are not in our countries. We are in someone else's. And we should not be so boastful in saying these are now our lands. We are merely guests here, explorers, working hard to integrate with the rightful stewards of these lands. Do you really think it is right for us to force religion on them as well?"

Diego looked surprised and answered, "We would not force it on them. But it is our duty as Christians to spread the Word of Jesus as far and wide as we can. It would be up to them to accept the Gospel. All we can do is teach it to them."

St. Denis could tell that something else was on his mind though. "What is it that you really want to talk to me about, Diego?"

"What are your intentions with my daughter?" he finally asked.

St. Denis stood and paced around the room. He knew it was a subject that would come up sooner or later. "I must confess," he began, "I did not know she was your daughter. But I believe the presence of your wife and mother today had something to do with you, am I correct? They would not have come without your permission."

"That is correct."

"Your daughter has been very kind to me. I am grateful for her visits and caring for me, bringing me food to eat. She is a lovely and intelligent young lady. You should be very proud of her, sir."

Diego nodded appreciatively and replied, "I am. But you are still not answering my question. If the Viceroy were to grant you your freedom, what would you do with it?"

St. Denis looked at him directly and answered, "I would do as he asked. But I would also ask you for your permission to marry Manuela."

"You would take her away from here? From myself and her mother?"

St. Denis sat down again and said, "Not without both of your blessings. But I must be honest with you, sir. I think…well, I know that I am in love with her. I do want to make her my wife."

Diego got up from the table and he began to pace this time. "She is our only daughter, you know that? She has been dragged around from one fort to the next since she was a little girl. She has the same adventurous spirit as you have. I admire that in you. You are right about one thing, Louis. This is not our country. I do not see you as an enemy. Only our governments declare this from afar, quite arrogantly I might add." He walked over to St. Denis and extended his hand in friendship. St. Denis got up and shook his hand in return. "I know my daughter holds favor for you. I see happiness in her that I have not seen before. If you win your freedom, you have my permission to propose to her."

Chapter 22

Nakahodot sat with Calanele in their home, warming themselves by the fire. She sat quietly combing her long, graying hair wondering when her husband would break his silence.

As he stirred the broken, ashen embers in the fire, he finally decided to speak. "It is much quieter in here now without Kewanee. I trust she and Tokala are well together?"

"They are a good match," Calanele sighed, grateful that he was finally speaking. "She still comes to stay with me some nights to keep me company. She is gone when I awake though." She laughed a little as she knew the reason.

"I do not like being away and leaving you here alone," he said.

"I am not alone, husband. Our boys are here too. The grandchildren are a joy and they keep me busy. And having our old friends from the Nashitosh for a longer stay is a blessing to me."

"They are not boys," he corrected her.

She sighed heavily once more and agreed, "No they are not." She put her wooden comb down and put her hand on his arm. "Is there really a need for you to go back? You said so yourself that they would release him soon. The other whites did not even stay with him. Why must you go?"

Nakahodot didn't hesitate in responding, saying, "Natchitos feels it is right and I agree with him. The Spanish men would not let him even speak to his friend the lieutenant. And I can sense my brother's anxious feelings on the matter. The lieutenant fought side-by-side with my brother. He stood with the Nashitosh. It is right that we return to stand with him."

Calanele was sad but she understood her husband's reasons. She resumed her combing and then asked, "When will you go?"

"In a week's time, after we are well rested, Bear Trapper, Buffalo Tamer and I will go with Natchitos. Tooantuh and Pakwa will ride with us as well. I will leave Nashuk, Notaku, Anoki and

Tokala to stay and hunt and watch over the tribes. We will not return without the lieutenant."

She became worried and asked, "You are thinking of using force to free him?"

"No," he assured her as he caressed her face. "We will find the small one who has no hair and persuade him to speak for the lieutenant. He carried the cross of the one they call 'Jesus'. Most certainly the small man would practice what he preaches."

Calanele quietly contemplated his words, even though she remained skeptical of the story of Jesus. However, she trusted that her husband knew what he was doing.

Back at Fort San Juan Bautista, St. Denis sat with Manuela as he ate an orange. As he peeled the brightly-colored fruit, the sensational aroma wafted into their noses. "This fruit always smells amazing," he laughed as she watched him peel it. "You never told me where you get so much of it. I have only seen one tree around here by the wall and it is a ghastly sight. I cannot imagine it to be an orange tree."

She laughed at him and answered, "Silly, that is a mesquite tree. The orange groves are not far from here. We have plenty of them. I am glad they appeal to you." He handed her a slice of orange with a smile. "Louis, tell me about where you live."

He was more than happy to answer as he hoped he would take her there one day. "It is beautiful, lush and green," he began. "Far different from this landscape. Yes, the mountains in the distance are majestic, but where we built the fort, it is…how should I say? It is enchanting." She smiled at the notion and begged to hear more. "The trees reach high into the sky and sway gently in the breeze. Even in the hottest of days, the shade is cool and soothing. And there is a magnificent river that flows gently through the middle of the village, with majestic cliffs and riverbeds dotted with cane and flora unlike you have ever seen. Everywhere you look is green and full of life. I very much want to take you there someday, Manuela."

"Oh yes, Louis. Please take me there. I want to see everything that you have seen." He set down the orange and reached across the table to hold her hand. She gladly placed her hand in his. His hands were soft and warm to the touch and it soothed her. "I want to go where you go," she said softly.

He cupped both his hands over hers and gazed at her sweetly. "Manuela, if I may be so bold. I have spoken with your father." She gasped, and her heart skipped a beat as he slid off his chair and fell to one knee. "I am about to leave for Mexico City to plead for my freedom. What your father has asked of me I feel is significant in securing my release. Then we would be free to do as we wish." He cleared his throat and he became parched in trying to get the words out. She waited patiently but a tear formed in her eye as she did. "Manuela, I love you." Butterflies danced in her belly as she heard the beautiful words. "And I want to spend the rest of my life with you. Would you do me the honor in becoming my wife?"

She leapt off her chair and into his waiting arms. "Yes! Yes, Louis. I *will* marry you," she exclaimed happily through her tears. She kissed him deeply for the first time, not caring if anyone would see. Then she opened her eyes and smiled at him and whispered sweetly, "I love you too."

They embraced for what seemed like an eternity when finally, she pulled away just slightly to wipe away her tears. "I never thought I would marry," she said softly. "We move from place to place and..."

"And what, my love?" he asked curiously.

She hesitated for a moment and then admitted, "I am not as young as I used to be."

He chuckled and said, "Of *course* you are still young." He brushed her long hair aside to reveal her blushing cheeks. "And so beautiful too. I am the one who thought this day would never come. I am not the young man I once was either. I would not trade this moment for anything though. I would wait two lifetimes for you." She kissed him deeply once more, relaxing in his arms. They finally sat down at the table and he handed her some more orange slices. "It reminds me of a story of a young couple among the tribes I live with now. One man's son from the

Nashitosh, Tokala, and Chief Nakahodot's daughter, Kewanee. They were deeply in love but were separated by circumstances beyond their control for over *fourteen* years."

"Oh, my," Manuela exclaimed. "This is a *sad* story."

"Yes, it was a very sad story. But it does have a happy ending. Once the Nashitosh returned to their homeland and reunited with the Nakadochito, Tokala was returned to his true love, Kewanee. I was witness to their wedding only months ago." He placed his hand in hers once more and said, "So, you see, my love. Not even time can stand in the way of true love. I would very much like you to meet them. They are a lovely couple."

"They had waited for each other all those years? Even though they were well beyond their age to marry?" St. Denis nodded with a smile. "It is indeed a true love story and very much like ours, Louis. I cannot wait to meet them."

Six days later, St. Denis arrived at the official residence of the Viceroy of New Spain in Mexico City. He was accompanied by Domingo Ramon, Father Margil and two guards.

They entered the chambers of the Viceroy and were directed to a small bench along the back wall. The room was adorned with nothing on the walls or any sort of decoration with only two windows open to the outside air which provided the only light. A small desk with a feathered quill rested neatly on the corner in its holder next to a small ink jar. A single chair in the middle of the room was positioned in front of the desk. St. Denis waited patiently as he casually looked around the otherwise drab chamber.

"Such a lovely court the Viceroy conducts his affairs in," the friar admired aloud. "Quite a charming room, is it not?"

Domingo looked at him crazily and asked, "Have you gone leave of your senses?" Just then, a door at the far side of the room opened and the Viceroy entered. "We must rise," Domingo whispered. The five men all rose in unison as the Viceroy shuffled across the floor.

St. Denis observed the old man closely and respectfully. He was dressed in a perfectly pressed uniform. He wore a blouse of royal red trimmed with yellow and the red stood out prominently against the dark navy jacket. Across his chest he wore a satin turquoise sash that signified the rank of Viceroy. His hair was neatly trimmed but graying around his sideburns and just above his wrinkled forehead. He neither smiled nor frowned yet sat with an heir of supremacy.

As he took his chair, he motioned for the men to take their seats. He unrolled a parchment on the desk he had been carrying in his hand. "The guards will wait in the corridor," he said in an old but commanding voice. "I only have need of the commander and the prisoner, as well as the good friar." He gazed for a moment at St. Denis, then said, "If you will, Lieutenant, come and sit before me."

"Of course. Thank you, sir." St. Denis rose and quickly walked to the chair in front of the Viceroy.

"I understand you are well-versed in our language?" the Viceroy asked.

St. Denis sat forward in the small chair and answered as best he could. "I am not as fluent as I would like to be, Your Excellency, but I am getting better with your language."

The Viceroy nodded and said, "I feel your Spanish is quite adequate. We will proceed without any need of an interpreter."

"Thank you, sir."

The old man quietly looked over the parchment before him, reminding himself of what he had already read before. "I trust your journey here was a safe one?"

"Yes, Your Excellency. It was quite sufficient, thank you."

"I must apologize in requesting that you make this long journey from the fort at San Juan Bautista. For the reasons of this particular case, I would have wanted to visit this outpost personally. But in my feeble state, I am no longer able to make such long rides."

St. Denis nodded in understanding and said, "I appreciate you saying so, sir. It is my pleasure to come and see you here."

215

The Viceroy coughed before answering. After clearing his throat, he continued. "I appreciate your professional candor. Let me be frank with you, Lieutenant. I did not summon you here to scold you, though I must act formally in this charge that is brought against you. So, let us deal with that first, shall we?"

"By all means, sir."

"You are charged with carrying unauthorized arms across our border and suspected of an intent to deal these arms to unknown cohorts. In a sense, the commander has suspicions that you, a French commander and former adversary of the King of Spain, would try to incite rebellion within our borders here in New Spain. What say you to this?"

"I am innocent," St. Denis quickly answered. "The charge is false and completely baseless. And might I add, quite absurd." Domingo frowned behind St. Denis, crossing his arms in protest.

"I would advise that you hold your opinions privately, Lieutenant. Saying you are innocent or guilty is all I need hear from you."

St. Denis bowed his head contritely and answered, "My apologies, Your Excellency."

"However," the Viceroy continued, "I am in agreement that these charges are groundless."

St. Denis' expression brightened immediately and exclaimed, "Thank you, Your Excellency."

"I have examined the weapons in question and conclude them to be quite inadequate. I doubt they would level even a goat much less a man." St. Denis tried to keep from uttering a laugh. "Allow me to speak frankly. May I call you Louis?"

"Of course, Your Excellency."

The Viceroy put down the parchment and leaned back in his chair. "I have read a great many things about you, Louis. Your achievements as an explorer are quite noteworthy."

St. Denis bowed graciously saying, "I am honored by your compliments, sir."

"I am told that you never carry a weapon on your expeditions."

"That is correct."

Raising an eyebrow, the Viceroy added, "Yet you carried one on this expedition. Why?"

St. Denis shrugged his shoulders and answered, "I felt it necessary in this case. I was traveling as a guest of my friends and native guides. My skills with a spear or bow and arrow do not match their skill. I thought I would be better equipped for the hunt for our daily meals if I carried a musket."

"Quite so," agreed the Viceroy. "I would be useless with a bow and arrow myself. Louis, it is these natives I wish to speak to you about."

"Yes, Your Excellency?"

The Viceroy cleared his throat once more before adding, "His Majesty has expressed a great interest in the writings of our former Governor Alonso DeLeon. An attempt was made many years ago to establish a mission in this so-called *Tejas* territory. However, the poor governor could not finish his assignment and fell ill, eventually dying. Unfortunately, as a result, his replacements did not share his enthusiasm for his exploits with the native peoples in these lands and the mission fell into neglect. Disease was rampant and eventually the mission was abandoned and destroyed." St. Denis listened intently as he knew he was getting to the point. The Viceroy sat forward in his chair and continued. "I have read these journals as well as documents written by the friar of this failed mission, Father Damian. It is why I have summoned the good friar, Father Margil, here today with you." He motioned for Domingo and Father Margil to approach his desk. They came and stood on either side of St. Denis. "Is it correct that you have much experience with these *Tejas* people?"

"If I may beg your pardon, I believe you are referring to the tribes that are called the Hasinai, Your Excellency," he said. "I have worked with and lived amongst many tribes over the years, especially the Nashitosh. It is their land where we have established a trading post east of the Sabine River."

"In your 'Land of Louis'," the Viceroy quipped. "Tell me, did you come up with this name yourself?" Domingo and the friar laughed at his humor. St. Denis smiled respectfully, biting his tongue and tapping his foot on the floor. "I am only making a little levity, my apologies. Please go on."

"It is quite alright. But yes, I have visited one other tribe that is in this territory you have mentioned; The Nakadochito. The chief is the brother of the chief of the Nashitosh. They were my travel companions when we came to your fort."

"And you speak their language?"

St. Denis nodded. "I do."

"Quite impressive," the Viceroy said in response. "So, you know their customs well then? And you have established trade with them?"

"I have, Your Excellency. And yes, I have learned their customs quite well. The Hasinai know the trail between our Fort St. Jean-Baptiste and your Fort San Juan Bautista. It is the trail of the ancients, as they say."

The Viceroy nodded and recalled hearing of it, saying, "The road of kings or I have once heard, The Royal Road."

"Yes, Your Excellency. It is this road that I wish to re-establish a trade route between our forts and points in between. It is the soul purpose of my visit to your fort. We did not come to be hostile. We came to do business, to establish a treaty."

"Yes. Yes. Let me come to my proposal, Louis. The King is quite interested in this wooded area west of the Sabine River, this *Tejas* territory, where you say the Hasinai dwell. It is his desire to again establish missions in this area. Spreading Christianity is of great importance to His Majesty and I agree with him. I am assigning this expedition to Commander Ramon here. Along with him and his troops will be the friar, Father Margil."

"Thank you, most graciously, Your Excellency," Father Margil piped up. He was too excited to stay silent any longer.

"What I ask of you, Lieutenant," he continued, "is to travel with them as a diplomat to these native peoples and serve as a worker of trade and a purveyor of peace on our behalf. Help us establish these missions and trade amongst the Hasinai, and I will grant you your freedom." He could see that St. Denis was carefully considering his proposal in his head. He could sense some trepidation in his expression, and he knew what the reason might be. "Before you answer, there is one other matter I wish to discuss."

"Yes, Your Excellency?"

The Viceroy smiled at him and said, "I understand you have found love during your unfortunate incarceration. In a most unusual place, I might add, but it has come to my attention."

"Yes, sir," St. Denis admitted. "I am in love with the Captain's granddaughter, Manuela."

"Domingo has told me her father has granted his permission for you to propose to her."

"Yes, that is true, Viceroy." He looked over at Domingo who was obviously curious as to what he might say next. "I have already proposed to her and she has accepted. She is my betrothed, Your Excellency."

The Viceroy smiled and laughed as he could see the surprise on Domingo's face. Father Margil smiled approvingly though. "The man wastes no time, Commander. You have to admire that. I am certain he takes as much care of his duties as he does as a gentleman." He looked straight at St. Denis and said, "My congratulations to you both. Senorita Sanchez is the daughter and granddaughter of a fine military and political family. It is a great sign of your character in being blind to political matters when it comes to love. As I say, true love knows no boundaries."

"It does, indeed," St. Denis concurred. "Thank you, for your kind words. If I may ask, Your Excellency, I would gladly accept your proposal to help with the missions, if I were allowed to take my bride home with me to our fort once they are established."

"My permission is not necessary, Lieutenant. I know you will do what you say and help us with this expedition. After which, I pray you will both be happy wherever you decide to live. And I pray for the commander with many blessings of grandchildren." He rose from his chair and Domingo snapped to attention and saluted him. "My thanks to you gentlemen in coming today, but I must retire. May Godspeed you on this quest."

Chapter 23

As they left Mexico City the next day, the friar was intent on showing St. Denis a marvelous site. As they rode north of the city, they came upon a hill where they stopped and dismounted their horses. In the distance they could see a colossal structure that stood high on a hill.

"What is it that you wanted me to see?" asked St. Denis.

"We will walk the rest of the way," Father Margil insisted. "This is considered holy ground."

As they continued to walk up the hill, St. Denis soon realized the structure was an elaborate basilica. As they drew closer, he became more and more impressed.

"This is what I wanted you to see," Father Margil continued. "Only completed seven years ago, this is the holy site on Tepeyac Hill, the *Templo Explatoria a Cristo Rey*."

"It is magnificent!" St. Denis exclaimed. "Truly a wonder, indeed. What does the name mean?"

"It is the Temple of Christ the King. Inside is the most holy image of Our Lady of Guadalupe. It is the site in which the Virgin Mary appeared to a simple peasant nearly two hundred years ago."

St. Denis was astounded. "I have read about this site but have never thought I would ever see it. I would very much like to go inside. May we?"

"Of course," Father Margil answered. "It is why we have stopped here. It is the best place to start our mission before we make our journey to the *Tejas* people. It is my belief that Our Lady will intercede for us and guide us on our mission. With God's grace, we will succeed this time."

They entered the church and knelt before the altar and prayed. To the side of the altar was the holy image of the Virgin Mother. St. Denis marveled at the beauty of the decorative basilica and the reverential care that was taken by its stewards. The columns that lined each side of the sanctuary were massive, reaching high toward the vaulted, intricately-designed ceiling. He was deeply moved by the experience and agreed it was the ideal spot in which to begin their mission.

As they knelt, Domingo looked over at St. Denis contritely and said, "Lieutenant, I hope you know that my actions with you when you arrived at the fort were not personal. You have earned my respect and I know that your intentions with my niece are honorable. I hope that you can forgive my actions against you."

St. Denis kept admiring the altar and the divine image of the Blessed Virgin and said, "Quite an appropriate place to ask, Commander. All is well between us, sir, I assure you. I see it as fate that I would come to your country for one purpose but to find something even more precious. I have met my future wife." He patted him on the shoulder as he stood, saying, "I would not have it any other way."

They made their way north back to the fort and after six days of riding, they finally arrived. Before they could even reach the gates, people streamed forth to greet them. Among them was Manuela who ran as fast as you could to greet her betrothed once more.

She flung her arms around St. Denis, kissed and hugged him and then said, "Tell me you are free."

He assured her with a grand smile on his face, "I am free, my love." She rejoiced in a loud voice and continued lavishing him with hugs and kisses.

Another young man came dashing out to meet them as well. It was a young friar from the monastery. "Father Margil!" he called out.

"Yes, Brother Teloni. What is it?" Father Margil asked.

Teloni pointed toward the river, trying to catch his breath and said, "They are waiting down by the river. They just arrived yesterday."

St. Denis heard what he was saying and asked, "Who is waiting?" Then he saw them walking up the slope. He recognized them from afar and he said to himself, "*Natchitos*." He lifted

Manuela off the ground and kissed her cheek in happiness as she fell back into his arms. "They have returned! I *knew* they would."

He ran out to greet the Indians as they slowly ascended the hill to the fort. "Greetings, Lieutenant!" Natchitos shouted.

"Greetings, my friends," St. Denis called back. They clasped arms in the traditional manner and St. Denis was overwhelmed to see them. "I am so glad that you have returned. I am very grateful to you."

"Have the white men freed you from the prison?" Natchitos asked directly.

"Yes, they have. And I know you must think the worst of these people, but I am here to tell you that all is well. This misunderstanding has been cleared up and I am free. I assure you they are not enemies. There are many things to discuss that you do not know. But first..." He looked behind him and motioned for the patient Manuela to come stand beside him. Natchitos and the other Indians watched curiously as a woman in a faded red dress approached them. "I want to introduce you to someone."

Natchitos and Nakahodot saw the woman approaching with a smile on her face and they looked at each other curiously. It was the first time Nakahodot had ever seen a white woman this closely. He observed her keenly and knew what St. Denis was going to say. "Has the lieutenant who stood alone and who was sent to a prison only to emerge standing with a wife?"

"You are very shrewd, indeed, Chief Nakahodot," St. Denis delightfully answered. "This is Manuela Sanchez. She comforted me while in prison and brought me food to eat. I spent my time getting to know her these last few months and now we are to be married."

Manuela spoke in her own language, "I am pleased to meet all of you."

Natchitos smiled and approached him once more, saying, "I am glad you took my advice, Lieutenant. You spent your time wisely."

The wedding was held two days later in the courtyard where they walked and talked together during his time in prison. She was dressed beautifully in a flowing white gown and veil. St. Denis was dressed very dashing, as were all the Spanish officers in attendance. Everyone that could fit into the tiny garden did and witnessed the significant, yet romantic union. The nuptials were held in the shade of the mesquite tree and a great cheer was heard throughout the entire fort when they were declared 'man and wife'.

Several days after his wedding, St. Denis sought out Nakahodot and Natchitos and asked if they would sit with him at a fire outside the fort with Father Margil and Domingo. They accepted and gathered at the fire.

"I wanted to speak with both of you," St. Denis began, "but to you specifically Chief Nakahodot. Father Margil tells me he has met you before just after my imprisonment."

Nakahodot nodded and said, "We call him the 'Small One'."

St. Denis told the friar what was said he and Domingo both laughed out loud. "I see no harm in that," the friar said, "I am a pretty short man."

Already having an idea of what the men were going to speak about, Nakahodot asked them anyway. "What is it that you seek?"

Domingo remained quiet and let Father Margil answer. "Chief Nakahodot, as you know already, I find your people extraordinary and I wish to meet more of them and learn more about your culture. The commander and I have been asked to travel back with you to your village, but with your permission. That is what we have come here to ask."

Nakahodot thought for a moment then responded, "Why have you been asked to go there?"

Domingo started to interrupt but Father Margil raised his hand in hopes he would remain quiet for the moment. He knew the importance and gravity of the conversation and wished for it to stay civil. Domingo relented and stayed quiet. Father Margil answered, "We would like to establish a relationship of trade and community very similar to what Lieutenant St. Denis has accomplished with your brother at the Nashitosh village. Many years ago, Father Damian attempted to establish a Catholic mission in an area near yours, but as you know this mission failed." Nakahodot nodded in understanding. "We would like to come back now and re-establish a mission at your village and hopefully at the villages of other tribes that surround you."

"Trade is always a good thing," Nakahodot replied. "The Hasinai have always been a welcoming people when it comes to trade but still with caution. I can only speak for the Nakadochito."

"I understand," Father Margil said.

"But you also say you want to establish a mission. Does this mean you are wanting to talk to the Nakadochito about the one you call 'Jesus'?"

Father Margil's eyes lit up and exclaimed, "Yes! Please tell me, how is it that you have heard about Jesus? Have you been taught before about the Son of God?" Nakahodot paused for a moment, then produced a small animal skin folded neatly. He unwrapped it slowly to reveal the crucifix he had been given years before and he offered it to Father Margil. The little friar marveled at the sight. He was astonished that the chief had been carrying one all this time. "Incredible," he gasped. "So, it *is* true. The governor *did* visit other tribes before his passing." He showed the crucifix to Domingo and St. Denis. "It *must* be one of DeLeon's. Only *he* could have been carrying this. But he never recorded the names of the other tribes. Oh, my goodness. This is astounding." He paused to gather himself, still holding the crucifix. "This…this is truly amazing. The Lord does work in mysterious ways."

Nakahodot nodded and said, "You are correct. It was given to me by the man named DeLeon. He promised to come back to spread this Word of God, but never returned."

"Yes, I understand. You have my sincerest apologies for the Spaniards not keeping their word. Those were different days, I am afraid. But now, the Viceroy has asked us to return to your lands. But of course, with your permission, great chief."

"I must give you a word of caution," Nakahodot continued. "My people are wary of what happened years ago at the Nabedache village. Many will be hard to convince, and some will be afraid of disease."

Father Margil nodded, saying, "I have prayed about this a great deal. We must have faith in God and hope our efforts will bear fruit this time. We will do our best to teach religion and bring trade to your people, not disease."

Nakahodot looked at the three men carefully, then over at his brother who was quietly taking in the entire conversation. "The lieutenant will be coming with you as well?" he asked.

"And my new bride," St. Denis piped up. Natchitos smiled at him, still feeling very proud and happy for his friend.

"You may tell your Viceroy that you have my blessing to come to the Nakadochito village," Nakahodot finally said. "And the lieutenant and his bride."

Father Margil and St. Denis were overjoyed. Domingo congratulated the men as well while the two brothers quietly observed their interaction. Natchitos and Nakahodot both saw it as a good sign that St. Denis had forgiven his former jailors and held no ill-will toward them. They only hoped that the rest of the tribe would be as accepting.

Chapter 24
Spring, 1716

A week later, provisions were gathered for the expedition to the lands of the Nakadochito. The caravan for the mission trip was assembled and the Indians gathered with them at the fort. The friar was accompanied by St. Denis and his wife, Manuela, her uncle, Commander Domingo Ramon, and fifty more infantry, craftsmen and settlers alike.

Manuela said goodbye one last time to her father and mother and a great gathering assembled at the gates to see the caravan off. As she embraced her mother once more, Diego and his father both said to the travelers, "May this road be traveled more and more with each day. We do not say goodbye, but farewell for now." They set out on horses, crossing the Rio Grande and headed northward.

As the days wore on, the terrain became hilly and the caravan moved slower. The spring rains slowed their progress. Creeks and rivers had swollen too high at points where they would normally cross over, so they worked diligently in finding narrower stretches in which to cross. Spirits were high when the skies cleared, and the sun warmed their faces.

A week later, the slow-moving caravan entered the forests of the tall pines. Nakahodot knew they were nearing the hunting grounds of the Pine Springs and that it would be a good place to replenish their food supply.

As they rode, Natchitos came riding up alongside him. "Brother," he said, "we should stop soon and form a hunting party."

Nakahodot looked at him wearily and agreed, "Yes, we will find much game in this land. We can..." He stopped his horse as he could sense something. He held up his hand for the rest of the caravan to halt.

"What is it, chief?" asked St. Denis.

Nakahodot looked curiously into the woods as far as he could see. He looked over at Pakwa and Tooantuh and they both nodded they too sensed something.

"Someone approaches," Natchitos said.

Trapper got off his horse and said, "I will walk out to them. The people must stay here."

Domingo trotted his horse next to St. Denis' and asked, "What is going on here, Lieutenant? What do they see?"

"I do not know," St. Denis admitted. "We may have crossed into someone's territory." The wind blew through the tall trees, knocking the branches into one another. The eerie quiet was too much for Manuela and she began to tremble. St. Denis immediately noticed her uneasiness. "It will be alright, my love. We will be fine."

As Trapper approached, he saw braves in the distance in the thick cover of brush and trees. Suddenly, arrows came zipping through the air and plunked into the trees all around Trapper and the caravan. He froze in his tracks, knowing not to draw his bow. The warning shots alarmed some of the horses and they became restless.

"Come no farther!" a voice shouted from the dense trees. "We are the Nadaco and you are on our hunting ground."

"Nadaco?" Nakahodot asked out loud. He looked over at Natchitos and said, "Wait here. I know this chief." He rode his horse out and stood next to Trapper.

Trapper looked up and asked, "Light Hair, why would the Nadaco be this far from the Sabine?"

"You should not call me that. They have traveled far to hunt." He steadied his horse and peered into the thick cover of trees. He looked about curiously but still saw no movement. He called out in a loud voice, saying, "Lahote!" His shout echoed through the forest with no response. Birds continue to chirp, and the trees swayed eerily in the breeze. He waited a moment more, then said, "It is I, Nakahodot."

Lahote appeared from the thick brush, raising his bow in defiance and shouted back, "Why do you ride through these sacred grounds? And why do you ride with the white man?"

"We are making passage back to the Nakadochito," Nakahodot answered. "The whites that ride with us come in peace."

"They do *not* come in peace," Lahote countered angrily. "Stand aside or be counted among them." At that moment, dozens more of the Nadaco emerged from the trees.

"They are going to attack," Trapper flatly stated.

St. Denis saw what was transpiring and called out to the Spaniards, "Men be ready!" He grabbed the reins of Manuela's horse and yanked the animal to his side. "Stay behind me as best you can. I will protect you."

"Prepare for an attack!" shouted Domingo.

Nakahodot pleaded with Lahote and called out once more, "Lahote, do not fire on these people."

Without warning, an arrow was fired directly at Nakahodot, striking him below his thick, broad shoulder. He winced in pain and went tumbling off his horse. Trapper caught him just in time before he hit the ground. He threw himself in front of Nakahodot to shield him.

"*Naka*," Natchitos cried. He jumped off his horse and scrambled toward his fallen brother.

"Fire at will!" Domingo shouted, and a barrage of musket fire and arrows started flying everywhere. Within seconds the area was consumed by chaos.

Natchitos knelt next to his brother as arrows sliced through the air all around them. He bellowed to Trapper, "Let us get the arrow out!" He shoved a piece of wood into Nakahodot's teeth and said, "*Bite* down, brother. Gather your strength." In one swift move, he yanked the arrow out of his chest and threw it to the ground. Nakahodot doubled over, groaning in pain with his hands over his head.

Natchitos and Trapper both stood over him and fired arrows everywhere they could. Men shouted with war cries and braves fell to the ground with every shot. Horses ran in alarmed circles, trying to run clear of the madness, while the soldiers sent an impressive barrage of bullets, cutting down the warriors one by one. It wasn't long before they gained the upper hand and the Nadaco began retreating far into the woods.

Natchitos and Trapper continued to protect the fallen Nakahodot as the Nadaco scattered. Nakahodot sat up, holding his shoulder, to see what was going on.

"Stay down, brother," Natchitos frantically said.

"Lahote will mount another charge," Nakahodot warned. "Be ready." He reached for his bow, but his shoulder ached too much. He winced in pain again.

Just then, Lahote came racing from the trees on a horse, shouting and waving his spear defiantly. Before he could throw the spear at Natchitos, he was cut down by gunfire and went tumbling to the ground. After Lahote had fallen, the rest of his tribe disappeared into the forest.

Nakahodot got to his feet and stumbled over to the stricken Lahote. He gasped in pain as he held his bloodied shoulder. He stood over the injured Lahote; his chest rising and falling in exhaustion and pain. He gritted his teeth, coughing up blood and sneered at Nakahodot. Tears rolled down from his weary eyes as he pleaded, "You let the white men into our country." He coughed and wheezed some more, gasping for air. "And now you stand by them as they come. *Why?*"

Nakahodot took in a deep breath and said, "They *outnumber* us, Lahote. By a hundred to one. Maybe even a thousand to one. Once they start coming, there will be no stopping them. We must learn to strike treaties with them. If we do not, all will be lost." Lahote coughed up more blood and rolled to one side in pain. "Please, let me help you."

"I do not *need* your help," he shouted defiantly once more.

Nakahodot shook his head and said, "We are old, Lahote. We are part of the old way. The new ways will pass us by and leave us here to die, but it does not have to be so for those that come after us." He picked up the arrow that Lahote had shot him with and said, "I will keep this arrow as a reminder of what you have given me. Go back to your people. I will instruct these men to let you go free. Remember that your life, and the rest of the Nadaco, was spared here today."

Eventually, Lahote was able to get to his feet and he stumbled into the woods and disappeared. Nakahodot was helped on his horse and the rest of the caravan re-assembled. They suffered no casualties but a few of the men were injured just as Nakahodot was. After making camp for the rest of the night, they set out at daybreak to complete the final ride toward the village.

Three days after the attack by the Nadaco, Nakahodot arrived with the caravan at his village. Shouts of joy rung out and people ran to greet them. Kewanee came running out to her father, along with her brothers and mother. She saw how Trapper helped him from his horse and immediately came to his aid.

"What has happened to you, Father?" Kewanee asked. "You come with many more people than you left with."

"Hello, my daughter," he said. "We had trouble with the Nadaco, but it is past now. Hello, my wife."

Kewanee got on one side of him and Calanele on the other. She smiled at finally seeing him again and said, "Lean on me, my husband." She looked over his wound and said, "You are falling apart on these journeys. I will tend to you. Who are all the whites you have brought with you? Was the lieutenant freed?"

"Yes, they freed him. He has also come back with a wife." Calanele looked over her shoulder to see Manuela standing with St. Denis as he introduced her to his friends from the Nashitosh. She had never seen a white woman before either. "I will explain to everyone about the whites who are with him, but now I must sit down."

The Spaniards were introduced to the tribe and given land away from the village to setup camp until the tribe had gotten used to their presence. Only the friar was allowed to make a home amongst the tribe. The troops and settlers did not argue and knew time was needed for the tribe to get accustomed to them.

"Are the whites here to stay?" Calanele asked Nakahodot that night, as he rested on his bed of soft pelts.

"I do not know how long they will be among us," he answered. "But they wish to live and trade with us as they have done with the Nashitosh. They wish to trade along the path from their village to ours and on down to the Rio Grande fort."

"They also want to teach their religion to us as they did before, do they not?" He could sense the defiance and worry in his wife's voice. "Are you going to let them teach this religion?"

"Do not worry yourself, wife. I have allowed them to teach it. But it is up to us to decide if we will follow."

Calanele stood her ground though and said, "My answer to this is the same as it was many moons ago. The women of the tribe will not listen to these words about the man on the cross. If a man walked the Earth, he would have had a mother. If he did not, then we have no reason to listen. They are just stories." She lifted the flap to leave him to rest but before she did, she added, "And remember what happened to the Nabedache at the hands of these people."

Chapter 25

St. Denis walked around the village with Manuela. He showed her the two creeks on either side and she loved the wildflowers growing in the open fields.

"You are right, Louis," she said. "The land is beautiful here. Much more so than I imagined."

"You will like the Cane River as well, dear," he said. "It is similar to this area but still has its own charming quality."

"When can we go there to make our home?" she asked.

"It will be soon, I hope. We must have patience. I am glad Bear Trapper is here to help with translating or else I fear it might be longer. I told the friar I would help him establish his mission, but once it is done, we will leave with the Nashitosh. I know they are anxious to get back to their home too."

They soon came across Tokala and Kewanee, who were also strolling through the wildflowers. St. Denis waved to them and said, "It is Tokala. This is the young couple I told you about."

"Good morning, Lieutenant," Tokala said.

"Good morning to you both. I had been wanting to formally introduce you. This is Manuela, my wife."

Kewanee smiled at her and said, "You are very beautiful. You have the same smile as I have."

She waited for St. Denis to translate and then she smiled gratefully. "My husband has told me of your story. I admire the faith and love and strong patience you have for one another. I wish for you many children in your home."

"The 'great spirit' has heard your wish," Kewanee said, blushing. She rubbed her hand gently over her belly.

Manuela beamed when she understood the news. "Oh, how wonderful, Louis. She is expecting! I am so happy for you both."

"Congratulations," St. Denis added. "I am very happy for you too." He turned to Manuela and said, "I must leave for now. The chief is meeting with the friar for the first time today. Pray we can make progress."

St. Denis, Natchitos, Father Margil, Trapper and Pakwa gathered inside the home of Nakahodot to listen to the friar's words. "What can you teach us today, Small One?" Nakahodot asked.

"Great chief," he began, "I wanted to ask about constructing a chapel first, so the people can understand it as the House of God. A visual representation will help them greatly."

Nakahodot raised his hand though and said, "No. I will not allow a chapel to be built. Not unless the people have accepted your teachings."

Father Margil was flustered, but he accepted his decision. "Very well. I respect your wishes. That means I will just have to work harder." He laughed a little at himself, but everyone else sat quietly. "First, please tell me what you learned from DeLeon."

"He claimed that this Jesus is the son of the 'great spirit'. The one you call 'God'. That he walked the Earth as a man teaching forgiveness. He said that jealous men put him to death, but he rose from the dead and now sits with his father in the heavens."

"You remember quite well, great chief," Father Margil said, impressed. While the men talked, Calanele sat outside the home quietly listening to them. "This is where I would like to begin with my teachings to the tribe. Jesus was a man just like you and me. He walked the Earth, he ate, he drank and slept just as we do. But God created him without sin. He is what we call 'perfect'. He did no wrong to anyone his entire life. And if wrong was done to him, he only expressed forgiveness to them."

"He sounds like he was a very wise man," Nakahodot said. "But what troubles me the most, is how a man can rise from the dead. We do not speak of the dead. It is our way. Nor do we believe that one can rise from the dead. This troubles me greatly."

Father Margil gladly answered, "That is the power of God. We believe Jesus truly is His son, thus not even death can conquer him." He produced a book and showed it to the chief. "This is called the Bible. It contains the teachings of many prophets, but most importantly it tells the teachings of Jesus Christ. I would very much like to teach your people the Bible. This is what we mean when we say, the 'Word of God'. His words are in this text."

"You have my permission to teach the people from your Bible. But the women will not sit with you."

"Oh, but they must," Father Margil insisted. "The salvation of Jesus is for all souls."

Nakahodot waved him off once more though, saying, "The women will not sit with you until they decide for themselves."

"Then how can I teach them if they will not listen?"

"They will decide on their own."

Father Margil shook his head. It was not going as well as he had hoped. St. Denis knew he was frustrated, but he tried to encourage him. "You are a preacher, good friar. Have faith that God will help you with this."

Calanele got up quickly when she heard the meeting was being adjourned. She walked briskly over to a hut where several women waited patiently to hear what was said. "Did you learn the mother's name?" Mitena asked.

Calanele frowned and responded, "He only asks about how the man rose from the dead. He is not asking the right questions. He keeps going back to the same story."

After the men had left, Natchitos stayed behind and asked his brother, "Why will you not let the women listen to his teachings?"

"Calanele is being stubborn. She will not listen to his words."

"Ah," Natchitos said. "The chieftess has already spoken then."

"You make light of this," Nakahodot said. "What would you do if it were your wife you had to convince?"

"You know the answer to that, brother. The same thing." Nakahodot laughed before he winced in pain. "You are not healing?"

"It will get better," he said. "You are looking to return to your village soon, I know."

Natchitos answered, "Yes, we have been away for too long. The lieutenant is eager to check on his fort as well. It will be soon, brother. One thing to consider though is your daughter."

He shook his head though, "Kewanee's home is with her husband now. She will go where Tokala goes. I know this." He got to his feet and tapped Natchitos on the shoulder playfully. "Besides, she will have an old uncle to look after her."

"Old?" Natchitos asked, befuddled. "Me?" He continued muttering to himself long after his brother had left.

For weeks, Father Margil taught the men of the tribe outside in the center of the camp, while the women looked on from a distance. "And Jesus told his disciples, 'Love your enemies, and make straight the way of the righteous man'."

Calanele shook her head as she filled another water skin at the creek. "Why do they keep listening to the Small One? Who can believe a story about a man who rose from the dead?"

Mitena nodded, but said also, "Even our husbands listen to them, Calanele. Do not some of the words of Jesus have meaning to you?"

"Yes, yes," she conceded. "It sounds like he said some very wise things to his people long ago. But why do we not hear anything about his mother? I am still not convinced that a man can walk the Earth without having a father you can see and touch. It is not real in my mind. It is still just a story."

One morning, Nakahodot once again called for Father Margil to visit him in his home. St. Denis, Natchitos, and Trapper came as they had done before. This time, Domingo was in attendance. "Thank you for inviting me, great chief," he said.

Father Margil sat down, still looking frustrated, and said, "Good morning, Chief."

"Good morning, Small One. Something is on your mind today?" Calanele quietly took her seat outside the wall of their home and listened in.

236

"Well, I appreciate everyone that comes to listen to my teachings, but I am still frustrated that I cannot teach the women. All are concerned when it comes to the salvation of Jesus."

Nakahodot held firm to his decision, saying, "The women will decide if they choose to listen."

Father Margil shook his head and answered, "What would help them decide? What are they looking for? I am not a miracle worker here. I cannot read their minds. I need...*something*. Anything to show me what I am doing wrong."

Nakahodot thought for a moment and then said, "There is one question that perhaps you could answer for them."

Father Margil perked up and asked, "There is? Please, tell me."

"They want to know about Jesus' mother."

"His mother?" he asked flummoxed. "Is *that* it? Well, of *course* I can teach them about his mother. It is one of the most key elements when it comes to teaching about Jesus." He wanted to kick himself for not thinking of it before. Even after visiting the shrine in Mexico City. He was so focused on teaching about Jesus, he had forgotten to mention His mother. "I feel so foolish in not saying it sooner. Yes, I can speak about his mother."

"Go on," Nakahodot said. Calanele leaned in closer outside as her husband finally asked the question she wanted to hear.

"Jesus' mother was as a simple peasant girl, who was chosen by God before she was even born," Father Margil began. "God kept her free from sin because she was to be chosen for the most singular privilege of grace. She was to become the mother of the Son of God. It was foretold by the prophets that a virgin would bear a son that would come into the world to save mankind from sin. This prophecy was fulfilled when an angel of the Lord appeared to her, saying that she would bear a son and call him Jesus."

Nakahodot stopped him though and asked, "But how can a virgin bear a child?"

"That is the great mystery that has plagued scholars for centuries," Father Margil answered. "But we go by faith that it is true. The child was conceived not by flesh, but of spirit; the Holy Spirit. The spirit of God came upon her. Thus, it is called the 'Immaculate Conception'." Calanele's eyes grew wide as she listened. "In simpler terms, she conceived without knowing a man, but of the Holy Spirit of God."

"Does this virgin have a name?" Nakahodot asked.

Father Margil smiled and answered, "Her name is *Maria*; The Virgin Mother of God."

Calanele gasped as her heart skipped a beat. She felt her whole body overcome by a warm, fluttering sensation. Her hands trembled as she stumbled getting to her feet. "*Maria...*I must tell them," she whispered. She quickly walked over to the home where most of the women were waiting. She flung the flap open and fell into the hut, gasping for air.

"What did you learn? What happened to you?" Mitena asked.

She panted as she caught her breath and finally said, "My husband asked the right question. Jesus' mother's name is *Maria*." All the women whispered the name over and over. "The Small One said that Maria bore a son as a virgin, not knowing a man, but conceived by the Holy Spirit of God."

Mitena seemed bewildered, yet amused, and asked, "She conceived and bore a son without knowing a man? How wonderful *that* must have been! Why did *I* not think of that?"

"I will go back and listen for more," Calanele blurted excitedly and raced back outside. The women spilled out of the hut and followed her over to her home.

Father Margil sat patiently as he waited for Nakahodot to say something. They soon heard a commotion outside and they all became curious. "Well," Father Margil asked, "do you think the women will listen to me if I tell them about the Virgin Mother?"

Nakahodot sighed and answered, "I think they already know."

The little friar jumped from his seat and went outside to find all the women of the tribe had gathered around the chief's hut.

Calanele approached him and said, "We want to know more about Jesus' mother, Maria."

All the men came out as well and watched intently as Father Margil spoke to the women, grinning from ear to ear. "I think I can help with more than just that," he told them. "Please, wait here."

Everyone waited patiently for him to return from his hut, when finally, he emerged carrying a rolled-up parchment. Calanele asked, "Can you tell us more?"

"Yes," Father Margil said, "but I think it would be better by showing you." He carefully unrolled the small parchment to reveal a hand-painted replica of the image that hung in the basilica on Tepeyac Hill. All the women gasped at the beautiful drawing of the Virgin Mother. "This is an image of the Blessed Mother that was given by God to a peasant man many moons ago. We call the image, *Our Lady of Guadalupe*. This…is the mother of Jesus."

One by one, the women dropped to their knees and bowed their heads with reverence before the image. Nakahodot marveled at the sudden transformation of them, including his wife. He looked over at St. Denis who was smiling. Then he noticed that Manuela was kneeling before the image as well.

"Now *that* is the power of God," St. Denis exclaimed.

Nakahodot walked over to Father Margil and said, "You may build your chapel."

The little man rolled up the parchment and smiled back at the chief. He said to the gathering as they all stood once again and said, "We will display this on the wall of our new chapel. Along with the Cross of Christ."

Nakahodot gave permission for the Spaniards to start construction of a chapel at their village. The soldiers and craftsmen, as well as the braves of the tribe, gathered together to work on the structure.

After more than a week of work, the chapel had taken shape and Father Margil stood off to the side admiring the results. St.

Denis walked over to him and said, "Looks like you *are* a miracle worker, good friar."

When the chapel was completed, Father Margil led the tribe to the edges of Lanana Creek and said to all of them, "Before we celebrate our first Mass in our new chapel, I will baptize all who have come to believe in Jesus Christ. I will baptize you with water from your flowing creek. Then we will christen the new chapel."

After all had been baptized in the waters of Lanana Creek, they gathered at the new chapel. Father Margil said to the people, "This is a blessed day for me and for all the Nakadochito in the eyes of the Lord. I will christen this mission church in God's name; calling it *Nuestra Señora de Guadalupe*."

Chapter 26

As the sun began to set, St. Denis went looking for his friends. Soon, he found Natchitos and asked him, "Well, should we share a smoke by the fire?"

Natchitos glanced at the side of the ridge that overlooked the village and spotted his brother perched in his favorite spot. "Maybe I have better idea," he told him.

"A better idea than a smoke?" St. Denis asked perplexed. He followed Natchitos up the slope and they both sat down next to Nakahodot.

"It is about time somebody came up here to watch these sunsets with me," Nakahodot quipped.

Natchitos stared at the beautiful colors in the sky and answered, "I wanted to see what you thought was so interesting up here. I thought I should do it since we are leaving tomorrow." They sat for a moment in silence. Nakahodot knew what was coming next. "You have my quiver?"

Nakahodot looked over at his brother momentarily and frowned a bit. Then he chucked his old quiver on his brother's lap. "Here. Take it. I will not be needing it anymore."

Surprised, Natchitos looked over the quiver with admiration. The drawing of the buffalo on one side was faded and had lost its red color. Otherwise, the leather was fine condition. "Oh, you looked after it good I see." St. Denis watched amused, impatiently waiting to see what would happen next. Natchitos then handed the quiver back to his brother. "You keep it. You are taking good care of it for me. Besides, you may still need it." Nakahodot took the quiver and set it down without saying anything. "But I do not understand why you are up here every evening while we could be having a good smoke by the fire right now. You should watch the sun as it rises in the morning like I do."

Nakahodot shook his head and answered, "I cannot waste time in the morning when there is so much work to be done. Be quiet and watch the 'great spirits' hand at work."

St. Denis was extremely amused and couldn't hold his tongue any longer. He smiled and laughed at them, saying, "You two are definitely brothers."

The End

Epilogue

Louis Juchereau de St. Denis returned to Natchitoches that same year of 1716 with his wife Manuela. He continued his explorations in various areas in the region until 1722, when he was named commander of Fort St. Jean-Baptiste. They remained in Natchitoches the rest of their lives, raising five children, one of which took over as commander after the passing of St. Denis in 1744.

Commander Domingo Ramon continued his expedition, also known as the *Ramon Expedition*, with Father Antonio Margil de Jesus, and established three more missions at the Hasinai tribes in the surrounding region.

A Zacatecan Franciscan, Father Margil returned to the mission at *Nuestra Señora de Guadalupe* where he continued to serve the Nakadochito until 1719. During this time, a terrible drought struck the region between 1717 and 1718, and both Lanana and Banita Creeks went dry. The crops dried up and the Indians and priests and soldiers thirsted for water. The tribe grew resentful and feared the same fate awaited them as what had occurred thirty-five years before at the Nabedache village. One night, Father Margil stayed awake all night in solemn prayer. The next morning, he went down to the dried-up Lanana Creek, knelt and said one last prayer. He struck the rock bank with his staff, and miraculously, two springs flowed forth from the rocks. The people were saved and from that day forward, the springs became known as the *Holy Springs of Father Margil*, or the *Eyes of Father Margil*. He is known as the most famous missionary to serve Texas and to this day is considered for sainthood by the Vatican.

The Spanish missions continued to spread in the area, including one on the eastern side of the Sabine River. The mission was called *San Miguel de Linares de los Adaes* and was positioned near present day Robeline, Louisiana. It was at this mission in 1719, that the *Chicken War* occurred. Tensions between France and Spain reignited, causing a small troop of soldiers from the fort at Natchitoches to retaliate at the nearest

Spanish outpost, which was Los Adaes. The handful of soldiers only found one priest and one soldier there and decided instead to raid the henhouse. The chickens scattered, causing one soldier to tumble to the ground from his frightened horse. The lay minister took advantage of the confusion and ran into the woods. Days later when he reached Father Margil, he warned them that 'hundreds' of French soldiers were on their way from Natchitoches and Mobile. Father Margil saw retreat as his only option and abandoned the mission and fled for another in San Antonio. The threat from the French never materialized and two years, and much progress in trade, were lost on account of the mishap.

Father Margil was then summoned back to San Juan Bautista in Coahuila, where he resumed his duties. The mission at *Nuestra Señora de Guadalupe* was restored in 1721 by the Marquis de Aguayo. The mission continued until it was abandoned in 1773 after the cession of Louisiana to Spain by the French.

During this time, the Mexican government ordered all settlers from the *Tejas* territory to move to San Antonio, but the settlers complained bitterly about this arrangement. In 1779, a Spanish lieutenant named Antonio Gil Ibarvo, gained permission to lead a group of these settlers to the region once more. At finding the deserted mission of *Nuestra Señora de Guadalupe*, he used what was left of the buildings to form a new settlement. He built a stone house for their seat and local government, which served as a trading post as well. The structure became known as the Old Stone Fort, and a replica of it still stands today on the campus of Stephen F. Austin University.

The spirit of the Nakadochito lived on into history. The evidence of this tribe remains today up and down the banks of Lanana and Banita Creeks.

As time went on and westward expansion continued, the tribe was forced to move to areas near the Brazos River after the Texas Revolution. By 1859, all that remained of the Caddo were moved to Oklahoma near the Washita River, in present day Caddo County.

However, the tribe holds its place in history just as the Nashitosh tribe did for Natchitoches, Louisiana. The small but determined tribe that descended from the Caddo stand alone as guardians and pioneers of what would become the center of the *Tejas*, or Texas Territory. It was known on all maps as a vital and strategic point along the road called *El Camino Real*. The town was named for the legendary tribe called the *Nakadochito*, or the *Nacogdoche*. The town is known today as Nacogdoches, the oldest settlement in Texas.